PRAISE FOR WHEN WE BLINKED

"Richly layered and compulsively readable, *When We Blinked* is an entertaining, insightful love story with real depth. Author Stephanie Mack deftly balances complex issues of marriage, morality, and modern dating with tender moments and witty dialogue to create a memorable and heartfelt romance debut. Faith, family, and female friendships provide the foundation for an engrossing second-chance love story between a couple you can't help but root for as they find their way back to each other. Mack is an impressive and engaging new voice in Christian women's fiction. A sparkling debut."

DEVON DANIELS
AUTHOR OF *MEET YOU IN THE MIDDLE*

"An addictive debut filled with depth: Stephanie Mack tells a captivating story that delves deep into complex matters of the heart and leaves you wanting to discuss the issues it explores with friends. This is relatable women's fiction!"

RILEY COSTELLO
AUTHOR OF *WAITING AT HAYDEN'S* + CREATOR OF SHOPFICTION™

"Full disclosure: I literally could not put this book down. *When We Blinked* is both an engrossing love story and a thoughtful journey of self-discovery. Author Stephanie Mack explores big themes—marriage, motherhood, faith, and friendship, just to name a few—with authenticity, grace, and ~~~~~~~~~~~~ umor. I can't wait to find out whi~~~~~~~~~~~~~~~~~~~~~~ will snap up the movie rights to ~~~~~~~~~~~~~

NATASHA BURTON
AUTHOR OF *101 QUIZZES* ~~~~~
*WHAT'S MY TYPE?: 100+ Q~~~~~~ ~~ HELP YOU
FIND YOURSELF —AND YOUR MATCH!*

"*When We Blinked* is a beautiful and honest look behind closed doors into a seemingly perfect marriage with very raw, real struggles ... refreshingly relatable on so many levels. From the start, I was wrapped up into the story and found myself laughing and crying alongside the characters in whom my heart was invested. This is a must-read, can't-put-down kind of love story that will also encourage you in your own journey."

ASHLYN CARTER
LIFESTYLE YOUTUBE CREATOR + PODCAST HOST

"An enchanting debut all but certainly destined for the big screen. Wickedly clever and hopelessly romantic, *When We Blinked* oscillates between perfectly imperfect Sera and Connor with an unapologetic message: the ability to love fully and freely can arise from the ashes of our deepest hurts and shame. Mack silences multiple stigmas as her voice flawlessly marries the wit and charm of Sophie Kinsella with the spiritual depth of Francine Rivers. I immediately wanted to know the conclusion, but never wanted it to end."

JENN MCBRIDE
FORMER MANAGING EDITOR, CBS LOS ANGELES
(CBSLA.COM)

"With the turn of each page, you'll fall more in love with the dynamic characters and become engrossed in this deep but witty story of balancing motherhood, a growing career, new dating life, and a romance rekindled in an unexpected way. I also adored the vividly crafted moments set throughout Orange County, which both made me feel at home and swept me away. I couldn't put this book down!"

LINDYE GALLOWAY
FOUNDER + CREATIVE DIRECTOR, THE LINDYE
GALLOWAY DESIGN STUDIO + SHOP

"Approachable and profound, *When We Blinked* is for anyone who has been brave enough to embrace a new beginning. Stephanie Mack has not only written an absolutely captivating (and fun!) love story, she has invited each of us to look beyond what is immediately visible and into the often-unseen hopes and hurts hidden within our own hearts. This book reminds us that beauty can indeed still come from ashes and that redemption is possible."

MARISSA HAYS
FAITH BLOGGER + MEDIA PERSONALITY

"*When We Blinked* is an instant favorite! It's all at once hilarious and heartwarming, raw and relatable. Through the eyes of our protagonists, we get an honest look at modern-day marriage with soul-baring heart, quick-witted humor, and inspiring hope. These characters and this love story will stay with you long after you've finished ... it's a debut that will leave you wanting more from Stephanie Mack!"

ASHLEY LAUREN TENORIO
AUTHOR OF *DAVEY* + FOUNDER OF ASHLEY & CREW

"Stephanie Mack is a relevant voice desperately needed in today's fragmented world. Her modern storytelling is endlessly relatable, all the while not departing from Christian values. Seamlessly bridging the gap between contemporary romance and inspirational fiction, she's built a timeless love story upon a solid foundation of faith. *When We Blinked* is flirty, lighthearted, and fun while also portraying the depth and complexity of marriage and dating relationships. From fast-paced dialogue and laugh-out-loud moments to endearing characters with real-life struggles, Mack's debut is one you will not be able to put down!"

MOLLY KELLEY
SPEAKER + BIBLE TEACHER

"Married love can be complicated and messy at times. This book perfectly captures the tangled juxtaposition of tenderness and heartache of married life in the most relatable way. The author beautifully depicts the dark and gritty realities contemporary couples face, while tempering it with lighthearted moments that will remind you why love always wins! It is a modern-day love story of redemption that will have you laughing, crying, and cheering for Seraphina all the way through!"

DR. TESS BREEN
LEADERSHIP + EMOTIONAL INTELLIGENCE EXPERT

"Stephanie Mack is a gifted author. *When We Blinked* is an engaging story, written from a Christian perspective, that reminds the reader of the power of redemption."

ERIC GEIGER
SENIOR PASTOR, MARINERS CHURCH

"I couldn't stop reading this book and didn't want it to end! Stephanie Mack transported me into a world I couldn't get enough of—from the gorgeous settings to the heartfelt sisterhood to the killer fashion! It's so easy to love the protagonists, to understand, empathize, and root for them. They had me laughing out loud, bubbling up with goosebumps, and genuinely tearing up *multiple* times! More importantly, the heart of this book is rooted in renewal, healing, self-reflection, courage, and leaning into your tribe. Oozing with positivity and humor, it is an honest and hope-filled look at the beauty and challenges of motherhood, marriage, family, and personal growth. This should be on any Christian's must-have book list, and I cannot wait to read it with my daughter one day!"

BARAKA MAY
SAG-AFTRA, STUDIO SINGER +
VOCAL DIRECTOR + ARRANGER

"Stephanie Mack masterfully crafts a story of redemption—not just the redemption of Sera and Connor, but the redemption of a literary genre. Finally, we have a faith-filled, hope-centered romance that brings reality and authenticity to today's readers."

KATIE QUESADA
SPEAKER + STORYTELLING COACH

"This beautifully crafted 'behind-the-screens' look at unfiltered life, love, and loss, and the toll it all takes on our hearts and minds, will leave you reaching for both a tissue and a highlighter. As Stephanie Mack fearlessly fuses fiction with reality, the pages flow far beyond a modern-day love story and into the truth of our intrinsic mental and emotional needs as humans. *When We Blinked* teaches us that the hope of healing cannot exist without the permission of pain."

CASSANDRA PRUET
COO, MENTAL HEALTH GRACE ALLIANCE

A NOVEL

STEPHANIE MACK

STEPHANIE MACK

When We Blinked is a work of fiction. While some elements are inspired by true observations and experiences, names, characters, scenes, and incidents are written products of the author's invention or are used fictitiously. Certain real locations and public figures are mentioned, but the story is wholly imaginary.

ISBN: 978-0-578-85533-2
Library of Congress Control Number: 2021903613

Cover design: Zak McIntyre
Author photo: Kimberly Hope Photography
Interior design: Natalie Lauren Design
Editor: Jessica Snell

Printed in the United States of America

www.stephaniemack.com

To my mom,
for giving me wings.

———————

To my dad,
for making me fly.

———————

To my Douglas,
for lifting me to my utmost
and always catching me when I fall.

TABLE *of* CONTENTS

PART ONE: Ask

PART TWO: Seek

PART THREE: *Knock*

ACKNOWLEDGEMENTS

PART ONE

Ask

ONE

SERAPHINA

I tapped the toe of my nude suede pump on the elevator floor, willing us to move faster. Piano music leaked from the ceiling, with zero calming effect on me. *This thing keeps glitching.* One day I'd be truly stuck, in the guts of this glass corporate castle. I breathed. If only we would rise at the rate of my blood pressure.

There. At last. Ascent.

I knew the meeting had started without me, and I was as tardy as I was jittery. I had failed to predict that my four-year-old would make herself a breakfast-time "beard" with the glitter Silly Putty Santa gave her for Christmas. Glitter would be the death of me. What had Santa (me) been thinking?

"Mommy, *it won't come off!*" Coco had cried, clawing at her cheeks, her anxiety heating up like the skillet. I'd been too busy reminding myself it had to be *exactly six* pancakes to avoid them being thrown back at me. Hot breakfast was my new practice, my way of saying, *We're still a family. I'll keep you warm. We're going to be okay.* I used to pour us all cereal and call it a morning.

You never knew what you had until you stood alone over a small open flame.

This morning, Coco wore a sloth nightgown, sloth slippers, and sloth eye mask pulled up onto her forehead—all Santa's fault, again. The sloth was her favorite animal of the moment. It changed every few months, but I was glad sloths were having their time in the limelight; it was easy to find paraphernalia. Lately, Coco loved to snuggle me in the early mornings and tell me she was my sloth, wrapping herself around my back like a cloak. It was the very best part of my days—the groggy moments before the dawn, when we both knew just who we were. Before she flipped and turned on me. Before my temper could flare. Mother and daughter, primal and pure. Come what may, as it would.

What did those wizards put into glitter Silly Putty? It would not peel off. *Make-up remover pads?* No luck. *Nail polish remover?* Too risky.

Hot water, I heard Connor say. *Rub it gently away with a washcloth.*

These were the moments when I sensed his absence the most. He always knew what to do in the face of kiddo catastrophe. Sharpie on our new vinyl floors? Magic Eraser. Gum in the hair? Creamy peanut butter. Lipstick smeared into our master bedroom rug? Folex, forever. I cringed now at comments I used to make about being a "single mom" when Connor was away on a golf trip. It was not funny and not even part true. Living alone, *being* alone, was cavernous and excruciating.

I was doing better, though; much better. My stomach didn't

hurt every day. My appetite was back for the most part. I could face my family again. I had resumed my full face-wash routine. I was going to spin class.

Fine. I was going to spin class, *sometimes.*

I still reached to twist my wedding band when I was nervous or lost, as if it would comfort or guide me.

It just seemed like an eternity since I'd had an empty hand. Or exercised like I used to. Or done much to take care of me.

My progress was slow. But I was in motion.

Hey. *Like a sloth.* You know?

Gripping Coco's cheeks in one hand, scrubbing her chin with the other, I watched the hot water work. Her face shined clean within seconds, spurring a billow of hope. *Maybe I really can do this,* I thought. I needed the reminder, each hour, especially here at the office, a planet away from my baby girl.

Finally, the elevator doors opened up to my floor and the rest of my life.

God, get me through this day.

Please don't let the team kill me.

May I slowly but eventually forget how it felt for Connor to be my sloth.

. . .

"You're late, Ser. *Again.*" He didn't even have to say it, my faithful work bestie. I could see it in the flat line of his mouth against his perfectly groomed hipster beard. Connor had grown one just like it, in fact, per my specific request. I'd always had to acknowledge that Beckham was objectively nice-looking, and always ahead of the trends, even if he drove me insane and felt, sometimes, like a son. I could never keep up with his antics. Or his women, for that matter.

"*Love your tie,*" I mouthed, taking my seat across from him at the front of the conference table. Morning light poured into the window and onto its mahogany shine. My punctuality was a growth area, and this bugged me, too. I vowed in silence to work on it. *Allow time for glitter.* "I'm so sorry I'm late, everyone."

Still, Beckham had missed me in my four years away as a stay-at-home mom. He had missed me, and we both knew it. Quarterly lunches and occasional phone calls simply were not the same. But we were back; *we were back*! The Dream Team! The Word Wizards! The Hotel Heroes of Syntax!

Even if he was my boss now, and still rolled his eyes at my names for us.

My ego had suffered worse hits lately. I was just thankful to be here.

He straightened his plaid lavender tie, jerking his head toward Phoebe and her presentation, as if saying, "*Be here, right now. Sit up,* Seraphina Lorenn."

"*Ahem*!" Phoebe, in her expensive-looking black skirt suit, shot up a brow and continued addressing our staff. We were a ragtag group of writers, designers, interns, and brand executives. "As I was saying, since Beck became national brand design manager and I took the global role, Mr. Hamilton has secured five new acquisitions across the U.S. to close within the next year."

"Mr. Hamilton? Is that what we're calling him now?" chided Sage, my intern, between chomps of peppermint gum. She helped us with writing and social media. I still couldn't believe I had my own intern, to keep me young and show me how to keep upping my Instagram Stories game. It was hard to keep up with the features. She was fresh out of USC. *Wasn't I still fresh out of USC?* We liked to compare the differences of my PR degree program and hers, the decade between them a chasm of digital evolution. My schooling felt practically obsolete—but we did still write actual press releases, as I learned to do back then. Well, Sage wrote them, if we were being technical. I made them sparkle and shine.

"Yes, we are calling him that," confirmed Phoebe. "And when you become one of the world's youngest billionaires, you can be called *Ms. Anderson.*"

It wasn't necessarily out of reach. Sage had over 500,000 followers on Instagram for her fashion and lifestyle blog. She was twenty-three years old. I was proud to call her my sidekick if not perplexed by her desire to work for us.

But there was nothing perplexing about Graham Hamilton. The Prince, we called him, though not to his face—head of the great Hamilton Hotels & Resorts Worldwide, Inc., headquartered here in Orange County, California. Graham was appointed CEO after his grandfather's death last year. Graham's parents died in a plane crash when he was young, and he was essentially raised at the company. He was also not far out of college—an Ivy League, naturally. Corporate Communications loved to remind us of his pedigree at every turn. I mean, he had "four years of real-world experience," and was now earning his MBA, so of course he was fit to be chasing mega-million-dollar properties and high-profile magazine covers.

"Coeur d'Alene, Cleveland, St. Louis, Chicago," Phoebe continued.

"Well," quipped Beckham. "Is The Prince going Middle-America happy on us?"

Giggles rippled around the room.

"You know he's not the closer," I said. "He's just the new face. He looks so much like his grandfather. Those handsome genes. Plus, the people trust Yale."

"Harvard," corrected Corey, Beckham's new assistant, about whom I still couldn't decide. "I did the research for that business feature you wrote. He graduated *magna cum laude*. He's fun to tease, but he's wicked smart."

Shoot. I was still easing in. Thank you for reminding me, *Corey*.

"Understated big cities, resort towns," Phoebe went on. "*Small America is the new black*. He coined that phrase on a conference call. But you might've noticed: that was only four properties."

Phoebe poised her thumb on the remote in her hand, scanning our group with her ivy-green eyes. Her thick red hair was chopped blunt at her clavicle and extra glossy today. Even in these awful overhead lights, she appeared fresh off a runway. "Meet our newest crown jewel, team—The Bentley at Jackson Hole. Now part of the Hamilton family."

Known by anyone in hospitality with half a pulse, the familiar dramatic mountain retreat filled the projector screen. The expansive wooden château was set beneath snow-slathered mountains dotted with pines. Were those actual ... moose? In the distance? It was hard not to gawk at the old-world majesty.

The high slanting roofs caked in white, the countless original windows, certainly a jacuzzi and fireplace in every room.

I gulped. Connor and I had always talked about seeing The Bentley someday.

Someday. I hated that word.

Ooohs and *aaaahs* emitted in chorus. Our senior graphic designer, Georgina, reflexively flipped to a blank page, beginning to sketch. Sage's eyes filled with visions and tweets. I locked stares with Beckham. We knew this was huge. Our National Brand Design Band was back together, and we were taking the stage. I practically fist-pumped right at him.

"Hamilton will be undertaking extensive renovations on the property, but we're keeping the historical bones," Phoebe explained. "You'll have the planned updates soon. We'll need the whole nine, ASAP, and this will be top priority. Full creative branding, taglines, website, brochures, press release drafts, the works.

"We need your maximum game, everyone," she proceeded. "The very best you all have. This is big for The Prince, it's big for us, and it's big for the whole company. This isn't just about a new property. This is the next generation. Everyone out there's got a hawk-eye on our every move."

We nodded.

I liked her more for referring to him as The Prince.

"Oh," she said. "One more thing. You two,"—a wild gesticulation in the air between Beckham and me—"you have to go see it. Next month. We can't catch this vision blind. February will be freezing, but there needs to be snow. Go the full week of Presidents' Day, so it's one less workday out of the office."

No. *No, no, no, no, no.* Coco's fifth birthday. I already knew it fell the Wednesday after that Monday because I'd started planning the party. My insides fizzled and churned. I couldn't leave her. Not yet, and not on a milestone birthday. Children were not invited on Hamilton trips—the ironclad rule, nonnegotiable. The trips were delightful and key, but always a full week, and also, frankly, exhausting. The dinners, meetings, writing, research, the really-hunkering-down. All of the local tourism. Even if I could wrap my mind around missing my baby's birthday, I hadn't left her for that long since she'd been born. I wasn't ready.

I can't do it. I couldn't.

"Um—" I began.

"Oh gosh, Phoebe," said Beckham, an apologetic lilt to his voice.

Thank goodness. My Beckham. My person. *He's going to take this one for me.*

"My twin brother's getting married in Hawaii that week, remember?" he finished. "Can we do March? I'm so sorry."

Disappointment flashed on Phoebe's sharp features, but just as quickly refroze, an easy feat given the amount of Botox in them. "No, we can't wait. It's the only week I can fly in for a day." She paused. "You, Sera. You're ready. Take an intern if you want. Beckham, start setting her meetings."

I held in the sigh that would surely betray my panic. I mustered the weakest of smiles and fakest of ra-ra-team gusto. Apparently this was happening, and I had to speak before Phoebe had reason to doubt me.

"Will do!" I exclaimed. "I'm on it. This is incredible. We've got this, Sage. I'll need your eye for social." She nodded her balayage layers, round cheeks aglow. She was, per usual, utterly darling and eager to please. I knew I was lucky to have her, if only three days a week.

The meeting continued, all of my teammates elated, while I sank lower into my executive chair. Plans for Coeur d'Alene and Chicago also sounded amazing, but those trips could wait until summer.

I get to write for a living. I get to write for a living. I get to write for a living.

I'd returned as a senior brand writer after a career gap smack in my prime. I should be purely grateful.

But my high-pitched mom guilt thrummed loudly and cruelly over everything else.

I would miss Coco's birthday.

But I needed this job more than ever.

God, this is bad. There's no way out. It really is only me now.

I once missed this place so much.

But in that moment, I couldn't believe how desperately I missed being a housewife.

. . .

I yanked my office door shut behind me, harder than I intended. Not like I could hide with these fishbowl windows that insisted on being so modern. When I used to sit in here, belly swollen, ankles thick, secretly wearing Ugg slippers under my desk, I'd imagine my return to work after Coco was born— *which we now know never happened*—and I'd wonder how I might hang a blanket over that pane so I could breast-pump in private. I cringed at the box of a nursing room down the hall, provided by corporate, and at email-requesting my time slots for something so sacred and personal.

Coco now beamed at me from the portrait on my office wall, chestnut eyes above her pink cheeks, lips pulled into a grin full of toddler teeth, sandy tendrils framing it all.

Coco. *My baby*. The motherless birthday girl. *Ugh*. I was the actual worst.

Rap, rap, rap. "Ser?"

I only ever closed my door when I was dealing with something personal (but only that which troubled me greatly) or deep in my deepest writer zone (which I could be, right now, if I were already dreaming of making The Bentley sing with my words, three minutes after our meeting, which I was not).

Beckham knew this. He didn't wait for permission to enter. "I am *so sorry*, Ser. I got to my desk and looked at the calendar. How could I ever forget the week you left me forever and never came back? It's Coco's birthday. You're freaking out."

"I'm not freaking out." I exhaled, crawling into my chair.

I was about to fold my arms on my desk and bury my head in their crook—for utmost effect—but the latest issue of *Forefront Magazine* stared right back up at me. At least it wasn't Graham Hamilton, but rather, a young woman, svelte and blonde. She looked like a sorority president, in the best way. Confident. Classy. Connected. "What's this? 'Million-Dollar Romantic Opens Our Eyes.' Is this a hint? Have I really become that depressing?"

Beck had a habit of leaving things on my desk for me. Sometimes fantastic things. Never subtle things.

"Not depressing," he corrected. "Just—a little doleful at times."

"Those are synonyms."

"Well, there's nothing *dolefully depressing* about Piper Maddock." He fell into my plush, royal blue office couch, grabbing a handful of Peanut Butter M&M'S from the crystal bowl on the side table, crossing his ankles above camel Gucci loafers. I tried to keep it cozy in here for when the hours grew bleak, and for Coco's occasional visits. "Have you heard of her? I thought you'd find her inspiring. The article is amazing. If I liked blondes, I'd track her down."

"Your confidence is astounding." I hadn't heard of her. Wide-eyed Piper could wait. She didn't look a day over thirty. She probably hadn't known anguish. How could she at, what, twenty-five? It was time to lower my forehead onto her face.

Wow, she was actually—*stunning*. There was also something centering about her, left hand on one hip, iPhone held out in the other. Set jaw, full lips, big brown eyes. Medium-length honey hair curled elegantly into waves. I also loved that she was wearing a hot pink wrap dress, a departure from the iconic business pub's typical male black suit covers. Mental note: *Read this later.*

"I don't mean to be a downer, Beck. Or late so often." I sighed. "I'm still adjusting, I guess." I'd only been back three months. And I knew I'd have to travel again. Just maybe not so soon.

"I'd go if I could," he promised. "Best Man. Twin. I kind of win. Sorry."

"You only turn five once!" I pointed out. "But you might get married *twice*." I held out my arms and pushed out my poutiest lip, pretending like I might cry.

He half-laughed. He wasn't budging. "You going to be okay?"

"Yes." *Maybe*, I would be okay. "Do I have a choice, Boss?"

"Can't your parents take her for the week? Make it special? FaceTime you in?"

FaceTime me in? I swallowed the gut punch. "Maybe. But Connor and I agreed to check with each other first if we'll be gone during our time with her. So. *Yay!* Extra communication with him!"

"I feel like he'll do whatever you want. He's, like, the dream ex-husband. You know that, right? Is this the worst thing ever?"

"It's not the best!" I sighed. "Shared custody feels like a root canal that won't heal. Her pink princess suitcase. My heart. A piece of it dies every time."

"My parents split when I was her age, remember? I know, Ser. It sucks. But also? It will get better."

I wasn't so sure. "Thanks, friend."

We sat in silence, comfortably, as we had many times before. Two friends who had learned side-by-side to convert our words into sales, to command respect for the marketing team, to lean on each other through highs and lows—life's "peaches and pits," as Coco called them. To rise through the ranks and form the strongest of ties, despite our divergent lifestyles, and all of the goals we shared. He'd never been my rival; he'd only ever been kind. I squealed when he called to tell me about his promotion, when I was in line at Disneyland with my mom friends and all of our kids. He'd been my professional ally since the day we started as baby interns together a decade ago. He'd earned a place in my heart. Even if I occasionally wanted to hit him.

I jiggled the mouse to fire up my computer and start clicking through my emails.

"The Bentley, though—wow," Beckham marveled as he stood up to leave. "Nobody writes a destination like you. I can't wait to read your stuff. 'She can bring emotional appeal and wanderlust to a glacier.' Was that the quote? And, I'm jealous. I hear their spa is unreal."

"Something like that." I smiled—though I never had quite understood that compliment, which came with the most prestigious business award I'd ever received. Weren't glaciers inherently wondrous? I think our CEO was trying to play on the whole "selling ice to Eskimos" thing and falling a little short. But I wouldn't hold it against him. He had us for the words. "Now scram! I've got a snow castle to sell." *To a whole bunch of very rich Eskimos.*

For a second then, I felt Beckham's eyes dance briefly across my desk to the family picture I hadn't yet put away. *Should've filed that one in the archives.* But I just couldn't. I almost never loved pictures of myself, especially pregnant, but I'd cherish this one always. We three wore white. We frolicked the beach. Coco was two. I was eleven weeks pregnant. I'd announced the news with that photo on social media. You could see the small bump beneath my cotton gown, but only if you looked closely. Connor had never looked better—strong arms, cute smile, brown hair wavy and soft. *Gosh, I'd loved him so much.*

Gosh, and I loved that baby.

"Read about Piper Maddock," Beckham added. "The best is ahead for you, Ser. And take a look at her product."

Romance. Hot pink. *The old me.* "Okay."

He shut the door with one final wink.

. . .

TWO

CONNOR

I cradled my cup of coffee from the old-school carafe in the waiting room, sipping the sludge as I watched for the door to open. The water fixture was nice. It looked like a waterfall and sounded like rain. And the sound of rain made me feel cleaner, as if it were washing away my sins. Lord knew I had my share. It also reminded me of the white noise app we'd used after Coco was born. *The feisty little pipsqueak.*

I'd never loved anyone more.

Except for her mother.

The feisty little pipsqueak original.

This was only my second session, but I'd already decided that I preferred clutching something while a stranger excavated my feelings. I probably didn't need the extra caffeine, because it made me talk more, and I had enough to say, to my shock. But I needed a buffer between me and my razor-focused inquisitor. It was unnerving and disarming at once, all that eye contact and attention.

Maybe I'd work on a prop. Maybe I'd bring a snack. I wondered if that would be rude. A sweatshirt? I could pretend I needed the Kleenex.

Today, it was coffee, hot and burned. *Same as Ser,* come to think of it.

She'd be proud of me, though. I never agreed to therapy during our marriage, while her beloved Linda was a celebrity name in our house. Sera was perpetually working on herself. When we were together, I so often wanted to shake her and tell her to stop. *To relax.* To stop being so darn introspective all the darn time. Enough with self-help and the Enneagram.

But now, sure enough, I admired it. Women weren't all like her and I knew this now. Sera was always brave enough to think therapy might have saved us. I wondered now if I'd been a coward. I had yet to conclude if she'd been right. So I'd tell her about my therapy at the right time. I still wanted to make her happy. I couldn't help it. It's partly why I was here. I couldn't seem to shake her, but it was time for me to move on.

I'd reeled over the decision between a male and female therapist but decided ultimately to go with a woman. I didn't want the slightest risk that a man might side with me because of our gender. I wanted the harshest truths delivered like cold salami, salty and hard to digest. I was ready to consider I might benefit from better understanding myself and making a few small changes. And I felt like a woman might be more inclined to *let me have it* when I needed it, the way Sera had always done.

I don't know; maybe that was ridiculous. But here I was, ready to meet with *Janine* for the second time.

Or as ready as I'd ever be.

"Connor?" Her voice echoed through the opening door,

with the calm, firm force of a flight attendant's. "Come on in."
I rose. Into her office I went.

. . .

Janine held impeccable posture in her oversized therapist's
chair. She was regal, my dad would have said, but I also detected
an edge. Light make-up, high cheek bones, gold skin. She looked
like a woman who vacationed in Nantucket but probably loved
true crime. Welcoming, yes, but you also did not want to mess
with her. Her thick, black-rimmed glasses were oversized, trendy,
her brown hair highlighted and pulled back into a low bun. Sera
never thought I was listening to the things she did to her hair,
but I always was. I knew all about highlights and hairstyles and
that a woman should never cut bangs in a time of crisis.

My official new shrink was very pretty, probably in her
mid-fifties, but not so pretty that I felt attracted or the slightest
bit less than comfortable. She had a warmth and a sense of
undeniable wisdom. I had liked her immediately.

"So, how was this week for you, Connor?"

It seemed like such a *general* question. I might be asked it
by a gas station clerk. I enjoyed being here but prickled momen-
tarily that I was paying so much for this. *Trust the process.*
Sera always said things like that. Her sister, Samantha, also a
therapist, was a strong influence on her. I wouldn't tell Sera that
I had asked Sam for therapy recs. We'd agreed it would be our
secret for now. Sera didn't know we still talked on occasion,
but was I really expected to lose her whole family along with
everything else?

"My week was pretty good. Work is busy, but I like it that way." I settled deeper into the tan suede couch.

"Tell me more about your job. What kind of law do you practice?"

"Estate planning. So, nothing too aggressive. But I'm a partner at my own small firm, so the hours can be long, you know?" I smoothed down the scruff on my chin. Women loved this thing, but it *itched*.

"Do you enjoy it?"

I did. Immensely. "I do. I work with big companies on their charity planning, but my favorite are the families. I ask them tough questions and walk them through important decisions. It feels meaningful, and the money is great—well, now it is. I feel lucky. Work has always come pretty easy." Except when starting the firm helped eviscerate my fragile marriage. There was, of course, also that.

"What about school? Did you always do well? Law school is no small feat."

Nothing lower than the one B in undergrad. *Theater Make-Up*. I'd needed some credits. Seriously, I wasn't *that* bad. "Yep, mostly straight-As, a couple A-minuses; and I never really thought law school was as hard as everyone said," I admitted. I rarely said that out loud because I thought it made me sound like a jerk. "Things seemed to go in my favor, even if it took time. I worked hard and got what I wanted. Which is why I think it was so hard when—"

I paused, thumbing the rim of my coffee cup. "When I worked as hard as I could at keeping Sera happy—and failed.

My marriage has been my biggest failure, and it still eats at me, every day. I don't see myself fully healing from this, but people keep saying it's possible. People say ... *this* ... will help. That it might've even helped sooner."

Well, I guess I'm not wasting these minutes. There I went. Straight there. *Hi, Janine!*

She flipped a page on her notepad and scribbled something I couldn't see.

What was she thinking now? Maybe that I was a handful? Maybe about cutting bangs?

"I want to tell you something," she said, after a hefty pause. "Something I believe about human beings as we try to let go of someone. An ex-lover, former friend, any person we once truly cared for."

I nodded. *Proceed, Your Honor.*

"When we miss somebody we loved, there are three layers interplaying together. Three different aspects of the loss, which each carry different emotions and representations. Does that make sense?"

"Sure. Layers." Like an onion, Sera would say.

"The first layer you miss is the *actual person*. Who they were to you; who they still are, as a human being. Their personality, sense of humor, vulnerabilities, all that you loved about them— mind, body, and soul."

This seemed to me a very obvious layer.

"The second layer you miss is the *version of yourself* that this person brought out of you—into the relationship, and the world. When your relationship died, so did a part of you. And your world. Usually, we feel complicated about this past self. We see the good characteristics the relationship brought out in us, but also mistakes we made."

To put it lightly, I thought.

"And the third layer is *the time in your life that this person represents to you*. You are mourning the time period filled with memories of Sera. She was a massive part of your life for over a decade. You're processing deep, complex loss. But we're going to work through it, together."

She jotted more notes and fiddled with an arm of her glasses.

"Now, to begin with genuine healing, I'm going to suggest something that might sound counterproductive."

I readjusted myself in the seat. I guessed we might be in for some *peeling*.

"Rather than harping on the end-goal of moving on—I want you to focus, for now, on *leaning in*, to the longing you feel for Sera. Rather than stuffing your feelings down, or pretending like they aren't there—I want you to invite these thoughts to the surface. Sit with them. See what they have to say to you."

This was getting a little *woo-woo*, but I supposed I was tracking. I didn't know if I loved it, but I thought I was willing to try. "So, like, pull out old love letters and watch our old favorite movies?"

"If you want to." She smiled. "I also love to say that the only way forward is *through*. Sometimes even backward, at first. Whatever helps you move through this, head-on, instead of skipping over your steps to genuine healing. We're doing surgery here, not slapping on a Band-Aid.

"And my question for you, Connor—to start—is this. Which of these three layers resonates most with you? Take a second. The person, the version of you, or the time period?"

I didn't need a second. I missed Sera. The human. I missed her so much. The end of us was a mess. There would never be doubt. But even with her shadowy moods and words that could bite me like teeth, I missed her. I missed her brain, her body, her heart.

"The person. I miss *her*. The things I fell in love with and the things that drove me insane. I miss the person." *I also think maybe I really hate being alone.*

"Okay, then," she said, edging forward, the faintest slack in her poise. "We will press into that. What do you think it would be like for you to tell me about how you met Sera, and the first things that drew you to her? The beginning of your relationship. What made you fall in love? Before we get to what fell apart."

My limbs tensed. I hadn't thought about those days in a very long time, and it might ache to dig them up. But there was almost nothing I wouldn't do to get rid of the anvil on my chest I still woke up to every day of my life.

"I can do that," I said, setting my coffee down on the matte-black pedestal table beside me. "I think I can do that."

. . .

Chapter

—— THREE ——

SERAPHINA

Less than punctual. Twice in one day. I threaded my car through the red beads of brake lights toward Haven, our favorite dinner spot. Monthly girls' night injected life into my veins, but the get-togethers were feeling harder to manage. Inspiration had avalanched that late afternoon, and I had to dump my thoughts into a blank-as-snow Word doc before they disappeared, or, I imagined, skated off to find someone else. Elizabeth Gilbert wrote about this in *Big Magic* and it had haunted me—productively—ever since. *Listen to your ideas when they come to visit you.* Otherwise, they will stop knocking, and run to find a more willing participant.

What a frightening thought.

So listen, I did.

My ideas usually knocked inconveniently, but I couldn't regret today's burst. I'd pored over The Bentley's existent marketing material and felt the corners of my mouth curl into a grin, like that villain at the Plaza Hotel in *Home Alone 2*, when he verifies Kevin McCallister's credit card is officially stolen.

Ahhhhhhh.

Trash! Well, maybe not trash, but the content was dated and dull, breeding ground for major upheaval. This was a prime opportunity for our team, for all of Hamilton. We could bring this historic property into a brand-new decade with the finesse of a deer and the speed of an Olympian skier. I'd popped in my AirPods and set to writing, snuggled down into Jackson Hole. I'd even brewed some peppermint tea. No one had interrupted me.

But then it was 6:15 p.m., and I was late to our ritual gathering.

Silently begging the traffic to flow, I rapped on my Volvo SUV steering wheel to the tune of Taylor Swift's song, "Lover." Romantic and indie with a sparkle of pop. I'd never see Taylor the same way since her new documentary, *Miss Americana*. Like most of the world, before that, I'd fixed her as a gangly, well-behaved country girl, no matter how many times she kept reinventing herself. Now? After hearing about her body image struggles, the cruelty she endured, the pressure to keep conforming? How she finally decided to become her own woman and use her own belting voice? I adored her more than ever. "I want to still have a sharp pen, and thin skin, and an open heart," I remembered her saying. *Amen.* Her music could still make me cry, but she also made me want to sign up for boxing.

My heels finally clicked up the glossy wood steps to our red velvet booth in the corner, the one for which we always waited, no matter how long. Our drinks already wreathed the oak table, their three goblets of deep red wine to my glass of Diet Coke. I hadn't had a real drink in some time.

How could I not swell with pride at the sight of these three, my best girls? My sister, Samantha, sat tall in the middle, her voluminous brown hair smoothly straightened down to her belly button, same brown eyes as Coco, flashing, but framed by dramatic faux lashes. She whipped heads everywhere that she went; she still turned even mine. That perfect face and her compact, curvy, muscular figure. She didn't see male therapy clients, simply because she didn't want to, but I'd always felt deep down like this was probably wise.

Red-haired Teagan and blonde-like-me Brynne flanked her now, like the bad devil and good angel in the old-fashioned cartoons, each whispering over a shoulder. As I grew closer, I noticed they were all staring deeply into Sam's phone, cupped in her hands like a prayer. They didn't even notice as I approached and squeezed into the booth in front of my soda.

"I'm so sorry I'm late!" I yelled above the thick jazzy music, snapping them to attention. Like a ninja, a black-suited waiter swooped in to drop down a grilled artichoke.

Teagan reached for a leaf, green eyes widening playfully. "Don't even worry. We're used to it."

"Oh, stop," said Sam, barely looking up from her screen. "We easily killed the last thirty minutes. I'm doing it, Ser. I'm taking the dating app plunge."

My stomach squeezed. She'd been my last gal standing. I waited a beat. "Sis! Are you serious?"

"Yes. How else on earth am I supposed to meet anyone? I'm always working, or watching Coco, or going to yoga. And three yoga date strikes? I'm *out*."

"What about Dominic?" He'd seemed promising. Spiritual. Kind. Employed. I reached for my own artichoke leaf. We were leaping right to the good stuff.

"Dominic was amazing. You don't meet a lot of finance guys doing yoga. But he left for business in Singapore. For a month. No thanks! Did you see how pretty the girls in *Crazy Rich Asians* were? He'll meet someone new in five seconds."

"Have you seen how pretty *you* are?" Brynne chastised.

"Thank you, Brynne," I said, looking to Sam. I hated when she couldn't see what we did. "So you're really doing this? Which app?"

"*Apps,*" corrected Teagan, scooping her leaf into the dipping sauce.

"Yes, it's all about casting a wide net," said Brynne. "Didn't Jesus say something like that?"

"Yep—'I will make you fishers of men,'" said Sam. "'*If you follow me.*' He was so ahead of his time."

"Just don't say you're going on Tapp," I begged. "*Pleeeease* don't say you're going on Tapp."

They exchanged the glances of three scoundrels deep in cahoots.

"*It's not that bad,*" they all insisted, at various volumes, with different words, more or less in plain unison.

"It used to be a hookup app, but it's not like that anymore!"

"My friend met her husband on Tapp!"

"It gives you the most matches per day and has the highest success rate worldwide!"

"You guys," I groaned. "Douche city! It's like a human vending machine. I can't. What about the one where the girl has control? Crumb? I love their marketing. Where your matches are cookies, your convos are crumbs—I mean, maybe it's supposed to be suggestive, but I'd like to think it's just cute and totally brilliant."

"Oh, it's one hundred percent suggestive," confirmed Sam. "Also brilliant. And adorable. I'm totally doing Crumb."

Extending her slender wrist, Brynne pried away Sam's phone. "She's also doing MatchMate, the original dinosaur. I'm making her. People think it's dorky, but I've been on some incredible Match dates. The guys *always* pay for dinner and they *don't* always try to sleep with you on the first date."

"Totally," nodded Teagan. "And their commercials? Come on. It's like those couples were made for each other in an honest-to-God Cupid factory."

Brynne swiped her oval manicured finger through the dating section of the app store. She looked so fierce in red lipstick, our resident dating pro. "Forever31 is another one hot on the scene. You have to be at least thirty-one."

"I bet the men *love that*." I rolled my eyes.

"I'm so sad Forever 21 filed for bankruptcy," Sam sighed. "Like, I'm actually grieving. I got this top there."

"Sam, I wish you would try the new app," Teagan begged. She worked in tech recruiting and stayed up on all things Silicon Valley. It made sense she'd have an opinion, and know about a new app. "It's the fastest-growing dating app in the U.S. right now. A bit more elite, but already up to 10 million users in only six months."

"It. Has. No. Pictures." Sam enunciated every syllable with a pop. "What kind of lunatic would sign up for a dating app without any physical evidence of the goods?"

My ears pricked. *Interesting.*

You know what? I would. *I totally would.* Along with 10 million other people, apparently. It was the swiping and tapping "hot or not" vibe of the virtual human buffet that made me want to bury my head in our backyard sandbox—not the inherent idea of online matchmaking. It could, in theory, be sort of mysterious and romantic.

"What's this?" I interjected, stabbing the artichoke heart we'd uncovered in record time. "Is this a real thing? A dating app. With no pictures? Like a chat room from the 90s?"

"I mean, things about it are old-timey, yes," explained Teagan. "You have to take an in-depth, 150-question personality test. And you have the option to include basic physical attributes, like eye color, hair color, height, weight. It also matches you by Enneagram number and Meyers-Briggs type. Such a time saver! It's all a step in the right direction, I think. Believe it or not, some people are fed up with swipe culture."

"Wait," Brynne said, waving a pretty, honey-colored hand in the air. Her regular spray tans served her so well. My own hands always ended up looking like the salon had given me leprosy. "This has been done before. I've heard of this. There have been a few of these apps along the way. They never last. The people want pictures!"

"It has been done," confirmed Teagan, swirling her wine in its glass. "But those apps failed because they didn't have the capital, they didn't have the marketing genius, and they didn't have *Piper Maddock.*"

Piper Maddock. *Wait, what?*

"Piper Maddock," I repeated. "Blonde? Beautiful? *Forefront Magazine?*"

"Yep," said Sam. "I don't want to use her app, but I wouldn't mind, you know, *being her.* Girl crush of the moment for sure. I think she's already worth $500 million. Dominic told me about her. She's twenty-eight and straight killing it."

That Beckham. Rascal. He knew how much I hated dating apps, mostly because of him.

I ruminated on this new information along with my bite of the heart.

"What's it called?" I asked Teagan. "Her app."

"*Blinde.* With an *e.* Which is both the archaic spelling of blind *and* slang among the youngsters for totally hot. It's genius. Gold. We need our million-dollar idea, you guys."

"Let's order," said Brynne. "But first, cheers! To Sam. And to Tapp, and Crumb, and ... ugh, these are hard to keep track of."

"MatchMate," Sam deadpanned, smiling, in mostly pretend agitation.

"And to Blinde!" said Teagan. "I'd do it in one hot second if I weren't engaged."

"Cheers!"

We clinked. We ordered. We caught up on work, and love. I told them about the new hotel property, for which they bought me a walnut-fudge brownie and lied to the waiter that it was my birthday. They assured me they'd help with Coco, if needed, while I had to be gone.

We talked about Teagan's wedding this summer—in Napa,

our gold, sequined dresses, her tulle waterfall gown with the pearled bodice, the contrast of texture and shine. We swooned about Ryan, her dreamy fiancé, who had been one of her tech placements, now the young CFO of a software company. Now one of the best guys we knew.

We spoke in hushed tones about whether or not she should invite Connor to the wedding, and I said no, I didn't think so, even though we all met in college. It was time to start loosening ties, even if I wasn't the best at actually cutting them. If you tied the knot, after all, maybe there could be some untying over a time period.

But dang it, I'd need a date, for this twinkly soiree in wine country. I didn't want to face it alone.

A final thought flickered and flashed as I pulled into my Newport Beach driveway. *I love this white farmhouse.* The picket fence, the pink rose beds, the black-shuttered windows and turquoise Dutch door. I'd do anything to keep it for us.

My sister, of all people, my level-headed, unwavering *therapister*, as I called her, had changed her mind about dating apps.

I wondered if I could change, too.

If only for one hot wedding date.

. . .

"Thank you, Mom," I said, scurrying into my kitchen. "*Thank you.* I hate not putting her to bed, but I know she isn't complaining." Our kitchen was bright white and steel gray, marble herringbone backing the Viking stove, the oversized island glittering with veined frosty quartz. The room made me thrill about cooking exciting new dinners. *Almost.*

Coco adored my mother, as did most people. She was hard not to love, even if things had splintered between us for a while after Connor had left. I knew she was hurting, too, but I had needed my space. She was endlessly giving, with the patience of a preschool teacher and the listening ear of a priest. She also had the dream marriage, approaching four decades of union. I might never admit to my mother the deep shame this alone caused me: my failure within our family, my breaking of our deep and abiding lineage of eternal love. I knew she and my dad still shed tears over my divorce. But she was becoming better, slowly, at not constantly bringing it up. Everybody was happier when we stuck with safer topics. Even tough ones like Coco.

"How was she tonight?" I asked.

Swiveling off the barstool, my mom carried her empty tea mug from the island to my porcelain sink. She and my sister had the same hair, hers still luscious at sixty. She remained a striking brunette who only barely had to touch up her grays and needed no cosmetic upgrades to her ageless face. She could pass for forty-five, easy. *Would not mind getting those genes, God.* She moved with such elegance, even in camo loungewear and trendy white tennis shoes she'd learned about from a blogger. *Glamma,* she liked to call herself, although it had yet to stick. *Gramma* it was, for now.

She was meticulously over-rinsing that cup. One of her classic tells.

I sighed. "What is it, Mom? Did she have one of her episodes?"

She turned around, brown eyes glistening, framed by faint lines and light. "I know you tell me about them, but—it's another thing to see them, Sera. We were going out to play and we couldn't find the right socks. They all hurt her or scratched her and … she lost her mind. I couldn't control her. I had to pin her down like it was a wrestling match. We were both crying. I'm—"

"Oh, Mom." I walked over, took her mug, and pulled her into a hug. "Don't cry. I'm so sorry. I shouldn't break our routine right now. We're working on it, with the therapist. Did she calm down?"

"Yes. Eventually I told her to *color her feelings*, like you said. The picture is there, on the fridge, if you want to see it. I'm always happy to help, you know that. She needs me. She needs *stability*."

That word. It stung me with shame. *No more girls' nights, for a while.*

"I'm trying, Mom. I'm trying so hard."

"I know." She wiped at her eyes. "Did you girls have fun? How's Sam?"

"Oh, she's the best. As usual. We had a ball. I felt twenty-five again. For an hour."

"You're a good mom, Sera. I'm proud of you."

I sighed. I knew I'd lost her pride in me a long time ago. I caught myself before blurting out the news of my trip to Jackson Hole. I wanted to tell Connor first, tomorrow. "Thanks, Mom. I couldn't do this without you."

"Oh, she also had some glitter stuck to her face? Just a few speckles, but they were on good. I think I got it all."

But of course! "Yes. We had a *morning*." I didn't need to say more. They'd had an *afternoon*, too.

I glanced over to Coco's drawing, a black tree dotted with ruby fruits. The sky was dark gray and etched with more black: angry birds, maybe, or rain. All of her sad and mad colors. I'd take it to my next session with Linda, our therapist.

"Tomorrow, as usual? I'll pick her up, meet you here at six?" My mom scooped up her Louis Vuitton Neverfull tote, always brimming with kid loot, always squeezing my heart.

"Yes. You're the best, Mom. Thank you so much for the extra help tonight."

I guided her to the door. We had settled into a schedule. I had Coco every Sunday evening to Thursday—then Connor had her every Friday, Saturday, and Sunday. Mondays and Wednesdays, I picked up Coco from all-day preschool on my way home from work. Today had been an exception. Tuesdays, Gramma picked her up early and they came to play at our house until six. Connor picked up Coco from all-day school every Thursday and brought her back Sunday evening.

Lather, rinse, repeat. My new divorcée tango. Things could be better, for sure.

They could also be worse.

After melting my own rainbow of feelings down the drain with a steaming shower, I slinked into bed wearing my new red silk pajamas. I was trying new things, when I remembered. I also tried my best to inch slightly toward the bed's center as I let go of the day. I was still hugging the left side hard, during most nights, naps, and mornings.

I reached for the book on my nightstand, *The Highly Sensitive Child: Helping our Children Thrive When the World Overwhelms Them.* The introduction alone had been revolutionary for me. Coco was not on the autism spectrum, as I had long thought. But there was an explanation for her fits, her persistence, her screams, her innermost craving of order. There were other kids like her. There was science and kindness and truth, answers to hold like a rare baby bird. Coco's brain sparked more brightly to stimuli than those of her four-year-old peers. She needed structure. She craved understanding. She absorbed emotions into her bloodstream until they curdled into a shriek—or bubbled into acts of pure graciousness that left adults on their knees.

To have an exceptional child, you must be willing to have an exceptional child.[1]

It had become my motherhood mantra. Coco pushed me to the very end of myself. Connor saw her like no one else did; he just saw her so much less now.

When I finished my chapter, I shut the book and reached down into my briefcase, which I always brought up to bed. *Old habits.* Sloth-like change. I remembered one remnant of the day, still scratching at the corners of my curiosity.

I curled up and flipped to page thirty-nine.

BLINDE AMBITION

With her revolutionary app, Blinde, Piper Maddock is single-handedly bucking the swipe-driven dating culture defined by tech-thirsty millennials. Founded on the belief that what we have to say, as humans, as connectors, as beings, will always be most important, as well as most reflective of our true selves, Maddock delivers a platform focused on the foundation of the original love note—on the foundation of the original world.

She brings us back to words.

Headquartered in Downtown Los Angeles with 50+ employees and growing, Maddock and her passion project have risen quickly to business fame and considerable fortune. The Yale alumna earned her Bachelor of Arts in Comparative Literature and her MBA from Dartmouth.

By charging a flat fee of $100 per user plus $9.99 per month, she keeps member investment high and her cash flow higher. The elite nature of the app is luring savvy daters in droves—and already proving to forge lasting relationships. High-powered professionals ages 25-42 with no time or interest in tapping through hundreds of photos during their days are instead focusing sharply on their 25 Blinde matches per week.

"If that's enough contestants for a whole *Bachelor* season, that's enough matches for users in a single week," says Maddock, a longtime fan of the ABC show and self-proclaimed hopeless romantic. "This is not a hookup app. But it's not a sappy soulmate app, either. This is for smart, young, vital leaders at the peak of their game, firing on all cylinders—who want to get the best return on their every deposit into the dating space. And from their every word."

Maddock frequently cites the psychological impact of swipe-culture on humankind, its numbing effects on our vision and pleasure sensors, the long-term emotional and physical anesthetization of having strings of romantic partners and infinite casual sex. Internationally acclaimed psychotherapist, love addiction expert, and TED Talk regular Esme Dayton has partnered with Maddock and will join her on her first speaking tour, scheduled for late next year.

"What if," Maddock challenges: "The greatest love is actually blind?"

I reached for my phone. I opened the app store. I found the hot-pink and white icon.

Get.

Install.

Tomorrow was a new dawn.

. . .

— FOUR —

CONNOR

I couldn't tell you the name of our exact location, but it was April 2005. A yellow bus shuttled us to the darkly glamourous party venue on a somewhat shady side street in Santa Monica.

"Hollaback Girl" boomed in the lofted space lined in sumptuous black leather booths and adorned with two open bars. The wallpaper was bold, geometric. The stench was bold, alcoholic.

I'd never get used to this scene. I already needed a breather.

I snaked my way through the dance floor, a pulsing mass of sorority girls and their dates decked out for the extravagant party's theme, "Used to Be Cool." *Dress up as something that used to be cool.* I loved it. As a senior, I'd been to my share of sorority events—the formals, the semi-formals, the disco and the 80s, and my least favorite, the Rubik's Cube theme, where you showed up wearing six different colors, and swapped clothing items with other party guests until you were monochromatic. The game didn't need to be raunchy, but it always was. Two hundred college kids with extra license to take off their clothes?

Why did I sound like a grandpa?

I scanned the booths. Most were full of their own mini-parties and drinking games, while others I didn't want to look at directly, for fear of losing my eyesight. Plenty of actual foreplay was unfolding on top of the cushions, right there in the party blacklights. *Gah.*

I was a grandpa alright.

I guess I could've dressed up as mine—but he'd never stopped being cool.

Then I spotted it. One booth, on the end, occupied solely by a little blonde elf, staring into the dark. She was alone, but not awkwardly so. She looked comfortable—*and pretty*, I saw, getting closer.

I had to scream over the bass even when I stood two feet from her. I leaned to her level. "CAN I JOIN YOU HERE?"

She looked up at me, an easy smile tugging on the corners of her full mouth, her natural pout shining red. It was too dark to see her eye color, but they were open and bright, and it didn't matter. She was something; that was clear. If this was Christmas in April, I wanted in.

I self-consciously remembered my costume.

Definitely should've dressed like Ole Gramps.

"OF COURSE!" she shouted back, scooching further back into the booth, scanning me up and down.

I sidled in next to her, into the alcove, where it was quieter and farther away from the mayhem. I no longer had to scream. "I'm Connor," I said, extending my hand.

As I did, as if on cue, a small purple bear fell from my wrist and straight into her lap.

"Oh!" She squealed, jolting, while I made it worse by reaching down for the bear and accidentally grabbing the inside of her thigh. *Shoot.* I hadn't meant to. It's not something I would do. But, of course, part of me also loved the idea because it was such a *beautiful* thigh, which made me incredibly nervous, so I pulled my hand away way too fast, as if she were radioactive.

Good Lord. Forget the bear. *I should just leave.* Right now.

But then, the elf with the mermaid-blonde hair to her waist started laughing. Hysterically. *Cackling.* Oh my gosh, this girl was losing it. She wiped underneath her eyes, blackened artfully with sparkles and smoke. "You're—" she wheezed. "Oh my gosh, you are BEANIE BABIES!"

I looked down to the ten pounds of bean-stuffed animals dripping from my whole body, Velcroed to every last crevice of my Adidas sweat suit and weighing on my every limb. *Yep.* I was Beanie Babies, all right. And I'd felt true pride at the costume until this encounter with Miss Sexy North Pole—who was very much still howling at my expense.

"You got me!" I said, hands up. "Don't tell my sister. I raided her collection. She once waited for a total of—at least 200 hours in line at the mall for these."

Her roars settled into a giggle. "I'm obsessed. I was probably waiting in line with her. Wait!" She stooped below the table and resurfaced, beholding the bear, eyes round. "This is the *Princess Di Collector's Bear.* You should not be wearing this here. I'm holding onto it for you."

"Keep it," I said, happy with her reply. "Sis is on the East Coast. What she doesn't know won't shatter her nostalgic heart into ten million pieces."

"Awww. Sweet. All mine!" To my amusement, she took the bear and shoved it into her party purse on a chain. "A memento. Of the worst night ever. I'm Seraphina."

I grabbed her hand and expected to feel actual lightning but instead felt the warmth of her skin, which was more like soft, balmy rain, and candied with apple-red nails. "What a pretty name."

"Thanks!" she said brightly. "I love it, too. But everyone calls me Sera. Or Santa, tonight."

Ahhhhhh, *Santa.* I studied her further. "You know who you could stunt-double for, this very second?" I observed. "Regina George in the Christmas talent show. Like ... *if I squint a little bit ...*"

Her smile spread. "You saw *Mean Girls?*"

"Of course. Sister, remember? She's eighteen months older than me. Plus, didn't everyone see *Mean Girls?* Already feels pretty iconic. Tina Fey, man."

"Right? She can literally do no wrong." She sighed. "But you know who can? Me. Santa is not so iconic to everyone, and I forgot this tonight."

"Huh?"

"My costume," she continued. "That's why tonight is so bad. I got set up for this one. And I didn't know that my date, a fraternity president, is the *president of the Jewish fraternity.* Absolutely no clue. I just thought, hey, Santa was cool when we were kids. Clever! *Haha!* But he got offended, and I don't blame him. And now I feel tone-deaf and totally awful that I embarrassed him. And I have to spend the rest of the night in this get-up, and I can't even take the first bus back because I'm on sober patrol."

For a girl who was, evidently, sober as ice, this Santa was awfully talkative.

And all I wanted was more.

"Don't be too hard on yourself." I shrugged, casually pressing down on my animals, apprehensive of shedding more of them. "How could you have possibly known?"

"Well, I could've done two seconds of recon when I learned his name." She sighed. "It's okay." She directed the point of her Santa cap to the dance floor. "I think he's doing just fine."

I saw the yellow Power Ranger making out with what could only be described as a Malibu Barbie. They did seem a perfect match, and it was absolutely my gain. *Go, go, Power Ranger.* "Yikes. I'm so sorry." *I wasn't.*

"So, Connor. I'm only a sophomore, but I haven't seen you around. Are you in a house?"

"Nope," I said. "Definitely not in a house. I'm actually here with my cousin. I know that sounds weird, but she said she needed the house points and had no one else to bring. She's also dancing with some other guy right now. But, you know, thankfully!"

"Well, aren't we two peas in a pod?" She laughed.

"Two beans in a baby?" I tried.

She wrinkled her nose, shaking her head. "You're funny, though. I like it. What's your major, Connor with the Jokes? Improv theater?"

"Close!" I shot back. "Pre-law. I was in the pre-law fraternity for a hot second, actually. But that was social suicide. Even worse than—dressing up as Santa for a date with the school's most popular Jewish boy."

"*Hey!*" she said, slugging my arm. But that smile was playing on her crimson lips again.

"What about you?" I asked. "Major?"

"Double major," she said. "PR and creative writing. I only wanted to study writing, but my dad says I need a backup plan. The infamous *backup plan*."

"What do you want to do? Write, safe to assume?"

"Yep!" she said. "Books. Articles. Narratives that matter, life-changing stories. Fiction, nonfiction, maybe poetry. Everything. I've wanted to be a writer since I was four."

"Well, sounds like you have it all figured out, Mrs. Claus." I hesitated. "You know, you're surprisingly down-to-earth. No offense, but—you don't really seem like the Delta Rho type."

"None taken," she said matter-of-factly. "Some of us are insufferable."

She was funny, and fast.

"*But,*" she went on, "some of us are also the best humans on earth, so don't cross one of my sisters, even the worst of us. Or I will have to hurt you."

I liked her loyalty and the rasp to her voice.

"I'm used to not blending in with them, though. I don't drink, for one." Her eyes narrowed above her sharp nose, splattered with the faintest of freckles, as if she'd revealed this information a hundred times and grown to anticipate the response.

"Me neither." I smiled, slipping closer to her. It was true;

I didn't drink. But I might have lied just then if it meant she might slip back.

"How come?" she asked, direct.

I raked my fingers through my hair, debating how honest to be, deciding to shoot straight for it. "Family reasons. My dad. It's destroyed his life and been pretty awful, so I personally have no interest. No judgment for any and everyone else, but—it's just not for me."

She smiled. *She slid to me.* Something intangible softened about her. Evidently, I'd passed, and it was better than acing a final.

"Me, too," she said. "My cousin. But also, I hate even saying this because it's complicated, but—I also have faith reasons. I'm waiting until I'm twenty-one anyway. Is that weird to you?"

Another test. Another certifiable straight shooter.

I studied her then, this spitfire Christmas decoration who had landed right in my lap—or, rather, I'd landed in hers. Her high cheekbones, the curve of her jaw, nails now drumming the table, maybe showing her nerves. But she still held my gaze in a lock.

Blue. Her eyes were cornflower, glittering blue, and she believed in something bigger than herself, like I did. I could feel it; I felt it then. I reached out to still her small hand. "Not weird," I said. "Not weird at all. I have faith reasons, too."

I felt the heat of her blush as she nodded, but she didn't flinch at my hand. "I love these girls so much. I love them to death. And I love having fun with them, but—I also love taking care of them." She paused. "I feel like they need me. You can't see it, but there's a lot of sadness in here."

I saw more than she knew; I didn't point out it was hard to miss.

"Speaking of which, gosh, *I'm so sorry.*" Startling, she gulped what was left of what I now assumed to be soda. She saw me staring. "Diet Coke. With grenadine. And watch, I can tie a knot in the cherry stem with my tongue!"

I knew she meant it playfully, but I gulped, and slowly, I watched.

"I have to go check the bathrooms." She held up her wrist, waving the yellow bracelet.

Sober patrol. *That's right.*

"It gets bad in there," she explained. "Lots of holding back beautiful hair, wiping tears over boys ..." Her voice trailed off. "Can I find you after?"

I nodded. "OF COURSE!" I screamed, exaggeratedly, stealing her intro line.

She grinned as I let her out, careful to keep my hands away from her thighs.

"I'll see you later," she promised. "*Beanie Babies.*"

She dropped the knotted stem on the table.

As I watched her saunter away, my winter dream in the middle of spring, there were three things I knew for sure about this girl with the face, the heart, and the wit. *Also the legs,* I noticed, as she evaporated into the crowd.

I needed to hear that laugh again.

I'd read anything she'd ever write.

And from that night forward, in my book forever, Santa would always.

Always.

Be cool.

. . .

What would those kids say back then, I wondered, the nine-teen- and twenty-two-year-olds meeting, flirting, so sweetly sharing parts of themselves with each other in the middle of one wild rumpus? What if they knew they were already falling in love? What if they knew they'd be swept up so quickly into each other that, within weeks, they wouldn't care to know where one of them ended and where the other began?

What if they knew they'd be boyfriend and girlfriend within a month, that they'd stay together the following year while he went to UCLA for law school, seeing each other on weekends and every single Tuesday night, for creative dates, for fancy dates, for nights eating pho and ice cream sandwiches while debating the fate of the world in his grungy Westwood apartment? What if he knew that those full lips really did taste like cherries, because of her loyalty to original Chapstick, that he'd never get enough of them, that he'd eventually be the only guy lucky enough to reach between those beautiful thighs? That one day he'd wake up and know unequivocally that he'd do anything in the universe to keep this goddess with the unusual name and get a lifetime of imperfect bliss with her?

What if they knew that the alcohol they both feared and avoided would kill the boy's father in his 2L year of law school, sending him spinning and barely finishing that semester, with only the girl to pick up the pieces and remind him he could go on, *he really could*, that he could pave a new way? That he could go into estate-planning law and help families leave a real legacy, unlike his own father's trail of poison?

What if they knew he'd propose later that year, her last of college interning at a magazine? That she'd cry like a baby while saying *yes* to the small purple bear with a two-carat oval diamond ring pushed snugly up one of its arms, with a hand-scrawled note around the neck that said, "Marry me, Ser. Be my princess. Every day is Christmas with you. Be my Santa forever. I love you. *I love you.*"

What if they knew they'd start to bicker when money got tight? What if they knew they'd have a hard time keeping their groove in the bedroom, that waiting for sex until marriage didn't guarantee sensual rapture and definitely not expertise?

What if they knew, somehow, about all the miscarried babies? What if they knew that she would start drinking, secretly? What if they knew she'd find his web browser riddled with plumped up, plastic brunettes, naked and pouting and bare, images she'd never shake, that would shatter her heart and her self-esteem?

What if they knew that their love of the ages would start to fracture apart, with the faintest of invisible cracks, that would split, then widen ...

... and break?

What if. What if.

What if.

"You're quiet," said Janine, still as a Monet cathedral, with no less nuance and depth. "Was that painful for you? To recount all of that? To tell me about your history with Sera?"

Obviously, it was terrible. I was done for the day. I started to squirm and avoided her stare. "Yeah. It was. It is. And seems our hour is up."

"Connor." She closed her pad, flooded with notes. "This is healthy. It's part of the process. You've been stuffing all of this down. This week, I want you to release your emotion. Process. Cry. Run. And I want you to do something else."

"What's that?"

"You feel a great sense of responsibility for your marriage failing, yes?"

I nodded to my new queen of the understatements.

"I want you to write Sera a letter. A heartfelt, uncensored letter you know she will never read. Writing is one of the most therapeutic tools we have. I think you'll be surprised at what you see on the page. Apologize for the times you know responsibility falls on your shoulders. You can read it to me next week. We can rip it up if you want, as a symbol of your moving on. A lot of my clients find this a very powerful step. It sounds like you've forgiven Sera for her part in things, yes? You don't seem to be bitter, from where I'm sitting."

I shook my head. I didn't need a law degree to tell me we'd still be married if it weren't for me.

"I think," she said, "that a big step in your healing is going to be forgiving yourself."

Well. A guy could dream. I grabbed my empty cup of coffee and stood. "Thanks," I said. "This is harder than I thought it would be. But I guess it's probably good."

"You're a good man, Connor," she said. "And yes—this is good. *Really* good."

. . .

Chapter

— FIVE —

SERAPHINA

"Mommy, can you stop singing so loud?"

I peered into the rearview mirror at Coco and saw her brown eyes staring back, judging me.

"Aw, but I love this song!" *Did I ever.* I wondered if she had noticed how many times her mom had insisted on looping these lyrics from "The Next Right Thing" since *Frozen 2* had hit theaters. That movie. That scene! The soundtrack, the whole sweeping story. I understood Elsa more of the two, but I'd needed Anna's strength lately.

And we both needed her *stability.*

Coco clutched her backpack, which was dazzled with sequin unicorns. "Can you play 'Into the Unknown' again?"

Also on theme. I obliged, glancing out the window to the final blur of lush ficus trees before we'd pull into her preschool.

"So, baby," I began, anxious as always when bringing up one of her tantrums. "Gramma said you got pretty upset yesterday. About your socks?"

"I never have comfy socks," she stated, all business. "The line on my toes twists around, and the material scratches me.

Can't you buy me more socks?"

Engage. Attune. Acknowledge. Empathize. Don't roll your eyes. Don't lose your mind. "Of course, I can. I'll take you shopping. You can pick them out. Does that sound good? That must have been so *frustrating*, being so excited to play and then *not being able to find any socks.*"

She turned her head, slowly, pulling a strand of golden hair to her mouth, one of her habits. She nodded.

"And the next time you're feeling *really, really, really* mad? What can you do instead of yelling at Gramma, or me, or Daddy?"

"I never yell at Daddy."

I winced. "Okay. With me or Gramma, then?"

She sighed. "I can go to my calm-down place and play with my calm-down things." Her lofted bed, fluffy with pillows, had been made into her own special hideaway, per Linda's recommendation. Most of the time, I was shocked by how well it worked: ten minutes up there was like alchemy. For these "times away" (the phrase "time out" was supposedly more "likely to trigger shame") we had a bucket of sensory toys and gadgets for anxious children. Slinkies, squishy toys, an hourglass, spinning balls, kinetic sand, and a Rubik's Cube. Oh, that impossible Rubik's Cube. I always flashed back to college, and invites, and Connor. *Sigh.*

"Yep!" I said. "And you can take your deep breaths. And Gramma and I can both squeeze your hands, the way you like. Also, you did a great job coloring your feelings. I loved your black tree."

I knew when I was overdoing it, slathering it on thick as

frosting. Grabbing every tip and tool and method known for parenting sensitive children, desperate to cover the bases for my baby and her skyscraper highs, her outrageous lows, her feelings the size of an ocean with the density of a barge.

I just didn't want to miss anything. I couldn't. *I wouldn't.* I couldn't bear the thought of not preparing her for the world, in her thinner-than-average skin, with her bigger-than-average heart. I would never stop doing everything in my power to help her understand the way her mind and body worked in tandem— and to help me understand, too. Linda was changing our lives.

Sensitivity isn't a weakness, Sera. Sensitivity is her superpower.

I pulled into the carpool line, inching my navy-blue Volvo between a boxy black Mercedes G Wagon and gleaming new silver Range Rover. Yes, it was a fancy preschool. We fit in, I supposed, but barely, by the skin of our zip code. The steep tuition was another reason I'd needed to go back to work. We weren't about to yank Coco out now, in the middle of an Arendelle ice storm.

"I love you, Coco. I know things are new, but you are being so brave. Your mommy and daddy are so proud of you."

She unbuckled and leaned forward to peck a kiss on my cheek. "I love you, Mommy." She pulled back, shy, in a pause. "Do you think you could tell Daddy to make me a calm-down place? I don't get mad. But my feelings sometimes feel really big at his house."

"Of course." I returned her kiss, my throat tight, quietly pulling the piece of hair from her lips. "I'll tell him. Have a great day, Coco Bean."

I watched her skip to her cherished swings. She liked the rhythm, the swoosh. I understood how it soothed her.

I swiped at my eyes as they blurred, flicking back to my favorite ballad. I wound to the 405 freeway.

As I drove to the comforting boom of Kristen Bell's voice, I suddenly saw myself three years ago; nestled into the coziest corner of our dove-gray Pottery Barn sectional, Coco sleeping upstairs, Connor working late at the firm. Without knowing it yet, I had grown adept at hiding expertly from myself and my grief. And this particular night I remembered with clarity. I could revisit the pain of that second loss, as if I were in the room, right there inside of another reminder that this body, my body, would never, *ever*, be good enough. Not enough to hold life, not enough for my husband—some days, barely enough to go on.

The clock chimed 11 p.m. as my eyes glazed over to my fourth consecutive episode of *Pretty Little Liars* and as many glasses of wine. Sparkly things that lessened the pain, before my vision went black.

Pretty. *Fun!* Scary.

It was hard to tell what was true anymore.

I heard Connor's key in the lock and my whole body perked, as it usually did, right through my zoned-out sludge. You could feel Connor's goodness coming into the room, any room. But he was gone so often these days, buried in his new firm. I was getting less and less of him.

"Hi, babe," he said softly, walking straight to me, hunching over the back of the couch. I knew he could smell the wine, and also knew how much it hurt him, the drinking. He hadn't taken a sip since his father's death more than a decade ago. I never used to drink either, but lately my edges needed softening in order for me to breathe. It only scared me a little that I was hurting too deeply to notice anyone else.

Except Coco.

My precious Coco.

Gently, Connor pulled back my greasy hair and wrapped me up from behind. "I missed you girls today. How are you feeling?"

"Fine," I said, voice hard, eyes forward, determined to ignore the tenderness of his gestures. But his kiss on the top of my head tightened my whole throat into a knot.

I shut my eyes as his soft lips pressed into my cheek. I felt them move to the side of my neck. Instinct and memory took over me, inciting a pleasurable heat in my stomach. I could still smell his John Varvatos cologne from the morning.

Then a sob almost escaped me, and I flinched. *I flinched.* And he jerked back, like he had kissed fire.

"Sorry," I said. "I'm just tired."

"Come up with me then?" he asked. His brown eyes were so tired, and sad, pleading with me to engage.

"Sure. I'll be right behind you."

I wouldn't be right behind him, though, and both of us knew it. I'd grip the remote for two more episodes, wondering if we'd ever find out who the killer was, dazedly drinking in my wine, and the fashion, the scandal, the hair.

When I clicked off the screen and the room went dark, I'd feel the hot tears on my cheeks. I would hate that I didn't know how to talk to my best friend anymore. I would hate how hard he was trying, and myself for shutting him out. I would hate that my body still felt too broken to picture myself having sex, let alone remembering how to enjoy it. I would hate that I still sometimes flashed back to screenshots of women I'd never be, nimble and fertile and young. The kind of girls that surely, deep down, my husband would take over me if he could. *How could he have betrayed me like that?* So many uncountable times.

Unbelievably, that night, that season, wasn't even my low point. I still hadn't faced my biggest heartbreak; I wouldn't until a year later. It was a brutal blur of a year, full of park playdates and managing Coco and my friends announcing new pregnancies. I was a zombie mom, but I kept my smile bright. No one seemed to notice when it would tighten.

When my rock bottom came, finally, I had to face that I couldn't hide anymore. Not from the mirror, not from anything. I saw myself, and it broke me. It was the darkest time in my life. I saw that I was pouring alcohol into my holes attempting to fill them, to ease my pain and anxiety—which worked, sometimes, for a breath.

But as time went on, and I was gasping harder for air, I knew I was pouring gasoline onto the flame. I looked up, by God's grace. I told Sam how bad things had spiraled. She helped me find my sweet Linda. I came back to life, one step at a time, after more pain than I knew I could handle. I had to. For Coco. *For me.* My deepest low was what I needed to rise, and rise, I did, one step at a time. I felt a greater strength carry me.

By the time I was ready to *fix things*, though, I'd lost Connor completely. He didn't survive our final rip of the windstorm. He had checked out. *All gone.* He wouldn't go with me to therapy. He had stopped kissing my neck. I found another trail of Internet filth. He said he couldn't turn things around, that he could never promise to kick the habit completely, that he felt like he no longer knew me. Which, I suppose, he did not. How could he possibly know me when I was running so fast from us both? He'd been sleeping in the guest room for months. He said it was because of my nightmares.

Couldn't he have tried to hold me?

Did I give him the chance?

He said he thought it was best if we finally considered what it might look like for us to go separate ways.

We missed each other, two ghosts of our pain. Like ships in the night, as they say. He was willing to fight when I wasn't, and then the reverse became true. We were two sunny halves of a catamaran, who crashed irreparably into a hurricane.

That was then, this was now. I tried to let the memories arrive on their own terms, and wash over me, do their work—and then not look back anymore. Linda had encouraged me in this practice.

"The present is all we have," she said.

We were only going forward from here.

I understood Elsa more than Anna; I did. The hiding, the running, the refusing to let people love you. The sharpness of your own magic, or your own untamable tongue. Your thing, *the* thing, which doesn't have to be your undoing, but might, for a time, seem to be. I understood the power of sisters who see us, who save us from night, and ourselves.

Apparently it was as simple as finding "The Next Right Thing."

If you say so, Anna.

At the very least, I could try.

. . .

The morning's seventy-five-minute conference call, with almost as many people, snapped me out of my somber memories and into the rest of my day. The energy in the office was high. I ran some of my initial ideas for The Bentley by everyone on the call: our branding team and executives nationwide. Everyone loved what I pitched, and I was relieved. This was the project I needed, *right here, right now.* So good for my soul; I could feel it. I even started shopping online for my wintery wardrobe. I'd need some new outfits for Jackson Hole. Professional Snow Bunny, *please.*

When the virtual meeting ended after roughly twenty-five years, I thought I'd earned a few minutes. I hunkered down at my desk to finish my profile for Blinde. I pledged not to overthink it.

HAHA! Good. Luck.

Rate the following questions on a scale of 1-5,

from Strongly Disagree (1) to Strongly Agree (5):

1. Generally, I am adventurous and take risks.

Hmm. Usually I'd say two-ish—but I was taking this test, right? *Let's give this one a four.*

> **2. I am a true romantic at heart. I love grand gestures.**
> **I believe in soul mates.**

What was the number for "Used to Be?" Three seemed safe-ish. *Okay.*

> **3. I am extroverted.**
> **Time with other people recharges me and brings me to life.**

Yikes. *Hardest-core introvert ever to breathe, about to hit dating apps near you.* But I didn't want to be matched with antisocial weirdos, did I? Especially without visual evidence. Why don't we select *two*?

Forty-seven more questions, in this section alone? Okay, Piper Maddock. She was nothing if not comprehensive. But I was thankful she, or her product designers, had seen the need for a robust website to go with the app. My big screen and mouse at the office made it so much easier to hack through the questions—and appear like I was actually working.

Still, I needed more coffee. I stood up with my *Mom Est. 2015* mug as Beckham walked into my door.

"Morning, Sunshine," he chirped, bolting straight to my couch, bright-eyed and ready to chat. "Well, that call was a doozy. But you were fantastic."

Shoot. I panicked. I still had the website up, and he had a clear view of my screen from where he plopped down his fit little rear. Frantically I reached for the mouse. Why did the tiny red upper-left-corner circle for closing out of the browser have to be *so darn tiny*?

Too late.

"Is that what I think it is?" he gasped, gaping at my computer and promptly dashing to me and my desk. "Ser, you rascal! You weren't going to tell me? I knew you'd love it. And signing up already? I am *so proud* right now. I think my work here is done."

I rolled my eyes. "Only because I love the idea of connection through words—instead of nudes," I added pointedly. "And the idea of bucking the swipe culture that's ruining the world and commodifying women."

"Hey—men, too," he jeered. "You can trust me on that. But you're going to love it. It's so efficient. And fun. Girl, we're getting you back in the *game*! Let's see."

He scrolled back up to the portions I'd finished, details they'd use on the backend to match me. The app allowed no last names, to circumvent Internet stalking. It openly permitted fake names, but encouraged first and middle names to sustain a degree of authenticity:

Name: Sera Lorenn

Age: 33

Location: Newport Beach, California

Relationship Status: Divorced

Hair Color: Blonde

Eye Color: Blue

Height: 5'4"

Weight: 125 pounds

Enneagram Number: 2W3

Meyers-Briggs: ISFJ

"*Seraphina.* Stop. Just put single. You can explain later."

"What? No! I'd rather be up front if that's a deal breaker for someone."

"Trust me. You're single. Done."

"But *technically,* if divorced is an option, it's the more *accurate* choice."

"Semantics."

"Important ones!"

He groaned. "Whatever. Would you be more likely to reach out to guy who was single or divorced? Be honest."

Hmm. I wasn't sure. Maybe divorced. Especially if he was a dad. Truthfully, I didn't know yet. I tapped my pen to my forehead. "Well, you're the pro, Beck. If you truthfully think single is better … fine."

"Let me just—look at what else you have going on here."

Assuming ownership of my keyboard, he changed me to *single* and sorted through my responses. At the top, a key section still flashed blank—the big introductory bio. The sell. My *pick me, gentlemen!* paragraph. The 150 words I had, to tell five million men why they should want to strike up a conversation with me, sight unseen.

"This is important," he said. "You should sit on this for a couple days. Give it your sparkle. Run it by me. It has to be *good.* You're competing with Tapp chicks and their … you know. Body parts. Really smoking hot body parts."

Wonderful. *This was wonderful.* "Did you have to say that?" I groaned. "Okay. I'll email it to you for approval, Boss."

He stood. "What pushed you over the edge? Was it really the article?"

I continued to the door, craving caffeine in my veins. "My sister, actually. She's finally doing it, all the apps, and I figured, hey. If she's game, maybe I can be, too. Plus, I need a date for Teagan's wedding this summer. Better start now, I figure."

He'd heard one thing as we strode the hallway. "*Your sister.* That Sam. How is our goddess of mental health? More importantly, when are you going to let me take her out?"

"Oh, you know. When a place called hell turns to ice."

"Well, then, chop, chop. Let's get you there, Elsa," he poked. "Come on. Am I really that bad?"

"You are," I said. "I adore you and I'd do anything for you. But you are really that bad. I honestly shudder to think of you in the wild."

He didn't argue as he ducked into his office and I paused in my journey to our twelfth-floor café. "Someday," he promised, wiggling his eyebrows. "I'm going to surprise the socks off of you. I mean—not today. But someday. I will." He flashed a mischievous smile.

"Great! I never wear socks, anyway!" I yelled, shooting a grin right back as I walked away. I liked to razz him for all of his escapades, but I'd seen his heart of gold. I knew for a fact he'd surprise me, and also, that I wouldn't be that surprised.

But this was still true: he wasn't going anywhere near my sister until he sorted things out.

I filled my mug to the brim. I had more than enough new action items to tackle for our prized acquisition. For the rest of the day, I'd have to submerse myself in The Bentley.

As soon as I finished that bio.

. . .

> Orange County native, former housewife, looking for love after heartbreak!

Good Lord. *Delete, delete.*

> USC Trojan. I got in for real. HAHA! Also holding to it that the Hallmark Channel's Countdown to Christmas will never be the same without Aunt Becky. It's just so sad. Do you think she'll ever be back?!?

Mom jokes. Why couldn't I stop?

This was so much harder than writing for big hotels or in the privacy of my journals. What could I possibly say about myself, so briefly, that showcased some humor, suggested some depth, hinted at my small duffel of carry-on baggage and somehow made me seem hot?

I rubbed my temples. Before I could question myself, I fired an instant message to Beckham via Office Communicator:

Seraphina
S.O.S.

Beckham
Oh, gosh. What? I know the existing marketing is a disaster.

Seraphina
No. Not that. This Blinde bio. I sound … gosh, everything I wrote sounds so desperate and cheesy. Am I really back here?? I haven't dated since 2005.

Beckham
Your innocence is endearing. I promise.

Seraphina
It's not. But thank you for lying.

Soooooo: I have a question. Do you think there's any way you'd …

Beckham
Nope.

Seraphina
Pleeeeeease!

Beckham
I'm not writing your bio for you!

Seraphina
But you're the one who wanted me to do this! And you're the best writer I know!

Beckham
Stop flattering me to get in my pants.

Seraphina
Barf. And, WORK PORTAL. Come on, Beck!

Beckham
Wait. Are you saying ... you want something from me?

Seraphina
Yes! Desperately.

Beckham
What if I want something back?

Seraphina
Oh. Shoot.

Beckham
It's a deal. One date with your sister? And I draft your bio.

Seraphina
OMG. You're the worst.

Beckham
I know, right?!

Seraphina
What if she refuses?

Beckham
You really think I'm worried about that?

Seraphina
I repeat. YOU'RE THE WORST.

Beckham
I know, right?!

Seraphina
Fine. UGH. Fine, fine, fine. But I want it by tomorrow morning!

Beckham
I can do that. My Tapp date for tonight just cancelled so I am freeeee.

Seraphina
That's the last I want to hear about one of your dates until after you've gone out with Sam and she never wants to see you again.

Beckham
Great! I can't wait! And YOU: Get excited. Your profile is going to make Blinde men see again.

Seraphina
LOL. Uggggh. Thanks, Beck.

Beckham
You're welcome! My win! Now get back to work!

Sam was going to kill me. But I'd worry about that later. For now, I had one more thing to attend to before I could concentrate fully. I took deep breaths before I picked up my office phone and pressed Connor's number, familiar as my own, like half a piano duet that I could never forget.

Three rings and his voice filled my ear. I'd always loved his voice. Smooth like good espresso and just as buzzing to my system, for so many years.

"Hey, Ser," he answered, unreadable.

I hadn't decided yet how I felt about him continuing with my nickname, but now was not the time to address it. "Hi! How are you?"

"I'm fine. Same old, same old. You?" The distance between us grated painfully under my ribs. I didn't even know what his *same old* was anymore. Not really, anyway.

"Good—things are great! Hey, listen. I need to talk to you about something."

"Of course." His tone picked up slightly.

"Obviously, I have Coco during the week. Every week." I grabbed anxiously at a Hamilton notepad and started to doodle.

"Yep."

"And we promised we'd check with each other first if we had a conflict, to make sure she gets the most time possible with a parent." A mountain range took shape on my paper.

"Yes, I still like that plan."

"Well, a work trip came up—and I need to go to Jackson Hole, Wyoming, next month. For a week. We're acquiring a new hotel. Do you think—do you think you could take her for the whole week? My mom and sister can help."

He paused, but barely. "I don't see why not," he said. "I'd love the extra time with her. It's no problem."

That was too easy, I thought. I hesitated before launching my final cannonball. "There's one more thing," I continued. "It's … I feel horrible, but it's the week of her birthday. The one after President's Day. I have to miss her fifth birthday, Connor. I hate it, but I can't get out of this. Do you think you can help make it super special? I already started planning the party. It's going to kill me that I can't be there."

Now the silence. Now the guilt. Now the tension ripe with unspoken insults, insinuations, and anyone's guess what he really wanted to say.

But then. He surprised me, again. "You're working this job for her, right? You're doing a lot to keep things going smoothly for her. For us. Go, Ser. Really. Do you even remember your fifth birthday?"

I smiled. Of course, I did. It was the tea party out of a dreamscape. My mom had outdone herself. Handmade doilies, blueberry scones, my grandma's finest china set. A setting in my childhood living room, fit for the queen. I'd plan something just as fantastic for Coco. She would have me there, in spirit, and her own grandma in flesh and bone.

"Gosh, thank you," I said. "Thank you so much. I was expecting—I don't know. More pushback."

"I'm here for you guys. You know that." *There.* The slight edge. No one knew it like me.

No one hated it as much, either.

That scratching on my insides was there again. "I really appreciate it, Connor. Thank you. I'll talk to you soon?"

"Sure thing. Have a great day, Ser."

I caught myself before the reflexive "love you" bubbled its way to my lips. "Bye. You too. Thanks again."

I clicked down the phone with relief, but not three seconds later, it rang again. My heart sank. *It was too good to be real.* I snatched it up, crumpling my little mountain sketch. "Yeah?"

"Seraphina Jones?" a woman's voice sang.

"Yes!" I straightened up in my seat. "This is Sera. How can I help you?"

"This is Allie, assistant to Graham Hamilton."

The Graham Hamilton? The Heir? The Prince? The Socialite? *Were men called socialites, too?*

"Hi, Allie," I said, mustering all of my chill. "It's so nice to hear from you!"

"Yes. So, Mr. Hamilton would like to schedule a meeting with you."

What in the. Wait. "Me? Why?"

"To discuss The Bentley acquisition," she said. "He grew up vacationing at the property. It's a very big deal to him. You're leading the upcoming trip, yes?"

Of course. Beck had scheduled our meeting at the hotel in February, and surely Graham had been skeptical. I was not senior enough to be leading a trip of this caliber. Graham wanted to meet me first. I resented it, but I understood.

"Yes! I am. My boss can't come, so I'm taking the charge. Probably bringing an intern."

"Well, bring her to this meeting too, if you'd like. But let's get a lunch on the calendar. How's Thursday, at noon? Starfire at The Mirabelle? Does that work for you?"

Um, *yes*, that worked for me. It was only Hamilton's finest property on the West Coast, overlooking the cliffs of Laguna Beach. Lunch would cost half a mortgage. Two days from now was aggressive, but I knew I could rearrange anything else on my schedule. I also knew I had no choice. "Of course! I'll be there. Make it for three—I'll plan on bringing the intern, Sage."

"Fabulous. I'll send you the meeting request." *Click.*

Did that really just happen?

What did one wear for high lunch with a prince? I knew I'd be needing Beckham again. *Darn that date barter I'd made.* I was going to need it, but when Sam heard about it, I'd be a dead woman.

Sisterhood sure had been nice while it lasted.

• • •

Chapter

— SIX —

CONNOR

She was gorgeous, unflinchingly so, with long hair the color of onyx and the whitest teeth I'd ever seen. Her eyes were sharp, foxlike and amber green; her matte lips, heart-shaped and nude. Pink blushed her cheeks, subtly softening the severity of her look. She was maybe out of my league, but Sera had always been, too. I knew how to disarm people, or so I'd been told. I could only hope this trait still translated into my dating life after thirteen years out of the game.

Not that I was fully ready to date yet. To be honest, I wasn't close. Hence my budding relationship with Janine; I was working through plenty. But I'd gone out on a couple of dinners in the last year, setups that didn't go anywhere. Sera was always lurking in the back of my mind.

My law partner, Seth, had been bugging me for weeks to go out once with his cousin. *Just a blind date, no pressure!* Her name was Hailey, a dental hygienist. "I just have a feeling you two would hit it off," Seth said. "I have a great track record with setups!"

"Look at me." I had pulled up on my suit pants, socks

mismatching, in spite of myself. "What about me screams, 'Set me up with your super-hot, hip, young cousin'?"

"She went on *The Bachelor,* you know," Seth boasted, and I hated that this intrigued me. Not because it made her desirable, necessarily, but because I had *questions* for her. How much say did producers have on their picks? Did Chris Harrison have an anti-aging routine he was willing to share? What were the typical details of everyone's contracts? Sera had made me a superfan; I could admit it. "She's a good girl, Con," he continued. "She wants a good guy, and we both know you're one of the good ones."

Thus, here we sat at Puerto, one of the hottest spots to hit Orange County in years, famous for their edgy spin on Mexican street tacos. I'd made the reservation two weeks ago, so maybe my game could be worse. Bright reds and yellows colored the dining room, which featured an open kitchen. Succulent planters filled the perimeter; round lights draped from the industrial ceiling. The setting was perfect, and I relaxed. I even remembered to stave off my *Bachelor* inquiries until we'd exchanged basic facts.

"So, a dental hygienist," I started, diving straight for the chips. "Your teeth are incredibly white."

She laughed. "Crest Whitestrips! They're the best. Don't let anyone tell you otherwise."

I nodded, grateful, impressed. "That's valuable information. Thank you."

"You're welcome." She sipped her skinny margarita, puckering her lips around the salted rim. "So how old are you, Connor? Can I ask that?"

"Of course. Thirty-five. You?"

Her face betrayed no opinion as she flipped back her shiny hair, so black it was almost purple. "Twenty-seven."

Whoa. Younger than I thought. *Too young for me?* I wasn't sure, but I also had a great poker face. "So, we definitely weren't in high school together."

She shook her head, laughing. "Or at the same concerts."

"Yeah, nope. Unless you love Coldplay?"

"Who doesn't love Coldplay?"

Ding! Common ground. We continued digging into the chips, both loosening up with each crunch. I tried not to feel like this beautiful girl's nerdy uncle. She was awfully cool in her black leather jacket and so many gold, layered necklaces. We decidedly weren't in the same league. Maybe barely sharing the sport.

"So, I'm sure Seth told you I'm pretty recently single." I figured I'd save us the dance around the elephant that now followed me into every room. "And that I'm a dad, to the best four-year-old girl ever."

Again, no reaction, or at least not a flinch. "He did. I love that! I love kids. I used to be a nanny. Have you been dating much?"

"Ah. Not much. Is it that obvious?"

She laughed. "I didn't mean it like that. Just curious."

"What about you?" I asked. "Do you date a lot? I mean, I assume. You're so young. And so pretty. Sorry, don't mean that in a forward way, just—factually."

Seeming charmed, she leaned toward me, elbows on the table, cradling her pretty chin. "Factually, huh?"

Do not make a bad lawyer joke. Do not make a bad lawyer joke.

"Factually."

"Is that weird, to tell you about my dating while we're—*on a date?*" she whispered across the table conspiratorially, cupping one side of her mouth.

"I'm a dad." I shrugged. "I can handle it."

Her laughs were getting louder, a good sign, I guessed. "Okay then, yes—I do date a lot," she said. "Mostly dating apps. They're so efficient. Weed out the chaff, you know? Tapp isn't as sleazy as everyone thinks, and I love Crumb, with women calling the shots. But lately, I'm so into Blinde."

I pulled my sparkling water closer. "I've never heard of that one."

"Oh, it's amazing," she effused. "No pictures! It's pricey, but it draws a really great type of person. It's strict, like—you have to talk to people for a certain amount of time before you can exchange contact information. But I've met some really great people."

"Huh," I responded, intrigued, and not the slightest bit bothered by hearing all of this from my date. It felt like a brave new world. This was what had happened, apparently, while I married my college sweetheart, had a baby, and founded a law practice. People built apps. People joined apps. People dated multiple people at once and went out on dates and discussed their experiences with these apps. It seemed preposterous and strangely natural to me, all at once. "How much does it cost?"

"A hundred dollars, flat fee, plus ten bucks a month."

I nearly choked on my chip. "Holy guacamole!" *Can't take the dad out of the dad.* "That's steep."

"Can you put a price on connection though?" She smiled, and I was fairly certain I felt the toe of her boot brush my ankle under the table. My body started to buzz, and I pressed into the date.

We ordered every kind of taco you could imagine—ostrich, bacon, sweet potato and black bean, street corn, carnitas, shrimp. I learned more about dental hygiene than I could've bargained for, and Hailey learned more about trust funds. I discovered that Listerine strips were the key to fresh breath on the set of the *Bachelor* and that now she never left home without them.

Seth was right. Hailey was awesome. She was my type of girl.

But after our date, amazing by any measure, when I walked her to her black 4Runner, and hugged her, and smelled the coconut in her hair, and the Listerine on her lips, I felt myself pull away before I even stepped backward. Away from her poreless skin, her midnight hair, and the tiny flower tattoo on her chest that probably didn't show in her lab coat.

I felt how unready I was.

I felt how un-Sera *she* was.

I hated myself for all of it.

I kissed her on the cheek, and I backed away. "It was so great to meet you, Hailey."

I saw in her eyes that she knew. This young bright buck was the dating whizz, and I was clearly the old man. So old, *and so not ready*. I also saw that she didn't hold it against me.

"You too, Connor." She stood on her toes to peck back my scruffy cheek, which touched me more than she knew. "You're going to be just fine."

I watched her drive away and I pulled out my phone. One text, from Sera.

> Coco wants to play at Grace's house after school Friday. You OK getting her there?

> Of course. No problem. Xo.

Xo? What was that? All the therapy? All Hailey's hot, young energy? *What was I even doing?*

As I walked to my Audi wagon, replaying my conversations with Hailey, one topic kept resounding. I opened Google. I searched. I studied. I got to my car and read more.

Taking it slow. Testing the scene. Easing back in, sight unseen.

Before I even turned on the engine, I'd dropped one hundred bucks on a blind investment.

. . .

Turned out Blinde wasn't kidding around. I didn't yet have the energy required to set up a profile, much as I was intrigued. The founder was making millions, and really shaking things up. I was trying the app, no doubt. I was just *tapped* on dating tonight, pun completely intended.

My apartment wasn't far from the restaurant, off Jamboree in a high-rise. Coco had loved it at first, all the glass and mid-century furniture, the big flat screen, with Disney+, obviously. But lately she'd seemed more withdrawn here, and it was breaking my heart. I was having her room painted pink, because she had purple at home. One each of her favorite colors. Anything that might boost her joy, ease her spirit at Daddy's new place.

At my concrete kitchen island, fit for a bachelor, I poured myself some granola, a habit that had always irked Sera. She thought my late-night cereal was an affront to her cooking skills, but that simply wasn't the case. I loved everything she made.

I just also really loved cereal.

I took the bowl to my office and powered on my laptop. I answered a few pressing work emails. I logged into Instagram and clicked over to Sera's profile. I always figured she could never trace back my profile views to a desktop computer. It seemed safer somehow. I liked to check in now and then. Did it have to make me a creep? Didn't everyone look up their exes sometimes?

No new posts since last week: she and Coco ice skating, in leopard beanies and white puffer jackets, holding hands, wearing huge smiles.

"My best girl," read the caption.

Did Sera feel as hollow as I did when she thought of what we once had?

Did she feel the weight on her chest when she opened her eyes in the morning?

Her pictures didn't look like it, and they never failed to sting. Her golden hair billowed, sky eyes dancing as always. I was a masochist and I knew it. On the day there was another man in a picture, with either of them, I didn't know what I would do. *Somebody hold me back.*

My thoughts were spiraling, fast. I shut my eyes and reached for Janine's wise words. What had she suggested again?

The letter.

Yikes. Did I really have to write an *imaginary letter* to my ex-wife—who had *been* my wife for almost ten years? Then again, what did I know? Maybe it would pull me out of my panic loop. No one else would ever see it. *Right?* Maybe it could be "therapeutic."

I pulled up a fresh document and watched the cursor flash like a car blinker. *Which way are you going to turn?*

My fingers started to move.

And then delete, type, and delete again.

It wasn't going to happen.

I shut my computer and reached into my drawer for a legal notepad and pen. This was much more my style. I would write it out freehand, in cursive, like once upon a very long time ago, when I would write love notes to Sera.

Here went nothing.

I breathed.

Dear Ser:

Two words were as far as I got. Absolutely nothing would come.

I flipped open my laptop again and lazily opened Safari.

Search or enter a website name.

I sat there awhile in my bedroom's harrowing silence. I fingered my palms and then clenched my fists, feeling my hands get wet. I was so alone, *always alone* these days. No one would know, not a soul. And if they did, who cared now? No one at all, which made me weirdly sad, the accountability to no other. Of course, it was possible (extremely likely) that the government was spying on everything, which did cross my mind sometimes. But I highly doubted they cared. There were worse crises unfolding; there were worse hoodlums to catch. They were focused on the real criminals, not on the average, white, bored, divorced guy looking at some light porn.

Maybe just lingerie pics.

Probably not just lingerie pics.

Now the cursor couldn't keep up with my heart rate.

Which way are you going to turn?

To the burn, the hit, the release. To the moment outside of myself, the white-hot space beyond pain. That's where I was going to turn.

"Naked"

"Yoga"

Slam.

Sudden anger surged through my bloodstream, replacing the lust in my veins. *Anger, lust, lust, anger.* Sometimes they felt inextricable, one never far from the other. But now, my frustration felt coursing and primal in a way desire did not. I was mad at the Internet, mad at the divorce, mad at Sera, mad most of all with myself. Furious at the computer in front of me now, clicked shut tightly, still hot. I'd throw it if I didn't need it, if it wasn't so dang expensive. I was picking another lane—at least for tonight, I was. I didn't need to hit the pillow feeling any more emptied or tired than I already did.

Truthfully, finally, *maybe*, the habit was losing its shine. The girls, the lace, the skin of strangers, the daughters of somebody out there. In my fits of guilt, I thought of Coco, and fought the urge to throw up. *What if she knew what I did?*

Maybe I really could stop. Probably not, but maybe. We'd been facing off for a while. Maybe I did have it in me to kill the thing that had nailed my coffin shut; the thing that would never give back to me all of the precious things that it stole.

Feeling barely victorious, I grabbed my empty cereal bowl and padded my way to the kitchen as my phone vibrated next to the sink. My sister's name filled the screen.

Isla.

It was such a good name, like her. Cool as a river and wise as the day, she never yanked you around. She flowed, and carried you with her, and you always knew where you stood.

There would never be anything quite like your sister to unwittingly provide a cold shower. I brushed off the X-rated test I'd just passed. I couldn't pick up her call fast enough. I wanted to hear her voice. *The voice of someone who loved me.*

"Sister! Ah, I miss you. It's late. What's up?"

"Is it?" she asked. "I just got off a twelve-hour shift. I work another tomorrow, so I wanted to catch you. How are you? I miss you!"

"Eh," I said. She was an ER nurse with three young kids. I'd never known a harder worker, other than maybe me. I cherished every one of her calls. "I've been better. I had a date tonight."

"And?"

"She was young, gorgeous, and sweet. And I'm officially older than time."

"With sayings like that, you are."

"Do you realize what is happening with the dating apps these days?"

"You're such a grandpa."

I pressed in my wireless earbuds. "But I have AirPods. So, I'm not like a regular grandpa, I'm a *cool* grandpa."

"And who bought you those for Christmas? Oh, me. So, she was too young?"

I sighed. "Not too young, necessarily. I just feel so old. So *divorced*. And I think I'm still not over Sera. Maybe I'm just not ready."

"You haven't been together in over a year, brother. And it was bad way before that."

"I know." I hoisted myself onto a barstool. "This girl was stunning, and smart. She gave me hope for dating, actually." I thought of Blinde but wasn't ready to mention it. "It's a lot, though, you know? I haven't dated since college. Do people just sleep together on every first date now? Obviously, that's not my style. So, do we go and make out somewhere? My car? My place? I have no idea how this all works."

"I caught maybe two of those questions, bro."

"I'm venting. It's fine. Just pray for me. You're good at that."

I heard her smiling. "I am."

"How are the kids? Can we hang soon?"

"They're annoying, and amazing, as always. And yes! Maybe in a few weekends? With Coco?"

I mentally scanned my completely empty, always empty, totally blank weekend calendar. "Definitely. I'm open. Let me know and

I'll plan on it." I paused. "Have you talked to Sera at all?"

Now she paused. "I haven't, but—I also don't feel like I should talk to you about her, Con. And vice versa. I want to keep my friendship with her, but I don't want to be in the middle."

"But you have to tell me if she meets someone. Sister code."

"What about girl code?"

"Blood. Water. You're practically a doctor, so don't even tell me that you don't know which is thicker."

"*Fine*, fine. I'll tell you if she meets someone. But I'm not giving you details." I knew she was telling the truth. "It wouldn't be the worst thing, you know. You need to move on, little brother. Not today. But eventually."

"Tell me something I don't know."

"Okay! I will tell you that you might need some help with the ladies, but also, you're not that old."

"Thank you."

"And I love you. We all do. You're going to be okay."

Everyone seemed to think I needed to hear that today. "Yeah?" I asked, not hating it.

"One hundred percent. You're going to be great. I'll text you about getting together. See you soon. Okay?"

"Okay, sis. Love you."

· · ·

After scrubbing my face and brushing my teeth, and *moisturizing* (which I did now), I snapped off the lights and tucked into my queen-sized bed. It still felt so big, but I'd live. I was inching my way to the middle week after week. I felt better after

talking to Isla. I sifted through my mental archives for the scene
of a happy memory that could lull me into sound sleep.

I landed on the white-sand beach of the Paradaiso Hotel on
Hawaii's Big Island. *Paradaiso* meant *paradise* in Hawaiian.
Sera and I both loved the word and every inch of the resort.
It was the first time either of us had stepped onto a Hamilton
property, for our honeymoon, and the week Sera fixed in her
mind that she had to work for them someday. She kept collecting brochures and marveling over details of the mind-blowing
five-star experience.

"Everyone needs writers," she said. "I'm going to find out
who theirs are. I wonder if they're in-house employees or an
outside agency?"

She would work for a low-budget local lifestyle magazine
first, but she'd end up working for Hamilton. It felt like wild
serendipity that they were headquartered in her home county,
where the Hamilton family originated. I loved this about Sera's
spirit. She had a way of finding the open window into her dream,
after years of peering in as an outsider.

One afternoon, splayed like starfish on our sumptuous lounge
chairs on the hotel's main beach, we intermittently napped and
read and splashed, managing to keep our hands on each other
for most of it. Every half hour, a butler would saunter by with
a treat on a real silver platter.

"Mai tai popsicle, Mr. & Mrs.?"

"Ice-cold towelette, Mr. & Mrs.?"

"Cup of sunscreen, Mr. & Mrs.?"

"Is there anything at all we can do to enhance your afternoon

*or your life, you heavenly pictures of youth and love, Mr. &
Mrs. Honeymooners?"*

There would never be any getting used to such service.
Groggy from a long nap, I accepted a mini ice-blended mocha
and watched my sunbaked bride as she soaked in the tropical
heat. She seemed transfixed, staring off toward the water—at
what exactly, I couldn't tell. But then I saw a woman, probably in
the second half of her thirties, ankle-deep in the whitewash with
a toddler boy on her hip. He was even tanner than Sera with a
shock of translucent blond curls. Three older girls, presumably
the lady's daughters, were bodysurfing the waves farther out.
Four, six, and eight-ish, I guessed.

"I'm a mermaid!" one shouted.

"I'm a dolphin!" cried another.

"I'm the sea witch, and I'm going to get both of you!"
screamed the third, plunging toward her sisters, arms high. All
three wore matching bathing suits, orange with hibiscus flowers.

"Penny for your thoughts?" I asked Sera.

She angled her face to me but didn't take her eyes off the woman,
who was a sight to behold, accessibly fit in an *I-run-around-with-
my-kids* kind of way, rocking a two-piece, making a visor look chic.
She kept on kissing her son between yelling sweet things to her girls.
I looked around to see which man belonged to her. You could see
her rock of a diamond from here, but I didn't see the husband. The
woman looked happy. She looked strong, and free.

"*That,*" Sera said. "That's what I want. That is my dream, of
all my dreams. Now that I've locked you down, you old ball and
chain." She reached for my hand and started stroking my fingers.

"What?" I inquired. "Kids? A huge ring? Oh, you want a *visor*. I saw a few in the gift shop."

"Stop," she laughed. "I want a big family. A whole bunch of kids. At least one girl and one boy, but maybe like three of each. Not soon—but I want a brood. And I want to be happy. Like her. She looks like a happy mom, doesn't she?"

I nodded. "She does."

"You're gonna knock me up so hard one day, Mr." She traced circles inside of my palm.

"We can go practice right now, if you want," I offered.

"Soon," she promised, reaching to squeeze my thigh, starting to stroke my boardshorts. "But I'm serious. More than working for a big company, more than writing a book someday—that's what I want. Okay?"

I grabbed her wrist and yanked her onto my chair, held her waist and squared her on my lap, side-saddle. Sera was flawless to me already but would manage to grow even more stunning with each uphill year that passed for us. Her black bikini hugged her tight body then, every muscle toned to perfection due to months of her engagement regimen and general lifestyle of super-health.

I thumbed the bronze skin where her bathing suit edge met the curve of her hips. I cupped her neck and pulled her face into mine. She usually couldn't stand PDA, but she'd been generous on this trip. Her lips, still salty, brushed mine. She bit my bottom lip softly.

"You know," she whispered into my mouth. "There are kids present. Back to the room?"

"Yes, please." I tucked a piece of wild butter-blonde hair behind her ear and nodded my head to the ocean.

"I'm going to give you that," I promised. "I'm going to give you the world."

We would head back to the room and not leave for another four hours. For a long time, Sera would make me happier than I ever dreamed I could be. I knew I gave her the same.

But I'd never give her the big family, the brood, the lightness on her feet in her thirties, or the darling boy on her hip who looked exactly like her. I wouldn't give her the dream. I wouldn't give her the world.

Instead, I'd shatter it.

I'd shatter it straight to dust.

. . .

SEVEN

SERAPHINA

Sera Lorenn

Single

Age: 33

Newport Beach, CA

Hi! My name's Seraphina. My friends call me Sera. I write for a living. No pressure to totally wow you in the following 30 seconds! I was born and raised in Orange County. Books and the ocean are two of my loves. Little Women *is my all-time and I think Laguna Beach is the best. I also love spin class and church. Sometimes they feel like the same thing. I believe in real love, too. "That can't eat, can't sleep, reach for the stars, over the fence, World Series kind of stuff." I have a young daughter. She's my world. I'm an old soul, new to dating apps. Borrowed music taste, usually. Sucker for the Top 40. Blueberries are the best fruit. Blueprints have tended to fail me. Oh, and my coworker who's making me do this says that I'm pretty. For a blonde. Would love to meet you! Xo.*

One hundred fifty words on the dot. Beckham, that over-achiever. I loved it. *I loved it!* I sounded witty enough without being too sassy, educated without seeming pretentious, romantic but neither clingy nor desperate. If a guy actually picked up on the *It Takes Two* movie reference, we might have a shot at forever. But, worst case, it was the perfect quote about love. So cute and cheesy you had to smile. Or least, my type of guy would smile. And that's why I was doing this, right? To find somebody I liked.

I also decided on my three of the fifty available "Blinde Breakers," the app's way of letting you show a bit more of your personality, a play on *deal breaker* and *icebreaker:*

Current Song on Repeat:

The Next Right Thing, *Frozen 2*

Favorite TV Show Ever:

Friends (Are there even other responses?)

Interesting Fact:

I twirled baton competitively back in the day. Fire and every-thing. Is that interesting? If not, I can recite (sing) all of the U.S. presidents in succession from the beginning.

The rest of my information appeared below in a graphic with clean lines and a modern font. Relationship status, religion, blood type, and SAT score. Not really, to those last two, but they might as well have been. There was a lot of personal detail about myself going into this app, and the thought made my head spin a bit. This was why people did Tapp. And Crumb. And Bloom.

And whatever. Pictures were simple. Words took time. I couldn't wait to see if Piper Maddock's methods had merit.

I'd also done my homework to answer questions I had about this sightless digital experiment with humanity.

First, what kept people from exchanging numbers or emails right off the bat? Sure enough, the app software was set to detect it, and would automatically redact it from your exchange, then give you one warning before kicking you off. It was all in the Terms of Agreement. Same with specific addresses and "meet me" locations. People were smart. The app was smarter.

Secondly, how did couples eventually meet and take their connection to the next level? "Go IRL" (In Real Life), as the app called it? Well, you had to earn it. This part fascinated me most. Apparently, in the research phase, Piper, her team, and their research determined that four thousand words was the average length of exchange indicating whether or not you jived with someone and had hope of a lasting connection. In real life, this would go by in a blip, a thirty-minute conversation or less. But with the written word, you were forced to delve into the meaningful—to share information, not waste words, and reveal your personality. Thus, once you reached a combined 4,040 words—20/20 vision for each party—the IRL icon would appear in your app. You and your match would then have the option to click it and advance to the next level—or hit *snooze* for another 4,040 words.

Lastly, what about sexting? Were there any rules about jumping into getting X-rated with someone and arguably missing the point of the Blinde revolution? Nope. Piper Maddock didn't blink at this possibility. She felt that if people wanted to use the app for that, they were free adult agents. But, also: she might humbly suggest a competitor rhyming with *snapp* to cut to the chase, and save yourself the money and brainwork.

Blinde was complicated. Also simple. Mostly genius. Piper wanted people to write to each other. It was all very wartime of her, and what a frontline soldier she was.

I was ready to close the app, my profile now live for three hours, since 7 a.m. that Thursday morning. But then, I saw the number *3* pop up in the upper-righthand corner, in my Blinde Dates section for messages. Three quickly turned to four and then *five new messages*. Were these actual … prospects? *Already?* Guys who had aligned with my personality test, read my profile, and actually wanted to *talk?* My heart rate picked up. My stomach panged. I was doing this. *Keep pushing through.*

I clicked on the first message, from FootballGuy34. *All right!* I guess we were going for screennames à la the AOL Instant Messenger days. Should I throw it back to my *jamesdeansmybaby* alias? It probably wasn't too late.

FootballGuy34: Hey! Baton twirling, huh? Sounds hot. I live in Huntington and sell commercial real estate. Seems like we could connect. Hit me up. ;)

I groaned. I audibly groaned so loudly I half-expected Beckham to bound through the door and check for my pulse. I didn't know why this particular message made me want to stop breathing. The hot reference? Picturing Main Street in

Huntington on a hopping night? The winky face? *Hit. Me. Up?* Ugh. Over four thousand words with this guy? Twenty-five seemed like enough. From here, I could choose between the open-eye icon, to "Wink" and see what could happen, or the closed-eye icon, to "Blink," and pass. I pressed on the latter.

Blink.

The next one looked better. Adam Blake. Fascinating—it was a reflex even for me to look for a picture. Adam Blake was sure a hot name, but he could be six five, muscled, and handsome—or my height and balding with glasses. *But did he have a good personality?*

Adam Blake: Hey Sera! I saw in your details that you went to USC. If you're 33, you were there in the glory days. I went to Stanford around the same time. I'm sorry for all the bad press lately. Also sorry about our band. I love your school. You'll fight back! I live and work in Irvine. I'm an accountant. I'd like to think I'm not nearly as boring as that makes me sound. No kids, but I've also been married. I didn't cheat, and I do have a full head of hair. I like to be honest about both of those things up front. Anyway! Your profile was funny. I'm more of a banana guy, but not a deal breaker for me. Joey's my favorite *Friend*. But I share my food.

I was smiling. This time, I was *actually smiling*! Well, *hi there*, smarty Adam from one city over! Stanford? Funny? *Friends?* Yum. *I better hop on this.* Three more minutes online and I swore I'd get back to work:

Sera Lorenn: Well, could you *make* a better first impression, Adam Blake? As long as you're self-aware about the Stanford band, I suppose we can be friends. I love your school, too. In fact, it was my first choice, but I didn't get in. Don't tell anyone! And I'm so sorry about the divorce. Ugh. It's so painful. Everyone's always said that, but until you feel it, you just can't know. And I'm more of a banana split girl, but … you're pretty funny, too. Ross is my spirit animal.

We exchanged a few more banter-filled, informative messages that kept pulling up on my smile, until I knew I had to hop off and prep for my lunch with Mr. Graham Hamilton. I *blinked* on one more creepy message and another with grammatical errors, both no-fly zones for me. I shot one reply to a surfer named Brett James who loved *Forrest Gump* (good choice) and realized I much preferred actual names to the pseudonyms (sorry, Gamer Guy '79).

There was no denying it. I felt lighter and taller as I quickly conquered my meeting prep. I even felt the perfect blend of sophisticated and sexy in the simple black skirt suit, white ruffle blouse, and patent pumps Beck had suggested.

You might say I was fit for a prince.

. . .

"He went to boarding school in upstate New York," Sage reported. She was rattling off facts to help me conquer lunch with charm and exactitude. "Never had any siblings. Raised by his grandparents in New York City after the accident that killed his parents when he was eight. Worked summers at Hamilton from age fifteen. Went to Harvard. He's working on his MBA from USC, but to be honest, I don't know why. No offense to our school. Do you really need to follow up Harvard? Especially when you're a billionaire?"

I shrugged. "Maybe he wants to prove something."

She nodded. We took in the Mirabelle's majesty on this clear day, the ocean view glittering in the high winter sun, vacationers roaming the grounds and napping by the famous round pool. Sage snapped pictures from artsy angles and asked me to take a few solo shots for her Instagram, @SomethingSage. How did she know how to pose like that? How was her skin so dewy? *Note to schedule an intel session with her.*

We walked into Starfire, coastal chic, painted white, packed out with highbrow brunchers. Maroon florals centered wood tables, with a gray fur blanket padding each matching bench.

"We're here for lunch with Graham Hamilton?" I told the pretty young hostess, who promptly scanned us with small black eyes, from our blow-dries down to our heels.

She snatched two menus with an air of reluctant approval. "Right this way."

As she guided us to the best table in the place, with wide views of the Pacific, I felt Sage squeeze my elbow. *Hard.* Just as my jaw started to drop. *Wow. What?* Speaking of jaws, manly square ones—*did my stomach just actually flip?* Was I thirty-three or thirteen?

I was not prepared for the handsome thing in a slim navy suit who stood up to greet us, grinning.

I'd never liked blond guys, to be honest. Maybe I felt too *doubly blonde* in their presence, or maybe they just felt too Nordic. But Graham Hamilton, that boy—which he really was, just a boy, at age twenty-six—he looked like a missing Hemsworth brother, with all of their height, build, and swagger. His sandy hair was parted to the side but messy enough to say, "I'm still fun." He had gorgeous green eyes, the kind that looked rimmed in eyeliner. I'd seen so many pictures, but they did not do him justice. He seemed so much more relaxed in his own skin here than in all his stilted headshots or the society clips.

He stood up, and then we both *smelled him*. Sandalwood. Fresh air.

And heat.

Sage nudged me out of my trance.

"Mr. Hamilton?" I managed. "Seraphina Jones. Please call me Sera."

He grabbed my hand with the cute, crooked smile to end all cute, crooked smiles. "Please don't call me Mister Anything. Mr. Hamilton was my grandfather. Call me Graham."

My shoulders eased. "It's an honor to meet you, Graham. This is Sage, my intern."

"*Something Sage*, right?" He winked.

Sage gasped. "You know my blog?"

He laughed. "Well, my ex-girlfriend loved you. We took your whole Santorini trip last year. You look young to have traveled so much."

"Well, you look young to be running the world's most famous hotel group." Sassy Sage. You had to respect her.

Graham waved a hand, as if dismissing his status and prompting us to settle in for the lunch. Sage and I dipped into our side of the table, and Graham took his seat on the other.

"You're probably wondering why I wanted to meet you." He jumped right in, looking me dead in the eye while grabbing his water glass.

"I was, yes," I admitted, centering myself for this meeting. "But I hear The Bentley is priceless to you. And you know I'm running point on the branding trip."

He nodded. "My last clear memories with my parents are from The Bentley. It's the only non-Hamilton property we'd ever visit when I was little. You can't tell from pictures how stunning it is. Genuine magic."

"I bet," I said, "The pictures are impressive. The existing words and marketing? Not so much."

"Ah, but that's where you come in, I hear."

That uneven smile, those see-through eyes.

He is a child. You have one!

"I've read your stuff," he continued. "Especially for the Mirabelle, and Shutters in the Hamptons. The stories you create, the images and emotions—it's incredible."

Incredible? Who, me? *Stop it.* Wait! *Don't.* Those projects were years ago, but I loved that he knew of them. *Stop staring right at his mouth.* "That's way too kind," I responded. "But thank you. I learned how to write business at Hamilton, and it's where I'll spend my career. It's a privilege. The properties speak for themselves."

Sage was already taking vigorous notes to my left in her

Moleskine notebook.

"Well," Graham continued, "Surely you must know the pressure I'm under with this new addition to our collection, then."

I nodded. "I do."

"The board loved my grandfather, tremendously. But there were plenty of others vying for my position of leadership. Let's just say I need to validate my position."

"With an MBA?" I risked.

He raised his eyebrows and reached for the breadbasket. "Maybe. Fellow Trojan."

He'd done his homework, too. I pretended to scan the menu before locking my gaze into his. "Graham, listen," I started. I felt a speech coming. "I know I'm not a brand manager or a vice president. But you said yourself, you've read my words. When I dive into a Hamilton property, I leave nothing untouched. No word out of place, no feeling unfelt when someone visits one of our websites to look at one of our properties. With every piece of collateral, our team won't just secure bookings. We'll create an unforgettable narrative that promises the experience of a lifetime. Which, of course, Hamilton always delivers."

He chewed off a mouthful of breadstick, looking surprised, maybe impressed.

"The Bentley is an icon, sure," I said. "Hamilton is an icon, sure. But even icons can't rest. That's what we're here for. We're going to make you proud, and we're going to keep the company young."

Now I needed some water.

"Today, and in the months ahead," I forged on, "I want to

hear everything that makes this property special to you. Because that will give us the heart. *You're* the flesh and blood of the company. *You* will give us the gold. If you're worried about whether I'm up to the task, you can stop. Really. I am all the way in."

His smile exploded then. "Well, I feel like I should clap, *Seraphina.* That was actually quite amazing." He narrowed his gaze. "You're smart, aren't you?"

I exhaled. I had a lot riding on this, too. "Well, I'm not dumb, *Mr. Hamilton.*" Were we flirting? I couldn't tell if we were flirting. I felt Sage's curious stare searing a hole in the side of my face.

"Listen, I don't doubt you," Graham said. "That's not why I brought you here. I just wanted to meet you. I don't actually have a lot of close allies here at the company, and definitely not many friends. Most people have the wrong idea."

"Surely you can see why, though," I said, less boldly.

"Age isn't everything," he said, on the defense. "Is it? Neither is my last name. How about we forget about all that—and just be teammates on this?"

If I'd have met the Graham I'd prepared for—superior, snooty, entitled—I'd have thought, *Absolutely no way.* But the Graham here was different. Instead, I was looking at a well-dressed guy, orphaned too young, *too handsome,* maybe—but who seemed keenly interested in a destination he adored as a kid; in doing his family proud. He seemed invested. He seemed to care. And a new part of me suddenly longed to impress him. This assignment just became personal for me, too.

I mean, maybe a *tiny*, small bit.

"Teammates," I said, raising my glass and my smile.

"Teammates." He clinked. We sipped.

For the rest of the lunch, we noshed on delicious seafood while Graham regaled us with childhood stories from Jackson Hole, *the heartbeat of the West,* as he called it. I mentally noted to use that. Sage kept scrawling like crazy, and before long, I forgot she was there. I enjoyed every second of this unexpected *meeting*. The ease of Graham's laugh, his insights into the company, the current state of the board. I breathed easier.

Teammates.

And, my brain, or maybe his pheromones, conveniently recalled:

Ex-girlfriend.

. . .

EIGHT

CONNOR

I folded the paper in half and reached for a sip of water. *What an emotional dumpster fire.* I had no idea what Janine was expecting out of a letter from me, but she had just heard it, served up hot off the press. Our marriage debacle, there in my hands, an offering of my radical shortcomings. Had it felt great to read? Not really. To apologize? Actually, yes.

She sat, smile thin, looking intently back at me, rapping her pen on her pad. She was wearing a navy-blue dress today, long-sleeved with an air of the nautical, hair in a bun, looking every bit the captain of this situation. I could almost see her thoughts grinding like the inner workings of a big ship.

I waited. I drained my water.

"There's a lot in there, Connor," she finally said.

Insightful, Sherlock. "I know."

"You've been doing a lot of thinking."

"I have."

She pulled at her necklace and tilted her head. "This exercise is powerful for a number of reasons, especially in unearthing the version of yourself you seem to look back and see—you during your years as a husband. You're mourning all your mistakes."

"I wasn't all bad," I said. "I'll be better the second time." My joke fell flat on the floor, so I reset my tone. "A whole year divorced is a long time. I've had all these months to reflect. I can see now where I failed."

"Do you realize how huge that is, Connor? It takes some of my clients *years* to reach that kind of clarity. Sometimes longer for men. No offense to your gender."

"None taken." I smiled, palms up in surrender.

She tapped her pencil some more. "I want to talk about the pornography you discussed. Are you comfortable answering some of my questions?"

Whoa. I froze. I had to know this would happen. But I hadn't really thought until *this very moment* about the fact that I'd actually shared those words with *another listening human.* Words I'd never spoken out loud, to anyone, ever before. Of course, she was going to ask. And what other choice did I have but to nod my head? "Sure," I said, reluctant. "I know it's probably important."

"Very," she said, emphatic. "We can learn a lot about you and your roadblocks to intimacy by digging into this part of you."

I hunched over, elbows to knees, mildly exhausted already.
Here we go.

"Let's start from the beginning," she said. "When were you first exposed to provocative pictures of women?"

I felt *much older* than thirty-five as I started relaying the story—my new jam, the old man polka—but it grew easier with each detail of the personal history that sounded like I was born in 1942, instead of 1984.

I was twelve at the time, to answer her question of *when?* Raised in a small rural town in Northern California, I played daily with a gang of five boys in our neighborhood. We raced around on our bikes, we rode to the general store on our real-life picturesque main street, and we talked about the girls we knew, and the ones we didn't. We talked about girls, a lot. We were a scrawny, smart bunch, with little meaningful female interaction, but we found plenty to pontificate about anyway. We were rich with our imaginations and regular with our gatherings.

We all went on to achieve success as adults—doctors, lawyers, and one politician. But that summer, the only thing that mattered to us was the stack of *Playboy* magazines that our leader, Brent, had found. Brent was all red freckles, wiry muscles, and sneaky charisma. He turned out handsome, I had to admit. Back then, on that August day, he told us about the nude treasure trove he had stolen from his much-older brother. He hid them at the end of our street under a water valve cover plate—which, looking back, didn't seem the safest of choices. I felt thankful now there was never a fire or flood. Regularly, though, we took turns going to look at the magazines.

I'd never forget the first image I saw. So strange how, more than twenty years later, she was still seared in my mind. Hundreds would follow and blur together in wanton flesh, but I could vividly remember that girl—in a neon green, tiny thong with her naked, voluptuous breasts—shawled in a boa constrictor. I could still sketch her to a T, if I could sketch at all.

My parents had been fighting for years by that time, but Dad's drinking was growing feverish and aggressive. I'd always thought he retired too young—cashed out from his lucrative barbecue-manufacturing business too early. He was bored, it seemed to me, retired at fifty-one. My sister, Isla, practically lived at her best friend Emma's house, drawn to the faith and stability over there that she'd eventually share with me, too. But in the meantime, I was home, alone with our parents a lot, and I wanted to hide from the showdowns. I needed to block out their toxic air, before it infected my bones—though sadly, it had begun to. I craved an escape from all the thrown things and frequent reminders from Mom that *she was only staying because of the kids.*

It was harder back then—no smartphones yet—but where there was a will for a preteen male, there was also a way. I turned to women, as merely a boy. Or rather, I turned to *images* of women on bulky computers and the TV, fantasizing and letting their plastic lure play with my soul. It made me feel guilty, embarrassed at times, but briefly enough, often enough, it made me feel wanted, too. I didn't care that it was only a fantasy. The pictures were a distraction, however fleeting.

The habit continued. I wouldn't call it an *addiction*, but maybe that showed my denial. I wasn't sure. All I knew is that when I started going to youth group my junior year of high school, with my sister and all of her friends—and kind adults welcomed me and new peers *liked* me and pretty girls even *talked* to me—I started to feel my dirty little secret clash more with the straight-As, clear-eyed boy I wanted to be. The boy I very much *was.* The one you took home to Mom. My habit wasn't me; I had a habit. And that was the year I first felt feelings of hating it. Especially once I started believing in something beyond myself. I didn't have a great father, but I learned that God could be mine.

Once a month. That was the honest answer about the average frequency of my "escapades," through college and into marriage—though that frequency crept up, towards the end. Sera would ask me this many times, after my propensity for sneaking off to peer at Internet women finally came to light. Several years into our marriage, she clicked on my browser history to search for the website of a friend's wedding. She liked to remind me of this. *A wedding. You creep. You traitor. We. Said. Vows.* She felt like it was on the same level as infidelity, and to be honest, it was hard to argue without sounding lame even to me.

I didn't know how to explain that it wasn't a daily thing, or even a weekly occurrence. Or that it was, even so, enough to slowly chip away at my core. That I felt *so bad* being with her if I had engaged with it recently. Surely, she must've known, before she found out. Our bedroom time was loving and pure, but I'm not sure it was ever the best we could be. Sometimes it was stilted, and cold.

I also didn't know how to tell her that, during times of stress, or emotion, or distance from her—or of my widowed mom calling me with her theatrical problems, *again*, her incessant tales of woe—that the urge would flare up higher for a couple of weeks.

I vowed to quit forever, several times, because it broke Sera's heart, but I never stopped fully for more than six months at a stretch. I was good at hiding my footprints, but not quite expert enough. Sera caught me several more times during the rest of our marriage. Once on her iPad, once the TV, once a Victoria's Secret catalogue I stole from our pile of mail. Once, she was eight months pregnant, and you can bet how that made her feel. It was so awful, so sad.

Why couldn't I just stop?

At the end of our marriage, after several terrible years as glorified roommates, Sera suggested therapy. She wanted to give us one last try, but I couldn't. I'd reached my capacity of our silence, our anger, our insults that sliced to the bone marrow like an icicle. I don't even know how often I was finding my own escapes then. It all just seemed too far gone. I couldn't fight for us anymore. I didn't remember what I was fighting for, and I told her so. Our last few fights were unbearable. She'd finally come my way, but I was already gone. I certainly couldn't look her in the eye and promise I'd never look at anything that I shouldn't, ever again. I didn't know how to promise her anything. I was also tired of hurting her. I was sick of myself, especially the self of our marriage.

So I moved out, because I had to. You walk away from what's dead.

Soon after, though, it was strange. I gradually stopped looking at anything online that I wouldn't send to my sister. Honest to God, the old pictures and habits now made me begin to feel queasy. They triggered my anguish and loss. They no longer turned me on.

So here I was.

With Janine.

Searching for something intangible.

But finally willing to look.

Outrageously, I had held eye contact with her for most of these revelations. *She is a dang good therapist,* I thought. There was no judgment behind her spectacles. I trusted her, I realized then, too. I trusted her and, also, I couldn't wait to hear what she'd say.

No bangs! Yet, anyway. I hadn't pushed her over the edge.

"Connor," she said. "That was so brave, and vulnerable. Thank you, for being so open."

"That's why I'm here, right?" I shrugged, but I didn't smile.

"Do you know what I hear, as I digest all that?"

"Let's see," I pondered. "I'm a freak? And a failure of a husband. I don't respect women, and I show clear and present signs of addictive behavior?"

She shook her head. "No," she said. "Not at all. I hear that your innocence was taken, when you were twelve. That's young, Connor. And I hear that you didn't even come close to having the parental support that you needed, that you deserved. You found something to numb your pain. And that *thing*, that world, became something you didn't know how to extricate yourself from, when you realized you needed to. So many men are stuck in that loop. Plenty of women, too."

"Do you think," I started, gathering the nerve to ask something I had wondered for years. "Do you really think a habit, like mine—can affect your actual sex life?"

"I don't *think* it can," she said, eyes sharp. "I know for a fact that it does. Anything either partner experiences, sexually, is brought into their intimacy."

It was the answer I think I already knew and feared I needed to hear.

"From what I hear, your formative sexual experiences were with these images," she said.

I felt the sudden need to clarify. "I never looked at anything really hardcore." It was true. "Lots of lingerie and *Sports Illustrated*, in the early days. And scandalous stuff most of the time. The actual pornography was less frequent. It did scare me, on some level."

"What scared you about it?"

"It felt like a gateway," I admitted. "To something bigger and darker than me. Something—" I exhaled. "I don't know. Something I might never return from. Something that might actually impact my ability to appreciate a sexy, flesh-and-blood woman. Like Sera. She's a perfect ten. What if I lost my ability to appreciate the real thing?"

"That's absolutely right, and insightful," Janine said. "It's all a gateway, unfortunately, but it's good to hear you never got too deep. I do want you to know, though, how much this has likely influenced your experiences of intimacy—with friends, with Sera, with anyone."

I frowned. I wasn't sure I bought that. "Come on, though," I defended. "Every guy looks at stuff. Right?"

"Most guys, at some point, yes," she said. "And what is the national divorce rate, and how do you think that's going for our society as a whole? Do you think adult entertainment is serving us well? Upholding families, uniting our country, nourishing whole, honest humans, fostering respect between the two sexes? Or do you think—just maybe—that pornography is more destructive than many participants are willing to realize?"

Janine. Janine and her *points*. She would've made a good lawyer.

"Have you heard of Brené Brown?" she asked.

Oh dear Lord, if Sera were here. "Of course. Sera worships her. She quotes her all the time. I remember one thing she quoted of hers, during our infertility. That you should never say, 'at least,' to someone in grief. At least you got pregnant at all; at least you have one healthy child. That stuck with me. It's so wise."

"She's one of my favorites—a mentor from afar, if you will," Janine said. "Her research on shame is unprecedented, and I love her distinction between guilt and shame. She says that *guilt* is 'adaptive and helpful.' Guilt is measuring something we've done against our values—and feeling uncomfortable. Shame, on the other hand, is the painful feeling of believing that we are flawed, and therefore unworthy of acceptance. That something we've experienced—done or not done—means we don't deserve to belong or be loved."

I didn't know what to say as I sifted through her strong words and let the weight of them fall on me.

"We were made for human connection," she continued. "When men lack emotional connection, when they feel lonely, they often feel sexual urgency. So they turn to pornography, or images, or lust, for a quick release. But that 'release' leaves them feeling even emptier than before—because it wasn't true connection at all. It was objectification of another person, experienced all alone.

"And you, Connor, likely felt *guilt* at how this habit measured up against your faith values and your desire to be a good boy—but more significantly, you probably felt—*feel*—shame over how it defines you. As a bad person, bad husband, bad guy. Are you tracking?"

I was.

"And that *hurts*. Along with the pain of your childhood and your struggles with Sera, plus the stress of work and infertility … well, no wonder. You returned to the dark. You'd already done it anyway—so, hey, what was one more time? Especially if it numbed the pain. Even if you knew the pain would return *ten times worse*."

I gulped.

"The shame cycle. Over, and over, and over. It can drown you alive. Last week we talked about missing Sera. But as we process the *version* of yourself you are mourning from the divorce, the mistakes—I think we should reframe how you see it. You did bad things, Connor. Things you can hate. Things you should probably regret.

"But you? *You* are not bad. You are not a bad person, or a failure, or worthy of hate. You are not your mistakes. None of us are. Thank God, right?"

Her smile was full of compassion.

I sat back, quiet, impressed. I'd learned more in this session about myself and intimacy than I'd learned in thirty-five years. Janine knew her stuff. I felt more clearheaded than I had in months.

Also, I wasn't alone in facing the hex of this particular demon. *What were all of us seeking?* Love? Connection? Each other?

God? All alone by ourselves, with our screens, and our insatiable souls? When you stared it all down to see it for the thing that it was, it lost its magic and power. Like the time Space Mountain got stuck at Disneyland and they had to turn on the lights, back when I was a kid. No exhilaration, no other galaxy—just a warehouse with a run-down roller coaster and eclectic, frustrated people from all over America. The ride had depressed me ever since.

I glanced at my watch. Time was up. I rubbed my damp palms on my jeans as she jotted something down on her pad.

"I wish I brought a notepad today," I said reflexively. "Can I do that, in here? Is that weird? You said so many helpful things I don't want to forget."

"Of course you can," she said. "This time is yours. And I can recap next time if you want. Also—" She ripped off a piece of paper and handed it to me. "I think you should check out this group. It's at Crossfire, the big church. It's not for addicts, per se, and the group itself isn't religious. It's for men leaving something behind and trying to find true intimacy. Some of my clients have really benefited from going a couple of times."

Renegade, read the paper, with an address underneath. Cheesy name, but I'd check it out. Maybe I would. I mean, if Gramps could squeeze it into his bustling social calendar and unstoppable dating life.

I turned to face Janine one more time before I walked out her door.

"Thanks, Janine," I said. "Thank you, for listening. I've never told all of that to anyone."

"That's what I'm here for, Connor," she said. "And may it

not be the last time you tell someone. You're going to find what you're looking for. I'm going to help you make sure of it."

. . .

Chapter

— NINE —

SERAPHINA

"Sage. You put together—*all of this?*" Dumbfounded, I riffled again through the report, which she'd taken the time to get spiral-bound in our production room. It was the most brilliant, comprehensive, laser-focused social media strategy I'd ever seen. I was holding fifteen pages of gold, for which I was fairly certain we'd paid minimum wage. The proposal included an influencer collaboration campaign. Social ads to yield new revenue. A list of 300+ travel and lifestyle bloggers who fit with the Hamilton brand.

Sage stood in front of my desk, morning light dappling into the window on both of us. She looked suddenly bashful after handing her baby to me with total confidence a few minutes ago. I'd been in her shoes, her exact Jimmy Choos, and my heart squeezed. *Am I too eager? Did I reach too far? Am I stepping out of my role? I'm too much. I'm too much, aren't I?*

"You're not too much, baby girl," I wanted to reach out and say. "Keep going, keep reaching, keep aiming. *Aim at the highest, and never mind the money.*" That last part was from *Little Women*, from Jo's father about her writing. I'd held those words tightly since first reading them when I was ten.

Not that Sage was hurting for money. She once told me that companies paid her up to $5,000 for *one post* about their products. I still couldn't grasp why she wanted to work for me, for less than fifteen dollars an hour, every Monday, Thursday, and Friday. Even a raise would pale in light of her freakishly young success.

But I wasn't going to mention it.

"I did," she said. "I know it's a lot, but I've learned so much. I know these girls, the influencers. I go to BlogLady with them in Orlando every summer. I know the analytics. I know the game. They have crazy influence, and their followers have crazy buying power. There's a classy way to do this; I know it. If we can tap into these bloggers as the company unveils The Bentley under our name, I think it could be really huge."

I loved her ambition. And her tan leather pencil skirt. It was bordering on the edge of unprofessional, but you wouldn't find me phoning HR.

I sighed. Her plan was brilliant, but there were roadblocks. "The board," I exhaled. "They are so conventional, Sage. Stuck like mud in the dinosaur ages. They can barely use email. Coco could write better emails."

She laughed.

"I don't know if they'll go for it, but I'll talk to Phoebe, and think about it. Gosh, thank you. This is *good*. It's excellent."

"What about Graham?" she asked, regaining courage. "I think he liked you. I mean—I think he *really* liked you, but he also genuinely seemed to respect you. What if we took it to him?"

I raised an eyebrow. He liked me? *Focus.* More importantly, was this pretty little genius going to put me out of a job?

"That's actually not a bad idea," I said. I was secretly bummed I hadn't heard from Graham in the week since our meeting, but this was a great excuse for me to reach out. I peered again at the report in my hands. "Sage, can I ask you something?"

She nodded and pushed up the sleeves of her neatly front-tucked coral blouse.

"What do you want to do? What do you want to *be*? You were already working here when I came back, so I didn't get to ask you my interview questions. Obviously, I would've hired you on the spot—but I'd love to know. What do you want to do with your life, and why do you want to work for a writer like me?"

Bashful again. Her wide brown eyes and watermelon lips, highlights swept up into a chic high pony. "Well," she said, as if sorting through her next statement. "I feel like I'm riding a wave with the Instagram thing. Don't get me wrong; it's amazing. But is it forever? I feel like it can't be. What, am I going to be forty-five and still posting to social media 24/7? I love it now, but I'd also like to build a more sustainable life. Hopefully I have a bunch of kids eventually. I want to be strategic about my long-term brand and career. I want to build a skill set to last."

I tilted my head. "Well, you're very *sage* to consider all that."

"I've always wanted to write," she went on, ignoring my horrible pun. "Since I was a little girl and couldn't stop reading. And, look at you. You're so much more than a writer. You create stories for these big, beautiful properties. You write, but you also strategize, and dream. You help give people these unforgettable memories."

She took a beat.

"I guess," she continued, "I want to be like you."

Something filled my throat that felt a bit like shock and a lot like surprising emotion. *Why would anybody ever want to be like me?* My broken family, my sloppy career gap, my obvious and ridiculous clashes with punctuality. Especially this young, ambitious beauty with the whole wide world in her palm? Then again, I'd always needed to readjust how I viewed myself. The company had begged for me back at the smallest mention that I needed work. I fought with all I had for my family—I still fought every day—to make Coco proud and provide for her. To make every day a little better than the one before, if it was possible.

It was something.

Wasn't it?

Joke. I should make a joke so I didn't start sobbing in front of my intern.

"Well, that works out great," I said, straightening up in my chair. "Because I could definitely stand to be more like you. I'll take your whole outfit, your hairstylist's info, your social media mind, and—" My voice trailed off and my mouth curled up. "Thank you, Sage. I'm here to teach you everything that I know."

Hmmm.

We'd just had a moment. Right? Was it possible—*was it totally out of line*—for me to segue this conversation into some personal questions I had spilling from the core of my mind into everything else surrounding it? Say—some questions about dating app etiquette? I mean, if Sage could put together a *social media plan* like this, surely she had some advice for an old dog like me braving digital puppy love.

Whatever.

Life was too short.

"Sage, can I ask you something else?" Then I hastily added, "This is decidedly *not* a pretend interview question. You can sit down, by the way. Help yourself to the M&M'S."

"Anything." Looking grateful, she fell into my couch. The clumsy plop was endearing, as if she'd been holding it in. It made me relax and proceed, especially as she reached for the candy. "How do you stay so thin with these in your office?"

"Divorce," I said, only half-joking. "It's a great diet. One I can promise you should absolutely never try in your lifetime."

"You're such a catch, Sera," she said. "And still so young."

"Well, I'm not that young," I mourned. "But I guess that's a perfect transition to my next question. Have you heard of the dating app Blinde?"

"Who hasn't?"

I really had been living under a boulder. "Well, I'm on it now—"

"OH MY GOSH!" She squealed and clapped. "You're dating? This is so exciting!"

"*Shhhh.*" I put a finger to my lips. "It's not *public* or anything. But I need some help. I'm going crazy."

"What happened?"

"Well," I said. "There was this guy. Adam Blake. Total dreamboat, right? Stanford grad, accountant, so witty-cute, I can't even. We talked for five days. *Five days!*"

"Okay."

"And then, out of nowhere, he *vanished*. Cold turkey, stopped responding. His account is still live, he still exists, apparently, but—gosh, it is so infuriating. I can't believe how much this has gotten into my head."

Sympathy colored her face. "Oh, Sera. You got ghosted. Welcome. You've officially been initiated."

"No! Why would he do that? I told him things. I told him *personal things*. About my divorce, about my job—" I felt the offense on such a gut level. Was it something I said? Was it something I *didn't* say? At least it wasn't my looks.

"You have to be careful with that," Sage cautioned.

"He told me things, too, though! It got *personal*. And *flirty*. We had chemistry. Don't you think maybe he got in a car accident? Or lost his phone. He probably died, right?"

"Nope."

"No chance? Why not?"

"I'm going to tell you the best dating advice I've ever received. 'If a guy likes you, you'll know. If he doesn't, you'll be confused.' Those words changed my whole life.'"

I pondered that. *Huh*. "That is actually really profound, Sage. I mean, *thanks a lot,* but—wow."

"I can't take credit. It was a meme. I'll email you more of my favorites."

"No, don't," I said. "I don't want the IT guys spying on my desperation. Okay. Fine. Send them—they already know. So, it's done? I shouldn't ask if he's okay? Again?"

"Sera, *no!*" she reprimanded. "Absolutely do not message

him ever again. Block him. You can do that on apps. Don't take it personally. Move on! You want some more advice, and then we should get back to work?"

She stood, and boss-guilt hit me.

"Aren't I the one who should be telling you to get back to work?"

Sage smiled. "Number one," she said. "Hold your cards tight. Don't reveal too much, too soon. As my dad would say, 'Guard your heart, from which all things flow.'"

I smiled. I liked her. We likely shared the same roots, and probably a similar father hero.

"Number two," she continued. "Just a hunch, but I'm guessing you haven't reached out to any of your matches."

But how did she know? "Maybe not."

"If you're going play the game, girl—*you've got to cover the field.*"

"Was that from another meme?"

"Nope. All Sage!" She curtsied. "Get after it, Sera! You're hot. You're smart. Plus, you're the best writer I know, so you'll slay on this app. Trust me. Message five guys tonight. And then, when you get ghosted again—because it will happen, sorry—you won't take it so personally. Because *you* reached out. *You* held the power. Thank you! *Boy, next.* And onward."

I smiled. "You really are good at this."

"I'm pretty good. Ask me anything. You help me learn everything here—and I can help you start dating again."

"You can call that a deal." I flapped her report like a fan. "Can I hang onto this, by the way?"

"All yours," she said, adding before she walked out: "Let me know what *Mr. Hamilton* thinks."

. . .

Where on God's earth was Beckham? It was 9:36 a.m. He was usually here over an hour ago, and definitely never later than nine on the dot. I checked his Office Communicator status one more time to see that his computer was still not on. I needed to run Sage's idea by him before I emailed Graham. I hated that I had to, but it was the unspoken rule. I'd already drafted the email, but I needed his go-ahead:

From: Seraphina Jones
To: Graham Hamilton
Subject: The Bentley - Social Media Strategy

Dear Mr. Hamilton –
Or Graham, if that's still preferred! It was so great meeting you last week. Truly an honor. I loved hearing more about your vision for the future of Hamilton and The Bentley. I wanted to see if I could set up a call with you and Sage to discuss some social media ideas. She has some fantastic insights, and we think you'd love to hear them. We'll fit our schedule to yours—let me know what your next week is like. Looking forward to chatting!
Thank you,
Seraphina

Was it too friendly? Too many exclamation points? We *did* have a great lunch. Right? Or was I so out of touch with the opposite sex that I'd imagined the ease and delight of our conversation?

Just then, with no knock of warning on my door, in bounded Hurricane Beckham, looking far more disheveled than usual—he usually had not so much as a stray eyebrow hair out of place. He also smelled of excessive cologne. *Was he covering something up?*

He pulled the handle behind him and wasted no time in *lying down* on my couch. Full sprawl. Feet up. Arms first cradled behind his head, then the heels of his hands pressed into his eye sockets, indicating distress. Black suit, black loafers, white shirt *partly untucked.*

"*Ummmm.* Yes, sir? Can I help you? Did you come here from under the freeway overpass? Can I get you a sandwich? A cardboard sign?"

His dramatic sigh could've shaken our high-rise building. It was certainly shaking me. "I don't know how to tell you this," he said.

My pulse quickened. No. *What did I do?* I'd fix it, whatever it was. "I'm working so hard on The Bentley stuff, Beck, I promise it's going to be great, and that's actually what I wanted to talk—"

"Oh, stop. You're amazing. Phoebe is thrilled with you. Graham Hamilton told her yesterday that you were 'utterly charming and superb at your job.' Direct quote."

Charming? *Superb?* So it hadn't been all in my head. "Well, that's great news!"

"So is this. Sort of. Ser—I think I'm in love. Actual, grand-stand, or whatever you call it, total infatuation."

"Huh?" I needed to hear that again. I felt my office had slipped from its axis.

He sat up and grabbed some M&M'S, which I would need to replenish soon. *Was this becoming a therapy couch?*

"I never meant for it to happen," he said. "I'd always just been intrigued. I never expected to actually—"

"No!" I snapped, before I could filter my too-harsh reaction. I knew where this was going. How did Sam not call me the moment their date was finished last night? How did I forget to call her this morning? I sighed; I knew how. My morning had been extra rough. Coco's favorite white uniform cardigan wasn't clean, but you would have thought I was declawing her with hot pliers rather than forcing her sweet little arms into the navy blue one. I felt lucky no one called the police. As always, her fit had jilted me and rattled my focus. *Sam and Beck had their date last night.* Sushi Roku, Fashion Island. The only details I knew.

"*Ugh!*" Sam had cried when I explained that I had bargained her in a trade. "That guy? What's with the Gucci loafers? He's beautiful, though, I guess. If you're into, you know, male models. He's total eye candy. And maybe I could get some fashion advice. You know what? Fine. I'll do it. You'll owe me, though!"

I yanked up my phone. *Be. Cool.* I fired a text to her under my desk.

> How was the date?!?!
> Hope we're still sisters.

"Beck, you do not love her. You think she's gorgeous, and smart, and charming, and unlike any other girl you've ever met—because *she is*. There is only one Sam. But she's *my* Sam. And I will give you my life before I let you smash her heart."

He shot upright. He looked better like this, I thought, as more of a mess. More human. Less weirdly perfect. "You're wrong," he argued. "I've never had a conversation like that with a woman. And I've had a *lot* of conversations with a *lot* of women."

"You are not helping your case!"

"Ser, she's incredible. She asked me things no one has *ever* asked me before."

"Yep. She's a therapist."

He shook his head fast. "No. I mean, yes. Obviously. But it wasn't like that. This was mutual. Give me some credit. I learned all about your childhood."

I made earmuffs out of my palms. "This is just weird! There are millions of other girls in the world, and you know you can have any one of them! Can't you pick one not related to me, who also *happens* to be my best friend?"

"I'm already like your brother. Why's it so weird?" He paused, pulling his lips together. "Can I ask you something?"

"Sure." I sighed. "What?"

"Is this," he started, "is this because I don't believe like your whole family does? Am I not—*Christian* enough?"

I was thrown by him asking me this, so dead-on, so unswervingly. We'd skirted faith as a topic for years. *Well.* Was it part of the reason? Of course not! Maybe? Honestly, I wasn't sure.

You know what? No. I was responsible for protecting my sister, and I knew too much of his past. It was as simple as that. "No, Beck," I said. "Of course not."

"I was raised Lutheran, you know," he said quietly. "And I do believe in God, for the record. I just don't always know what to think about the whole thing."

I breathed. It was complicated, and this wasn't the time nor the place for the conversation.

Plus, thankfully, before things could get any more serious, Beck was smiling like a schoolboy again, and popping more M&M'S into his extra-unshaven face. "I would convert for her anyway," he said. "You know what? I'd go to *church*. Me! Church! Can you even? We could all go to brunch after! Doesn't that sound like *fun*?"

He threw two M&M'S at me and I caught one. "Honestly, what sort of spell did she cast on you?" Even as I asked, though, I knew. Sam cast a spell on everyone. She was the prettiest girl anyone who knew her had ever met—but more significantly, the most good.

"Give me a chance," he said. "If she'll give me a chance, will you?"

"Sam's a grown woman. But don't count on either. Ugh— now things are weird, because I already have to ask you something important about work."

"Anything. We can totally keep it professional. *Sis*." He winked, tossing up one more candy and catching it in his mouth.

Maybe Beck wanting me in his best graces wouldn't be the *worst* thing for me on the job. I told him about Sage's social media plan and asked if I could run it by Graham. He told me I could, of course.

"Are you only letting me because you want to marry my sister?" I asked.

"Ewwww," he joked. "Who said anything about marriage?" He feigned disgust, rising up. "I'm saying it because you're incredible at your job, and I trust you. And because Sage is a major hitter, and we both know we don't deserve her. You know, like you don't think I deserve Sam."

I moaned. "It's not like that. I just don't think you guys are—"

"It's fine, it's fine." He held his hands up.

"And thank you," I added. "For letting me email Graham."

"Thank *you*," he said. "Keep me posted. You're nailing The Bentley stuff. And I care about you so much that I'm not even going to make a joke about nailing your sister."

"*Goodbye, Beck.*"

This was a dilemma I had not foreseen. Mind whirring, I sent the email to Graham. Still no text back from Sam. I needed some M&M'S. Maybe some coffee to wash them down alongside my meltdown.

When I returned from the café, there in black, bold letters, already, burned a response from Graham in my inbox. *That was fast.* My stomach grew hot.

From: Graham Hamilton
To: Seraphina Jones
Subject: Re: The Bentley - Social Media Strategy

Hi Sera,
It's great to hear from you. My schedule's pretty crazy right now, but how about dinner next Thursday? Water Grill, 7 p.m.? Bring Sage if you want.
Or ... you can just bring you.
Always,
GRAHAM

Wait, *what?* I was tired. I was a mom. I was no longer twenty-six. But I knew *flirting* when I encountered it. And I was now certain this gorgeous heir to some kind of kingdom was flirting. *With me.*

What could I say in response? *Never write anything in email that you wouldn't mind seeing on the front page of the news.* My dad's voice always chimed in my head at the best and worst times.

People had business dinners all the time, I reminded myself. This was absolutely no big. Best not to overthink it.

From: Seraphina Jones
To: Graham Hamilton
Subject: Re: The Bentley - Social Media Strategy

I'll be there!
Sera

Sage had said to hold back, right? I followed up with a meeting request. The exclamation point left it friendly. The succinctness kept it professional. The choice not to acknowledge the flirting left it mysterious. But—*wait now.*

Was it too cold?

Too late.

Dinner with The Prince. No big.

Bzzzzzzzz. Bzzzzzzzz.

Finally, Sam! *I mean, Lord.* I felt bad for Beck. Someday he'd find a good girl to settle him down, but for the very last time—that girl was not going to be my sister. Her three texts came in like popcorn:

> Ser. OMG. He is wonderful. How come you never told me how sweet his heart is? And that face!!! He obviously knows what to say, but ... now you're the one who's going to kill me. I liked him.

> I liked him a lot.

> Do you think he'll ask me out again???

. . .

PART TWO

Seek

TEN

CONNOR

There's a part of my brain, the lawyerly side, that scoffs when people say things like: "I don't know how it happened." And then I roll my eyes higher when they continue with: "Once I was in so deep, I didn't know how to stop."

Shady deals. Hiding money. Having an affair with your secretary. Lying about your age. Not wearing any underwear with your jeans.

But then, of course, I look in the mirror, into my culpable eyes, and at the bad angel perched on my shoulder for thirty-five years. I see my *Bachelor* addiction. I see the Werther's candies stashed in my office desk. I see, most of all, of course, the things that shattered my marriage.

I see the string of justifications that made me do what I did next.

I see how something went, quickly, from:

"I can't believe this is happening."

To:

I can't believe my luck.

• • •

One nondescript Wednesday night, feet kicked up on my coffee table, I finally finished the Blinde questionnaire. The NFL playoffs provided the ambient noise. The questionnaire was a doozy. By the time I got to creating my viewable profile, I was all out of steam. Honestly, almost over it. But the app now had more information about me than my own mom. It had robbed three hours from me that I would never get back.

So, I would finish the profile. Not to mention I was already one hundred dollars deep.

I personally didn't love the idea of using my actual name. Or mentioning Coco up front. Maybe my inner attorney was extra protective. Should I use a cheeky alias, or use my real name? Or use a fake name that sounded real? The app didn't seem to care. It was all about the connections. *What's in a name? We think nothing*, it said in the FAQ section.

LawyerGuy84? Blah, it was lame and predictable. But I couldn't think of anything else.

So I would just pick a *real* name.

Jack.

I would be Jack, for sure. I didn't need to think further. It had been one of my favorites since *Call of the Wild*. Mainstream, but manly and cool. I could even be Jack London, which would be kind of adorable and hilarious.

But adorable and hilarious in a grandfatherly way?

No. Something else. I tuned into the football game for a beat. Todd Lawrence, a good-looking quarterback for the Packers, seemed to be a big deal. *Lawyer, Lawrence, London.* I loved it. *Done.*

Jack Lawrence

Single

Age: 35

Irvine, CA

Am I really on a dating app? I guess I'm on a dating app. Still not sure if 35 is officially middle-aged. I feel like it's up for debate. I enjoy a good documentary and a great hike. I work hard. Could probably play more. I believe in a thing called love. Whatever happened to The Darkness? They were amazing. Anyway. Hi! Just a guy here for the right reasons.

Favorite Game:

Uno

Favorite Romantic Comedy:

Hitch

Career in Another Life:

Broadway Star

I sat back. *Eh.* That was my honest summation of me as a prospect. *Ehhhh.* It was not my best work, but I was just so tired. Plus, wasn't it all about the backend matchmaking magic—every box I had ticked to call forth all of my soul mates? Once I received my matches, then I could really shine. I'd save the good stuff for later. Sera had never *loved* my laconic texts. Love letters, in the early days, I could do. Digital communication had just never been my forte. This app would have to pull from my depths, but I was up for the challenge.

Or, I would be tomorrow. For now, I was going to sleep.

Todd Lawrence's team sadly lost.

But I refused to see it as a foreshadowing of my defeat.

. . .

I padded to my coffee machine the next morning, eye on the piping, full pot tucked under my walnut cabinets. Sera had kept our Nespresso machine in the split, which was only fair. I'd given it to her as a present. I just didn't know how desperately I was going to fall in love with it. The flavor, the nuance, the depth. I was a full-on evangelist, but still hadn't gotten around to buying a new one. Even Coco loved to line up the shiny pods in elaborate patterns.

I missed it. I missed so much.

After setting my oatmeal to boil, I took a seat at the kitchen island with my phone and my UCLA mug. I tapped through a few work emails and read from the meditation book I started my days with, when I remembered. "Lead me into the land of uprightness." I liked that. If more lawyers adopted that mindset, maybe we wouldn't have such a rep.

The Blinde app then grabbed my eye. Because, how on earth could it not? *Seven notifications?* Written messages. From real women. This was getting so real. I probably wasn't ready. My fingers trembled a little, and not from my middle-grade coffee. I gulped, and I opened the thing.

Scanning the names, I started to grin. I wondered what it said about a person who used her real name—or at least a real *sounding* name—versus one who made up an alias? Blinde should have one of their many psychology experts run a report.

I'd specified that I didn't want any matches born after 1990. I knew this officially now. *I drew a line for her.* Thank you, Hailey. And Coldplay.

AttorneyGal88

OC Mama

Redheaded Reader

If nothing else, the app was on point. From the names alone, I saw commonalities.

Macy Rose

Allie Victoria

All right. The normal names. Interesting. None of them rang a bell.

Yoga Babe

Okay, that one creeped me out a little. Had somebody tapped my Google search? Probably. Or maybe I just really loved yoga girls.

And.

There.

It.

Was.

In plain bold font, like the rest, but the only one that made me lose my actual grip:

Sera Lorenn

Crackkkkk went my fake-glass screen cover the second my phone hit the floor. Dang it. *Those things were fifty bucks.*

Sera was dating online. *She was right here in front of me.* The woman who was my wife a few short years ago was looking for love, or romance, or companionship, or whatever, *it didn't matter.* She was on the active search for something that wasn't me.

Something curled inside my stomach. Jealousy? Anger? Rejection? Fear? I tried to name the feeling, as I knew Janine would encourage, but I wasn't sure there *was* a name for this. Or maybe there wasn't *only* one feeling. I was pretty sure I felt all those things. Even though I was right here, too—scanning strangers with hope.

Really, though. *Sera?* Messaging guys? *On an app?* Reaching out to some generic loser named *Jack?* I hated this Jack. *What did she even know about him?*

The phone felt hot in my hand now. The new plastic slice down Coco's face was the only thing that kept me from throwing it.

How was I going to play this?

I could ignore it. Delete it right now. *Blink, red trash can, goodbye.* She'd probably never notice.

I could actually *read* her message—and reply with humor and grace. Acknowledge the mild sting and the massive awkwardness. *Haha! It's me, Ser! I used an alias. I see we're both dating again! Well, um, good luck! Talk to you soon!*

My oats were burning. The yeasty smell filled the kitchen as I scrambled to take them off of the heat. I scraped what I could into one of my sturdy clay bowls. I worked slowly, methodically, as an option C took shape in my mind.

I was Jack.

Jack was me.

I could respond.

As him.

I mean, just once. *Obviously.* I could see how Sera would play around in dating app world. It didn't have to go anywhere. I could just—keep an eye on her. For a quick message. Or two. And she could see how I would play, too.

Only she wouldn't know.

Technically, it was dishonest, I realized.

But we were once married, I reasoned!

I opened her message.

Sera Lorenn: Hey, Jack! I'm Sera. Which I guess you can see. I'm new to dating apps, too. Broadway Star, huh? What's your favorite play of all time? And *only since you put it out there, Mr. Right Reasons*—Are you a *Bachelor* fan?! What do you think of this season? Firefighter Finn is amazing, I think. But I kinda feel like his mom. Just thought I'd say hi! We both live in Orange County.

Of course. Of course she was charming and witty with the perfect amount of flirtatious energy and immaculate grammar. Guys were going to love her. Sera was created to win this app.

Let's see. She sent her message last night, so plenty of time had lapsed to keep me from seeming desperate.

Let's see what *Jack* was made of:

Jack Lawrence: Hi, Sera! It's so nice to hear from you. Can I go back and revise my career in another life? Chris Harrison. I definitely want his job. Did you know he's worth $12 million? Firefighter Finn is awesome. But, unpopular opinion: I think Hannah Q. is his soul mate. I am definitely *everyone's* dad on that show. Anyway. Thoroughly revealing my fandom here.

I paused before I continued. It was risky, but I saw a temptation here. Naming our daughter had been a small fight. Sera desperately wanted to name her after Cosette in *Les Misérables*, which we did. Coco for short. When she first brought it up, though, I had *no clue* who Cosette was. I'd barely heard of the play. I could see the disappointment in her eyes that I'd seen many times before. It was a thing for us, generally speaking. I wasn't as *cultured* as she was. She'd taught me to love so many wonderful things. For instance, I learned that *Les Misérables* is incredible. Still. I would never be the guy planning the date to the Getty or knowing all of my *plays*. My Broadway star aspirations were mostly a joke, and simply from my love for dancing. Oops. I should've just put *backup dancer for Bieber.* I was a total Belieber.

The thing was, though: I might never be the guy knowing all of my plays. *But maybe our boy Jack could be!*

I took a good look at her profile before responding. I had my play and then some:

I'm not very original here, but *Phantom of the Opera* is up there—and *Les Misérables* is my top choice. I just don't think it gets any better. Unless we're talking *It Takes Two*. Now THAT'S World Series kind of stuff. Where are the Olsen Twins now, do you think?!

Sent. 7:08 a.m. I had to hop in the shower, or I would be late to the office.

Ping. Another match? *Jack was on fire!* Errr … I was on fire. I could still be *me* to the other girls. I didn't have to pretend. Yikes. I was getting a headache.

It was not another match. It was Sera again. Somebody wasn't so worried about the timing of playing it cool, which was so very her, and adorable.

Sera Lorenn: I love Les Mis!!!!!! I named my daughter Coco after Cosette. And OMG, I am dying. You know that movie?! I personally think the Olsen twins falling out of the spotlight is one of the greatest tragedies of our generation. Where did you go to school? I don't see it on your profile. Do you really believe in soul mates? Is that too many personal questions? XX.

My daughter. We also called her Coco after her dad, *Sera.* Some of this didn't feel awesome. *Stay in the game,* I told myself. *You're doing great. You got a double X!*

And look at all those exclamation points!!!!!!!

I shut my computer. I'd respond later, at work. I needed to give this some thought. I didn't include my college because it was ages ago, wasn't required, and frankly felt pretty irrelevant. But if this right here wasn't a moral dilemma—I didn't know what was.

What would a good lawyer do? *Lead me into the land of uprightness.* Gah. Why today, God, *why?*

How long could it last, though, really? My ex-wife, my actual wife for almost ten years, talking to me, online, without knowing it was me? A couple more messages, tops. Something would out me soon, and I didn't want to lie.

And yet.

I blinked my eyes shut, to blackness, and let my heavy head relax in my hands, elbows cold on the countertop.

I saw Sera on our wedding day. Ivory satin mermaid dress hugging every beautiful curve, cathedral veil behind her. She had done her own makeup, sexy and dark, like the night we met. Not light and coy like most brides. Cascading, soft, blonde hair, completing the look. But the thing is—it wasn't a look. Because it could never be replicated. Everyone gasped when they saw her that gold August afternoon. No other woman would ever be at her level. At least not in my mind or eye.

Maybe Yoga Girl was smoking hot.

I'd always wondered what it would be like to date an attorney.

I might get to know Macy Rose, and she might even be one of my soul mates.

But none of them would ever be Sera.

What was the worst that could happen? I knew I had to find out. Maybe I was willing to read between the lines for a second.

Sometimes, to do the right thing, you had to rewrite the rules.

Maybe you had to invert them.
And turn upright—
Upside down.

. . .

ELEVEN

SERAPHINA

I sipped on the Thursday afternoon pick-me-up Sage had
delivered, the caramel macchiato comforting me and crack-
ling in my brain. Sunshine spilled onto my back, relaxing
my shoulders as I clicked through the PowerPoint slides. I was
firming up the casual presentation I'd show to Graham on my
iPad that night.

At least, I hoped the night would feel casual. I was nervous.
For sure.

The Bentley was truly a magical property, so classy and timeless compared to the weird world we lived in. Sage had pulled
ten sample influencers we would target for partnerships, and I
struggled to differentiate some from the others. They were all
stunning, no doubt. Half had bluntly chopped lobs (long bobs)
while the others had wavy extensions even longer than my very
long mane. Big sunglasses, half the time. Celine or Tom Ford
or Gucci, or some lesser-known brand they were paid in droves
to promote. They all walked around with enormous designer
handbags and incredibly tiny legs. Sam could easily be one of
them, a wildly popular one, but I didn't tell her this. Nothing

could interest her less. She was barely on Instagram, but she loved to psychoanalyze all of it.

I, however, could be brutally honest about these enchanting female entrepreneurs:

They made me want what they had.

Or at least, the illusion of having. There was something undeniably mesmerizing about the whole thing. They influenced me, they did. At least a smidge. And, well, I sure hoped so, because I was banking on them influencing thousands of people into believing The Bentley was cool again. We were targeting people like me—late twenties to mid-forties, with their annual vacations, high-class taste, and disposable incomes. Well, I used to have disposable income. I was confident Graham would love the idea. The board? We would have to see.

Ready for a respite, I opened my email. I made a habit of closing it down when I needed to be in the zone. The constant previews popping up in the bottom right corner were too much of a temptation to bear. At least my dangerous M&M'S were across the room.

From: Brynne Callaway
To: Teagan Anderson, Samantha Jones, Seraphina Jones
Subject: Teagan's Bachelorette Party!!!!!

Hi Ladies!
Are you ready?!?! Nine more days!!! See the itinerary attached. If this plan looks good to you guys, I'll send the official Evite. Everyone's already saved the date, but I want to

send the details at least a week in advance. LMK!
P.S. DID YOU HEAR SAM IS INFATUATED?! Sera, you must
be dying. I'm personally just bummed his identical twin is
getting married. SO. HOT. I can't believe there are two of
them! Let's give him a chance, shall we? We'll plot his murder
together if he hurts Sam.
XX,
Brynne

Brynne was the sassiest second grade teacher for miles. Her students worshipped her and so did the parents—neither an easy win in the Newport school district, where standards were up in the clouds. She used to be an actual princess at Disneyland—Aurora *and* Cinderella—making little girls' dreams come true with her uncanny resemblance, somehow, to both. Her fairy-tale goodness was the crux of her charm, but also the reason nobody suspected her fierce side. She took zero prisoners. She was our teacher, our protector, and our planner, as she was for her students. Still single at thirty-two, but she never seemed to mind. Unattached, but rarely alone. She was on *all* of the apps. She'd definitely broken more hearts than she'd had heartbreaks.

I clicked the attachment to see that the plan was vivacious and detailed. I would expect nothing less. One night at the Sultry Hotel in Beverly Hills. Saturday afternoon by the pool, dinner at a celebrity steakhouse, dancing at the hottest new club. Sunday brunch on the hotel rooftop, then shopping at the Beverly Center before we made our way home. She insisted a limo drive us up there and back. It seemed excessive to me, but you know what? I could use a weekend of *excess*. I also loved that Brynne was our group administrator. At work and in my personal life, it was always me. I cherished her reliable efforts.

From: Seraphina Jones
To: Brynne Callaway, Teagan Anderson, Samantha Jones
Subject: Re: Teagan's Bachelorette Party!!!!!

Brynne—I LOVE IT!!!! It's perfect. Thank you so much for organizing everything. I cannot wait for a weekend with you all. You know what I don't love? Beckham and Sam. Ugh, I hate that even their names look rhymey and cute. But if she's happy? I'm happy. I'll even bring the Ben & Jerry's when he breaks her heart.
Love you guys!!!

I knew it wouldn't be long before my sister clapped back:

From: Samantha Jones
To: Brynne Callaway, Teagan Anderson, Seraphina Jones
Subject: Re: Teagan's Bachelorette Party!!!!!

I agree, Brynne—you're the best. It's perfect. I can't even wait! And Sera, I'M RIGHT HERE. Reading the emails. He's sweet to me, you know. Sweeter than at least 10 "good boys" I've dated. People can change. I know you believe that. We're going out again this weekend. :)

BTW, did you tell them you're on Blinde now, Sissy?! Wooooooopsies!

No. Way. *She. Did. Not.*

I was so not ready for the pelleting questions. *Gah.* Maybe I deserved it. I was trying to get on board with Sam's romance. I was *sort of* trying to get on board with her romance. They were talking constantly, she and Beck. And the thing was, when I dug into it, I didn't hate them together. I hated the idea of him bringing her down, or worst of all, breaking her heart. There's nothing I wouldn't do to protect her. Blood would always be thicker than water. Even my boss's (fancy, high-alkaline, seven-dollar bottles of) water.

I absently picked up my phone to see that I had three Blinde notifications. I smiled, tapping eagerly on the pink button. I was testing the sea with a couple new fish, one in particular who'd intrigued me with a few things he'd said. *Jack Lawrence.* Still no response from him, though. I probably scared him away with my multiple questions. But, you know what? *I wasn't there to waste anyone's time*, as a *Bachelor* contestant would say. I needed to know the big stuff up front, even while strategically playing my hand.

I scanned through the messages, trying not to feel crestfallen. One promising dentist in Tustin revealed he'd been married three times. It might be a double standard, but *three?* By thirty-four? I couldn't help but see it as a red flag. There was only one Ross from *Friends*.

The other was an avid snowboarder—me, too!—but his diction was very bro-heavy. I'm sure he was super sweet, but I could already picture me snapping my fingers, inviting him to keep up with all my *hilarious* jokes. Was that snobby? *Was I a snob?*

As I finished blinking my *noes*, I received a new notification. My stomach lurched. Maybe there *was* something to making the person wait. Eight hours seemed everlasting and each one had made me grabbier for Jack's response, like my younger self in a Limited Too:

Jack Lawrence: Hi! I went to UCLA. Deal breaker? I do believe in soul mates, 100%. But to be honest, I also wonder if maybe we have more than one, if maybe we're all more complicated than we know. I think we all have a hundred different sides to us that every new person, and only that person, has the ability to bring out. So, yes to soul mates. But I think we have only one lobster.

Looks like you write for a living? Anything I would've read?

Would love to ask you three more things. But is that too many personal questions?!

What made you go on this app?

Who would you want to play you in the movie of your life? Is that cheating? You don't have to look like the person!

Dogs or cats? I don't want to say this is critical, but, okay. I might block you if you say cats.

Take your time!

Jack

I caught myself smiling again, even bigger this time. *Be. Cool. Be. Sage.* I wasn't designed for this. I didn't know how to play games. I was drawn to this guy. A little sarcastic, grammar on point, obviously smart, and yes, I could forgive the UCLA. I'd spent tons of time there during Connor's years in law school. Everyone knew the Trojans could never compete with their neighborhood, and everyone knew they were geniuses.

I popped over to Jack's undetailed profile to peruse it for the fifth time. No mention of kids, at age thirty-five. But he did like Uno. It seemed an odd choice for a guy in his thirties. Settlers of Catan or What Do You Meme? seemed more like something you'd broadcast. I wanted to respond right away but felt wary of seeming *thirsty* (did people still say that?) compared to his no-rush response times.

Draft now. Send later. Perfect.

Sera Lorenn: I guess I can jive with UCLA. :) I actually feel a kinship to Bruins because of the rivalry. I like what you said about soul mates. INTERESTING. Going to give that more thought. And, no, I doubt you have seen my stuff. I wrote for a magazine, years ago, but now I work at a big company. They're good to me. I will answer your questions—but only if you answer them, too. Plus, three questions from me. Fair?!
I guess you could say I'm looking for a new beginning. And in the spirit of full disclosure ... wedding season is coming, with all those plus-one invitations. I don't want to be alone.
Good question! Is it totally obnoxious if I say Margot Robbie? Wishful thinking, of course, but we are both blonde. Not to

mention her talent. Is she the most gorgeous talented woman
alive right now??
CATS? Ew. I would love a Goldendoodle named Sugar.
What do you do for work? Tell me a documentary you liked
recently?
Do you want kids?
Sera

I caught myself before flicking it off into cyberspace. I would wait. It felt—*nice*. Being asked questions. Thinking about the answers. I reread my response three times, to make sure I wasn't *giving away my heart* too fast. I didn't think so. My answers were light—except for the honest part about being alone. But I didn't mention my divorce or the depths of my recent hard years. This was unicorn fluff in comparison. I didn't name my company, either. Not to mention, I could be using a total alias for all Jack knew. I put the app away, pledging not to peek again until the workday was over.

I circled back to my email and saw six more messages from the lively bachelorette crew.

My eyes widened to moons, though, at the name of Coco's teacher below them. She'd never emailed me before. The class mom did, sometimes. But everything important came home in Coco's folder, tucked inside of her backpack by a volunteer parent or aide. It made me laugh, reminded me of a secret messenger service, *classified information* being smuggled home by our kids without them ever being the wiser.

But this did not make me laugh. These words were shot straight to me. My stomach sank into my seat.

From: Lindsay Taft
To: Seraphina Jones
Subject: Cosette's Behavior at School

Dear Ms. Jones,

I hope you are well. I didn't want to have to write you this email, but the administration and I agree that it's probably best. There have been some friendship problems happening between Coco and some girls from her class during recess. Today, she was hitting another student repeatedly and trying to take off her shoes. The playground aide intervened. Later, while they were in line to return into class, she continued to argue with several students. She grew loud, and belligerent, and we had to send her to the Head of Preschool's office to cool down from her hysterics.

She was fine and delightful again when she returned to the classroom, finally, but it was all rather upsetting. We care for her and adore her. But this episode—and several recent ones like it—lead us to believe it's time for a meeting with you and her father.

Can you please let me know your availability at 3:30 p.m. on a weekday in the near future, and coordinate with her father as well? We think it's important to open a dialogue with you both.

We've also asked that she take a break from these particular girls. I hope you trust my judgment that this "break" will help her reset and return to the friendships after some space, if that seems feasible. For now, I think a separation is best.

If you have any questions, please let me know.

Blessings,

Lindsay Taft

Lead Teacher

Classroom 2

St. Joseph's Preschool

949-555-3957

. . .

Silver rain slushed at my windshield, blurring Bristol Street as I inched through the gridlock. So much traffic, so often. Orange County was feeling more like L.A. all the time. Today's weather had taken a turn for the worse, along with my afternoon.

I didn't want to do dinner with Graham anymore. I didn't want to do anything, with any other human but Coco. I wanted to bake her favorite macaroni and cheese, let her eat bubble-gum ice cream and play with her whisper-fine hair as I tried, with all of my strength, *for the one-hundred-thousandth time*, to just understand my baby.

I'd never understood her, not fully. That was the truth, one I'd only ever admitted to Connor and therapists. I had never known precisely *what to do, what do I do?* from the day she crashed into the world, screaming, at the crescendo volume of her newborn lungs, without stopping for six months.

Coco felt every small thing, internalized the infinite universe, but it was impossible to know when she would blow. No one could tell, not even me, when her feelings would—immediately and without warning—exceed her capacity to hold them inside. She was almost violent in her zeal for fairness and truth, which her body always seemed to define before she did.

Without understanding how to process her overwhelming emotions, Coco so often flailed. And, in turn, so did I. *We'd never done this before, though.* We'd never been thirty-three and four in the face of an unknown world. I didn't understand her.

But I would never stop trying.

I'd drafted and redrafted my email to Connor six times, with the forward from Coco's teacher:

> OMG. UGHGHGHGHGH. Read below. Hitting at school?!?! Lord, help us! She hasn't told me anything about friendship troubles! How's your week next week? I'm so sad. We need wisdom. And chocolate.

It's how I would've responded for years, but we didn't talk like that anymore. We hadn't in a long time. I settled on:

> Hi Connor –
> I just got this email from Coco's teacher. Gosh, I'm so sad to hear this. She hasn't mentioned anything to me about trouble with friends at recess. Has she to you?
> Any chance Tuesday at 3:30 p.m. would work? My mom will have her so I can meet you at the school and probably head home for the day.
> Let me know,
> Sera

He responded quickly, confirming the date. I knew I'd feel anxious to see him, but I was far more anxious about our daughter's ostensibly precarious state. There was no arguing the recent upheaval of her existence. It had to be playing a part. It was probably playing *the* part.

I pushed it out of my mind. For now, I had to figure out how to appear sharp, and poised, and not like a soaking wet dog as I walked into dinner with Graham.

I spotted him quickly at a table toward the back of the restaurant. I'd only been here once, a memory that made me grimace, but I still gawked at the setting. The décor looked like the Restoration Hardware Modern collection had crossbred with an old pirate ship. Stuffed marlin, old barrels, and classic maritime art covered the walls, while woven ropes, glass-blown chandeliers, and sections of funky wallpaper looked down on guests from the ceiling. It was rustic sailor chic at its best. Their fresh seafood was unbeatable, but more importantly, so was their cheeseburger.

I felt the instant *hug-or-handshake* debate from the second I saw Graham stand up in his dark gray suit. On impulse, I went in confidently with my grip. He met me there, holding it to the exact fluttery point that I felt it deep in my belly.

"It's great to see you again," I said, forcing a smile and taking a seat. "This is perfect."

"I love this place. Thank you for meeting me." He was even better-looking than last time.

"Thank *you*," I said. I spotted the bottle of expensive white wine already opened between two glasses. I hated these awkward moments when I was reminded that I no longer drank. I reached into my purse for my iPad.

"Right to business," he said, playfully. "Let's go!"

"We can wait. Just want to be ready for you." I smiled. *Forced again.* I felt distracted, and off. I swigged my water, priming myself.

He studied me. I could feel it. I could viscerally feel his dreamy green eyes boring into me.

Even worse, I feared he was actually *seeing* me.

"What?" I asked, self-conscious, raising my hand to my cheek.

"You okay over there?" One side of his mouth lifted into that uneven smile.

"I'm great," I responded, too brightly.

"Are you sure? You can relax. I really want to hear the ideas."

"It's not that," I said. "I feel great about the ideas. I just—" I hesitated. I didn't know where the edge of *appropriate* was when it came to getting personal with The Prince. I had to be careful. With the professional line, and my heart. "I had a hard afternoon. No big deal. I'll feel better after some food."

"Work? Personal? You don't have to tell me. But do you need to go? We can absolutely reschedule."

"No, no," I insisted, waiting another few beats before waving my hand. "Some problems with my daughter." I finally let out the big breath. "She's four. She's having trouble at school. We have to meet with the teacher and I'm coordinating some stuff with my ex."

Ex. Would that word ever not taste like vinegar?

Graham's face softened. His gaze danced. "You're a mom?" he asked, smiling.

"I am," I said. "The proudest mom. As mom of a mom as they come. I have the Volvo and the book club and *everything*." I wondered if he regretted his flirtations with me thus far. I tried to determine his energy, peering over the top of my glass.

"Well, I was a nightmare in school," he said, appearing unfazed. "Maybe I can help."

"Yeah? You? Boarding schools, Mr. Ivy League?" Somehow, I doubted it.

"Of course," he said. "Especially after my parents died. I didn't get a lot of personal attention, if you know what I mean. I was raised by my grandparents, and let's just say they were—busy."

I winced. Coco. *Didn't get a lot of personal attention.* "I'm so sorry," I said. "About that."

"Oh gosh, don't be," he said. "Ancient history. I'm just saying. Your daughter will be okay. Kids are more resilient than you think. They're incredibly strong. And I can tell you're a good mom."

"Oh, stop," I said, hoping that he would not. "What makes you say that? I work so much."

"My mom was the hardest worker I knew, before she died." He shrugged, a sadness glossing over his eyes. "She helped make the company what it is. Also? She was usually tired, and always played with me anyway. Not that you look tired." He grinned. "I'm just saying that if you work hard, and you're tired, and you love your daughter to death? You're probably in the top two percent of moms. I have a way of seeing things as they are."

An upright waiter in a crisp white shirt set down a pile of calamari and two lumps of crab cake.

I salivated, eyeing the goods. "Well, thank you for that. Don't mind me." I dove in.

Within minutes, I let an undeniable fact settle over me in the golden glow of this wonderful guy seven years younger than me: *I felt better around him.* My anxiety eased. My distracted mind, if only briefly, shifted from my worries and things-to-do, into the present moment. I still felt like a mom tonight. But Graham was making me feel like a mom in the best way possible, in the way he continued to ask me about it, with respect and kindness in his green eyes.

"Since I'm getting personal," I said. "That wine looks incredible. And I don't want to seem rude for not drinking it, so—just in case you're wondering, it's because I don't drink. Gosh, I'm so sorry, but I felt better telling you."

His eyes widened. "No, don't be! I shouldn't have assumed. What do you want?"

I told him a Diet Coke and he raised his finger. He was such a hot gentleman.

"Do you care if I ask why you don't?" he asked. "I know that's personal, but I respect it, no matter your reasons."

He was so charming. *Well, why not?* I could be vague. "I went through a hard time a couple of years ago," I told him. "Let's just say I'm better without it."

"Well, you're pretty wonderful now, so—I'll just have to take your word for it." He pushed his own glass away.

Between sips of soda, I ordered the cheeseburger without hesitation. He picked the seabass with butternut squash gnocchi. When I finished presenting the social media plan, as we waited for our dessert—he suggested we shared two—I could tell he was impressed.

"This is amazing," he said. "Please make sure Sage knows how much I appreciate it."

"Of course," I said. "She's really something else."

"She's lucky," he continued, "to be learning from you."

I blushed. The sexy ambience and his words were reaching my cheeks and my bloodstream. "So, what do you think?" I asked. "Will the higher-ups ever go for it?"

He pulled on his chin, probably evaluating the odds. "I'll do my best. I love it. I'll give them a heads-up, but you and I—Sage, too—we can present it to them in Jackson Hole next month. Together."

He loves it.

Together.

Okay.

He's twenty-six! And amazing. *And every bit as delicious as this crème brûlée.*

I shivered, feeling a chill. "I can't tell you how happy I am to hear that. I feel so good about the whole strategy. If the board allows it, it could change everything."

"I agree."

We scooped away at the rest of our sweets as our saucers of decaf coffee arrived. *I could get used to these Graham meetings.* We were even comfortable in the silence.

"So, I spilled my secrets," I said, savoring the dark chocolate cake. "Tell me something about you. Tell me something the people don't know about Graham Hamilton."

He tilted his head, pointing a forkful of ganache in the air.

"Okay," he said. "But only if you promise to stop referring to me in the third person, for the love of God."

"Sorry!" I laughed. I didn't realize I had been doing it.

"It's fine." He licked his lips. "Let's see. I can tell you, but—I'll have to kill you if you tell anyone. No one will ever find you. We're talking really, really dark stuff."

"I'm a vault." I pulled a fake zipper over my lips and pretended to toss the key.

"Swear?"

"I swear."

"OK, then." He angled forward and lowered his voice to a sexy hush. "I hate traveling for work."

Reflexively, I snorted. *"Nooooo."* I mimed earth-shattering shock, but it really was quite a bummer. It was essentially in his job description to circumnavigate the globe like a rocket.

"It's true." He sighed. "I've clocked almost five million miles. Always first class. Best hotels, obviously. But it's exhausting. And lonely. I hate it. I hate it so much."

"That's rough," I laughed.

"I know, right? You see why you have to keep it here at this table. In fact, maybe I'll just keep *you* here. All night. Just to make sure." He pushed a hand through his sand-dune hair. I didn't hate the idea of having a secret with him, and that jaw, and his adorable nose. Also didn't hate his cute comments.

I poked at the last raspberry drizzled in chocolate. "So, what are you going to do about this secret of yours? Seems like a pretty hefty part of the job description."

"Right now, yes," he said. "And for my grandfather, yes. But I'm hoping I can pave a new way. And if not? I'll do something else. I can't do the travel forever. Especially when I have a family one day."

My heart squeezed. "You want a family?"

"Sure," he said. "I'd like a whole bunch of kids."

The restaurant blurred around me and I lowered my eyes to my lap. I flashed back to the last time I was here in this restaurant, on the other side of the bar. My growing fifteen-week belly. I was over-the-top annoyed at the lingering nausea. I'd ordered the burger to settle my stomach. Now, today, all days: I would give away anything to have that nausea back.

Connor had held my hand across the square tabletop, as if trying to bridge the distance between us that underscored everything then. We were making an effort. *We were still trying at that point.* We discussed baby boy names, giddy and hopeful despite our long, painful road. We were having a son. Deacon and James were at the top of our list.

"You will make a great dad, Graham."

He perked up at that. "You think?"

I swallowed a taste of my coffee and looked him in the eye, smiling. "I have a way of seeing things as they are."

We parted ways at the valet with a hug. Graham was good. He was pure. He wasn't what people thought. Did I have a small crush? Maybe. Did he have one, too? It was possible. Did it matter? *Where could it go?* I liked his presence, and we seemed to be working well together. We both seemed to care a great deal about a lot of the same things.

At the very least, I was thankful to have a new friend.

. . .

I spooned Coco tightly for forty-five minutes in her four-poster canopy bed. I prayed for her while I stroked her eyebrows, her lids, her cheeks, her chin, and her jaw line, with the faintest brush of my fingertips. She was so still when she slept, so innocent and so clean. *How could she hit anyone? How could I be her advocate while acknowledging her imperfections?*

Before heading off to my nighttime duties, I turned onto my side in her bed with my phone. I curiously opened up Blinde. I'd sent my response to Jack before leaving the office.

I smiled. He had replied.

He was looking for a new beginning as well. He hinted at a hard breakup. Ryan Reynolds would play him in the epic of his life story, because "that guy was handsome" and cracked him up both with his acting and the way he sparred on social media with his wife. Dogs, *of course.* He dreamed of a Siberian Husky.

He worked for a small family business. *Free Solo* was a documentary that blew him away. He loved Yosemite; so did I. He had nieces and nephews that lit up his world, and yes. He'd like more kids in his life someday. He had three more questions for me:

What is your favorite food? Name three words to describe your childhood. What would you say if you could talk to your ten-year-old self?

I cozied down into my bed, feeling warmer after this day, and also feeling okay.

Feeling more than okay.

Two charming men. One single day.

Maybe fishing wasn't so bad.

I'd cried quietly in my office only hours before, but there weren't any tears on my pillow that night.

. . .

TWELVE

CONNOR

By the next week, Sera and I were talking on Blinde every day, sometimes every few hours. Time was tapping away like nothing, and the messages escalated more quickly than I ever could have predicted. I was seeing why this app worked. The platform was like a concentrated alternate universe where you wanted to bare your soul, and it let you connect with fast-forward velocity. Most of the time, we continued our game of tossing three questions back and forth to each other. I was starting to crave her quirky, cute answers, and wonder what she would ask next. Embarrassingly, I was learning new things about her. I never knew she wanted to visit Iceland before kicking the bucket. I didn't know she worried about getting Alzheimer's someday, like her grandpa. I didn't know she sometimes panicked from signs she saw in her mom. Some things hurt me to hear, because the real me was no longer privileged to this information. And then I felt the guilty pang of pretending to be someone else.

But the bigger part of me didn't care. The bigger part was so happy, in any capacity, to feel closer to her once again. I'd found a realm where we didn't have the pain of our history; a space where we had a fresh start.

Even better, I hadn't told any glaring lies yet, nor did I plan to. I was getting creative, for sure, but I was careful in steering us away from revelatory topics. It turned out there was plenty of ground to walk without exposing the telling details of your life. I was fascinated by this. I was fascinated that I was *hooked*. I was fascinated that I was falling so fast.

Again.

For the love of my life.

It couldn't go on forever, but I would hang on while it lasted. We had weirdly never talked on this level, this frequently, in years. Our conversations had the charge of a crush, the banter of wanting to captivate the other person and make them cackle out loud. For me, of course, there was also the anchor of knowing I had loved her for most of my adult life. I was checking my phone like a crack addict. Sera was flirty. Sera was smart. Sera was irresistible. Even better, I already knew all her flaws! I held the best of both worlds in the palm of my hand! It was greedy. I knew it. But also, it felt incredible to see this sexy new side of her, to have a piece of her back.

If I had started therapy to move forward, I was at least partially petrified that I was regressing with every new day. I hadn't seen Janine since I'd initiated my little *experiment*. I feared what she was going to say. I knew she wouldn't approve. I'd have to tell her next time.

The truth is, I was shocked by how far it had gone already. We were likely approaching the 4,040 mark, and, well, what then? I would vote to hit Snooze, and I hoped Sera would, too. We could slow down a bit, and I could use the next few thousand words to come up with a plan. We would soon be at the point where she'd be hurt if I disappeared.

I suspected we might be there now.

I had to focus, though. I had to focus on how to be normal and keep my phone out of sight when I saw her in fifteen minutes. It was a quarter after three. We were meeting at Coco's school.

I was going to see my college girlfriend.

I was going to see my ex.

I was going to see my crush.

. . .

With her curly black hair, top-knot headband, and Cupid-wide eyes, Miss Taft was new at most things. Newly married, new to teaching, clearly new to meeting with parents. I didn't fault her for this. I liked her. We all did. But I knew from the second I walked in the door that this meeting was going to be rough, that this twenty-four-year-old teacher was about to take us to school.

I arrived first to the classroom, where Miss Taft was already sitting. I reached out my hand and smiled as warmly as I possibly could. "Thank you so much for making time for us, Miss Taft," I said. "We're both grateful for this."

Her smile was tight. "Of course," she said. "Call me Lindsay."

I crouched into one of the child-sized chairs in front of her. Two folders sat on the table, one for me, one for Sera. *Cosette Wilson*, read the front. Coco had kept my last name.

Sera sauntered in then, her Chanel Chance perfume hitting me in a welcome waft of fresh air. My heart picked up, but I envisioned the beat slowing down. I heard, somewhere, this could help. I stood to hug her, and she looked surprised.

"Hey!" She stiffly patted my back and sank into her seat. I could see her unease and feel her sharp edge. This incident was upsetting to her. That much was terribly obvious, but she wasn't any less gorgeous because of it. Her blonde hair looked fresh and sleek, and her black skirt-suit fit her body in all the right places. Her blue eyes sparkled, as always. She carried the black leather Burberry briefcase I gave her for her twenty-fifth birthday. "I'm so sorry I'm a few minutes late."

What a sight we were here, looking like kids in detention. I knew we both felt like it, too. Lindsay glanced dutifully down from one of us to the other, back and forth, like a metronome.

We waited for her to speak.

She cleared her throat. "Thank you for being here today. I trust you know that we don't call a meeting like this unless we feel it's crucial."

Did she have to keep rubbing it in?

"Why don't you tell me a bit about how Coco's doing at home?" she said. "I know about your … situation. How do you think she's adjusting?"

Sera and I glanced at each other. I thought I should let her go first, but she said nothing. She looked frozen into a panic. I knew she took this so personally.

"She's been a little quieter, to be honest," I said. "Calmer, but more withdrawn. Also asking hard questions—"

"Like what?" Sera interjected.

"Oh, I don't know." *I'm on your side, Ser. We are on the same side of the table.* "Things about our new setup. 'Do you miss our house, Daddy?' 'Can we have a family date soon?' 'How come there aren't more *divorced kids* at school?'" *How come I don't have any brothers or sisters? What do you think of Mommy? Do you promise you still love me?*

"Coco is incredibly sensitive," Sera said, apparently ready to talk. "She feels everything in such a big way. Obviously, our divorce has been a huge upheaval for her. We're doing everything we can to love her and understand her and pour into her. We have a wonderful therapist who's helping us, too."

"That's good," said Lindsay, bobbing her head, hands clasped. "Kids have different reactions to divorce, but it's always a pivotal life event. Some kids feel deep sadness and loss. Some feel angry. Most are trying to figure out where they fit. Their stability has been shaken."

I felt Sera bristle.

"Some," Lindsay continued, "become aggressive or lash out behaviorally. I just wanted to talk to you both today about how we can work, as a team, to keep guiding Coco in a healthy, productive way."

"How is she in the classroom?" I asked.

"In the classroom? She's usually wonderful. Trouble focusing, sometimes, but she's incredibly bright. She could write her name before most of the class, and she can count higher than anyone. Her drawings are—detailed. Advanced. Often, likely, expressions of her emotions."

No surprise there. "And on the playground?" I asked. "Can you tell us more specifics about the incident? I know we're the biased parents, but—she usually doesn't lash out in that way, with her peers. It might help us to hear the context."

"Of course," she said. "She has her best friends, Grace and Lucy, as you know. They play together most days, and they tend to get along great. They can, however, be a bit exclusive."

"We emphasize kindness and inclusion at home," said Sera. "We really do."

"I'm not saying it's mean-spirited, I'm just saying—it's good to widen the circle," said Lindsay, drawing one in the air with her finger and pursing her lips. "Coco is well-liked by all of the kids, but she can be a bit *particular* about who she plays with."

"Okay," I said slowly.

"Anyway, the three girls were playing *restaurant* out at the playground kitchen. Another boy and girl, West and Sophie, wanted to join them. Coco said no. There was only room for three. Which isn't exactly *all-inclusive.*"

This isn't Cancun, I thought.

"But maybe there was only room for three," Sera said. "Coco is very spatially aware."

Try to listen, Ser. Let's get the rest of the story.

"I understand," Lindsay said. "And what West did next was not okay—his parents received an email, and we're addressing it separately. He started taunting the girls, and then pointed at Grace and said, according to the recess aide, 'She's ... fat. She's probably making pies. I don't want to eat at her restaurant anyway.'"

"*She's. Fat?* A four-year-old boy said that? To Grace?" Sera was starting to simmer.

Grace was the cutest, most wonderful kid. Half-Korean, and maybe carrying baby chub, but she was *four years old*. I was starting to think this *incident* did have a villain, and it wasn't our daughter.

"Yes, I know it's awful," Lindsay said. "But violence is never okay. Here or anywhere. Coco went up to him and told him he couldn't say that, that he needed to say sorry. He got closer and then—she started hitting him. He started to cry.

"And then Coco said Sophie could play with them if she wanted, but she had to take off her shoes because it was a *no shoes* kitchen. Sophie was alarmed by the whole thing, but Coco started trying to take her shoes off. Your daughter caused quite a scene."

"But she was defending Grace," I said. "Her best friend, who was bullied." And, well, the best kitchens had rules. Wasn't it inclusive to want to protect her?

"We don't take that word lightly, Mr. Wilson," Lindsay said. "He said something unkind, but West isn't a bully."

"But Coco is?" Sera's voice was rising, but now I was cheering her on. "I'm confused. She's in trouble, she is a *problem*, you want to talk to us about how to *parent* her, because she stood up for her friend?"

"Like I said," Lindsay said, "Violence is never okay. And I know Coco's been going through a lot at home—"

"So, you won't say *bully,* but you will say *violence*," I said, ignoring her jabs at the state of our family. "Just to clarify." We were doing our best. I appreciated the concern, but this meeting was starting to rankle me.

Lindsay looked ruffled. "*Neither*," she said, "are okay. But it's our policy that physical contact necessitates a trip to the Head of Preschool and a possible meeting with both of the parents."

We all took a beat. Things were feeling heated in this brightly lit, premier classroom, striking the oddest balance of sophisticated and juvenile. Everything was snow-white or primary colors, meticulously sorted and organized. Absolutely state-of-the-art. I had to remind myself that we didn't want to be kicked out of this place.

Or. Did it matter? Coco came first.

Coco *always* came first.

I made sure I was calm before speaking. "We respect your procedures, Lindsay. We really do. Coco hit a student, yelled at an aide, tried to take off someone's shoes. You've given us the facts. She deserved a punishment. We'll address it accordingly at home."

They still wanted our tuition. I knew this much was true. Even preschools meant business.

"We're a team," said Lindsay. "I love your daughter. I want to see her happy and thriving."

Sera softened. "We know that. And trust me, Lindsay, I know more than anyone what a handful she can be. I'm so sorry about the hitting, and the scene—we will also discuss every moment of this with her therapist. And I'm happy to contact the other mothers if you think it's necessary. I just wonder if, sometimes—"

"Things aren't always so black and white," I finished. Sera glanced at me. I hadn't felt that flash in a while, the subtle warmth of her pride.

I couldn't deny it; the rest of the meeting was awkward. We tied up the floundering ends of the *altercation*. Our folders held an official report that needed our signatures. I knew we would deal with Coco. I also knew part of me was proud of her protective spirit.

"One more thing," Sera said. "You said there have been other instances like this. Hitting? Belligerence? Gosh, I'm surprised. And so sorry."

"Well," said Lindsay, casting her eyes down. "I was referring more to the exclusion. Her particular ways. She can be very single-minded. Like I said, other kids like her. She's exceptionally likeable, in spite of her—*quirks*. We just want her to thrive here. We really do."

Quirks.

"Thank you," Sera said, pulling her emotional cards closer to her chest—*which was looking good*—and straightening up like the powerful woman she was. "For clarifying. We'll talk to her about all of it. We appreciate your investment in Coco and shared concern for her during this time."

She reached for her briefcase. I reached out to shake Lindsay's hand.

Well.

I guessed we were done here.

. . .

"Do you know what that reminded me of?" I asked when we reached the parking lot. The evening was warm for January, the ground wet from earlier rain. I sensed we both wanted to bust out laughing like we would have, back in the day. Disagreeing with strict authority when it *clearly* it had total blind spots.

"What?" She was smiling so big. Her eyes gleamed. She knew I could've cited one of several examples.

"When I came back to pin you at Delta Rho, your senior year. My meeting with the Panhellenic Board. That girl—Hannah?—the Greek President. She was *so not ready* for my arguments as to why I should be able to do it, even though I wasn't in a fraternity."

Her hand ceased to dig through her briefcase in search of her keys. She tilted her head. "You never told me that."

"Yes, I did." Of course, I did. Didn't I?

"No, I would've remembered that. I thought you just asked permission, and they said yes." Her dark brows narrowed, and I studied her face.

She was gorgeous. But still not as striking as everything inside that mind. *This was her.* This was Sera. The girl who'd been telling me everything lately. The girl who wanted a Goldendoodle and thought fake cheese was an affront to society. She was wrong about one thing, though. They could be sisters, easy, but I'd take her over Margot Robbie any day of the week.

I broke our eye contact. *If she only knew.*

"Yeah, it was kind of a thing," I said. "They said I had to be an official Greek member to proceed with the ceremony. I didn't have a real *pin* to give you. I asked what a pin signified, and they said a '*promise.*' Can you believe it? She said that to me."

She was loving this.

"I said I had given you an actual *engagement ring*, and that I would be presenting it to you, again, as part of the ceremony.

I asked if she thought most of the fraternity boys were willing to make that kind of public commitment. I asked if she thought that qualified as a *promise*. I asked if she thought it was in line with Panhellenic's values and belief in diversity to discredit one of their member's relationships simply because it was outside the system. If it was okay to *deny* her this obvious right. Let's just say I lawyered her into the deal."

She withdrew her keys, sticking out her lower lip into what she called her *compassion face*. "That's actually really sweet, Connor."

"Ah. Well."

"Thank you. You were—fantastic in there. Truly." She paused, as if she were pondering something. "Would you—you can say no, but would you want to come over and talk to Coco together? About all this? I think it might be good for her. I know it cuts your workday short—"

"Yes. Of course. Let's do it."

"You can stay for dinner, too, if you want. Nothing fancy, though! You know me." She shrugged, with a touch of sass. I wondered if she felt some relief at not being a wife anymore. "My mom will be there. She loves you, you know." She opened the door of her Volvo. "Thanks again, Connor."

See you at home. "You too, Ser."

· · ·

We decided to wait until bedtime, after Sera's Italian sausage and wheat spaghetti dinner with a side of asparagus. Every bite was delicious. She threw it together quickly but had undersold it, for sure. *I had never needed anything fancy.* Did she know that was true? Sera's mom had hugged me fiercely when she saw me tonight, as if it might be the last time. I missed her; I truly did. She had been a healthier, more reliable mom to me in the last decade than my own had ever been to me, period. I searched for any small sign of dementia in her throughout the evening, but I detected nothing, at all. She was as sharp as glass, youthful as ever in a slouchy, burnt-caramel sweater, tucked into her jeans. I silently noted that we had some good years ahead, but also, that we should cherish them.

I knew bedtime would feel intimate, so I was surprised when Sera suggested it. But we didn't want to bring up the playground ordeal in front of her mom. She grew livid about things like that and was wildly protective of Coco. I wouldn't put it past her to go yank her out of the school and leave behind a dose of her mind. We'd left enough damage in our wake. Best to handle this as a family, imperfect little threesome that we were. Maybe not broken. Just rearranged.

After tucking Coco into her lavender bedspread, we each took a side under the canopy, her two bookends. We'd each already heard her side of the story. I couldn't figure out why she hadn't told us the mean things West said to Grace. We'd talked about the hitting and shoes; we'd both told her it was not okay.

We relayed to Coco everything Miss Lindsay had told us. We asked her if it was true. In so many probing, parental words: *Did that mean boy have it coming?*

Coco hugged her stuffed sloth and smoothed its fur as she pondered. She looked down, hard, as she stroked. She was searching for words. Like Ser, she always either found the right ones, or the ones that would pierce you forever. Sometimes, she surely found both.

"I was sad for Grace," Coco finally said. "I didn't want you to think that she was fat, too. I didn't want her to be embarrassed."

"Honey," Sera said. "We would *never* think that about Grace. About *anyone*. You can trust us."

Coco shrugged. "It's a bad word. I really don't like that word. West is mean."

"You do *not* have to play with West anymore," I emphasized.

Sera took Coco's palm and flipped it to face the ceiling. She started tickling her soft forearm. She loved when we did this. *Up and down, up and down.* "How did it feel in your body when he said that about your friend? Where did you feel it?"

With her opposite hand, Coco reached up to her chest. "Here," she said. "*And here.*" She held her hand on her stomach and shut her eyes tight. "It hurt me. And Grace looked like she wanted to cry. So—I hit him."

I swallowed a laugh.

"I'm proud of you, Coco, that you know where you felt your feelings," Sera continued in earnest. "But what do you think you can do next time? It is never, *ever* okay to hit someone. We must keep our hands to ourselves, no matter what."

"I know," she said. "I'm sorry, Mommy. I said sorry to West and Sophie, lots of times. I can take my deep breaths. And then, go tell a teacher?"

"Exactly!" Sera exclaimed, clapping once. "Exactly. We love you, Coco. We're not mad. Mommy and Daddy will *always* be here for you."

"Just no more hitting," I said. "And no more shoe-tak-ing-offing!" I reached down to tickle her feet until she howled, breathless, and begged me to stop without meaning it. *Her giggle.* I craved that giggle.

We read her a new *Fancy Nancy* book and sang her Sera's creepy Delta Rho rush song that sounded only a little like a lullaby but had, against all odds, grown into a family favorite. We kissed our daughter goodnight.

"This all meant a lot to me," Sera said as she walked me to the door in her sweats. Also noted: *I still loved her in sweats.* Tiger print, tight on her rear. "Thank you. So much. Again."

"Of course," I said. "I think the more we can do together as co-parents, the better. We can give Coco—wait for it—"

"STABILITY!" we whisper-yelled together, cracking up, not wanting to wake her up.

"Ugh, that word," Sera said. "But I know."

"You were so good with her at bedtime. That was amazing. All the stuff about feeling her feelings?"

"All Linda," she said. "I know how you love hearing about *Linda.*" She stabbed my shoulder with two of her fingers.

"Stop," I said, smiling. "I believe all the good things. You seem happy, Ser. You look great."

"I do?" she asked, looking flattered, putting her palm to her chest in half-teasing shock. "I am, lately. I think work has been good for me. I love it. I really do. I miss Coco, but it feels right, you know?"

"I do," I confirmed. I wanted so badly to tuck her hair behind her ear and pull her into a hug.

So I did.

"Good night, Sera," I said softly, careful not to hold her too long or obviously breathe in the scent of her hair. I held her shoulders squarely at my arms' length. "I think we're doing fine."

"Yeah," she said. "I think so, too. We have an exceptional child."

. . .

I crawled into bed still in wistful surprise at the way this Tuesday had turned out. Ser had invited me over. We tucked Coco into bed. I knew it would be a rarity, but it also felt like a peace offering. I was thankful, riding high.

As had become my new habit, I checked Blinde once more before turning to fall asleep. I was waiting for Sera to answer my next three questions:

Tell me one of your biggest dreams.
What has been the saddest realization of your whole life?
What is your favorite color? (How do I not know this yet?!)

I (Jack) had sent the message at lunchtime. Usually, lately, Sera would have responded by now. But then again, she was with *Connor* for the whole afternoon and evening. I didn't see her use her phone once. Maybe she was distracted by *Connor.* We did have a wonderful night. Maybe our best in years.

Was I disappointed by her lack of response?

Or was I glad to have her attention?

It was getting harder to tell.

. . .

THIRTEEN

SERAPHINA

There was something about Connor's *otherness* yesterday, and last night. The way he carried himself, his confidence in our school meeting. I'd known him only as an extension of me, for *year after year after year*. Since I was nineteen years old. Like a ponytail, or limb. Necessary and glorious! But a part of me—a part that sometimes also annoyed me or gave me a headache. Seeing him walk around as a man in the big, free world, climbing into his always-clean car and driving away a little too fast—I don't know. It was weird. It was nice. *It was hot.* How did other women see him, I wondered? His left dimple, thick hair, sweet brown eyes?

Was he dating again?

How did I feel, if he was?

I wasn't ready to think about it. *Switching gears.* I owed my Jack a new message. Jack who had taught me that I actually knew how to flirt. How to feel sexy by using my words, my most favorite secret weapon, one I'd never had the chance to show off with a man before, at least not with such specificity.

Jack, Jack, Jack. What was I going to do about Jack? *What was I already doing?* With every word, I was inching closer to liking him more than I could control.

Our banter started off like conversational tennis. "You tell me this, I'll tell you that." Serves and volleys, some lobs and slams. There wasn't a lot on his profile, but I had so much faith in the system. I'd pored over every line of fine print and knew that Blinde background-checked everyone. You were required to enter your full name and driver's license number into the database. No criminals were allowed. Between the personality profiles and next-generation algorithm, I'd trusted the app from day one.

And then, message by message, in a long string of days, Jack began to wear down the high wall of cards that I was playing so carefully. He was full of interesting questions and answers, ranging from the totally random to increasingly deep. I found myself needing more. I found myself smiling again. I found myself thinking about him. I found myself starting to picture him.

I found myself wanting to meet him.

Hunkered down at my desk, I stabbed at the last few bites of my Trader Joe's salad. I was sneaking off to a therapy appointment with Linda on my lunch break today, but I still had a couple of minutes before leaving the office. I opened Blinde on my computer to write to Jack:

Sera Lorenn: Hi, you! I'm so sorry for my late reply. It's been a crazy couple of days. I love these questions! Here you go: OK, I have so many dreams. I can't pick just one, so you're getting two. First, I've been trying to get on *After the Final*

Rose since 2010. What does Chris Harrison want from me? A kidney? Take it! Take both! Seriously. Secondly, I want to write a book. Someday, I will.

I lost something very small, precious, and enormous to me two years ago. The realization that it was over. I've never been the same since. Would love to tell you more someday, maybe.

Yellow. It's the happiest color, I think.

I know that's a mix of details. Thanks, for listening, and making me smile so much lately.

Tell me: Age of your first kiss. Color of your socks today. Favorite day of the week.

XX.

No sooner had I hit *send* than a new notification appeared on my screen:

CONGRATULATIONS!

You and **Jack Lawrence** have reached

4,040 words in your Blinde Exchange.

Please select IRL to indicate you are ready to exchange contact information and meet IRL—or SNOOZE to reset for another 4,040 words. Bear in mind that you can only hit SNOOZE one time before choosing between IRL and moving on to new matches.

My heart rushed. 4,040 words? *Already?* How was that even possible? I scrolled back up through our conversations. I scrolled. *And scrolled.* Okay. It was, in fact, possible. I didn't want to make this call, though. I would let him go first. The app wouldn't advance you to the next level unless both parties hit IRL. What would he choose? What did I want? Was I ready, or not?

I could be ready, sure—but I also had a ton going on, with work, and with Coco, and with this weird Connor hangover still hazy in my peripheral. I wouldn't mind waiting until after my Jackson Hole trip. I was about to turn off my computer when a new message sprang into our chat:

> **Jack Lawrence:** Is it just me, or did 4,040 words together go by insanely fast? Sera, DO WE TALK TOO MUCH? I'm torn. I would love to meet you, but I'm leaning toward Snooze? I don't know? It's going so well? It's such a great way to get to know someone (you!) and I'm really busy at work the next couple weeks. But, truly, I am; I would never just say that. What do you think?
> I'm really sorry for whatever you lost. Reading that made my heart ache. Yellow IS happy—you're pretty yellow in my mind! And stellar dreams, girl. Both of them. I'm cheering HARD for you.
> I was six. She chased me. What can I say?
> Black.
> Thursday. It's almost Friday! By Friday the weekend is basically almost over and there's nothing else to look forward to.
> Just one question for now: What's been the best day of your life?
> Jack

11:38 a.m. I had to go. I *really* had to go. But I wanted to close the topic:

Sera Lorenn: We definitely talk too much!!! I agree. Let's wait. My next few weeks are wild, too. I'll give your question some thought. Gotta get to an appointment right now.
HAPPY THURSDAY EVE!!! ;)

Snooze.

I snatched up my phone and walked out of my office, checking my work email one last time in the elevator, which thankfully was on better behavior lately. *One. New. Message.*

From: Graham Hamilton
To: Seraphina Jones
Subject: The Bentley Deck

Hi Sera,
Whenever you have a sec, would you mind sending me the social media deck you showed me the other night? Let's set up a call with you, me, and Sage next week to discuss. It's already in pretty great shape, but we can fine-tune, start planning the presentation, and do one run-through before the trip. Hope you're having a great week. I had so much fun at our dinner. Meeting?! Dinner meeting! Like I said, you are such a hot mom. GOOD MOM! Oops. You are such a good mom. ;)
Graham

Before I lost my courage, I fired the ball back.

From: Seraphina Jones
To: Graham Hamilton
Subject: Re: The Bentley Deck

Hi Graham,
Of course! I'm out for lunch but I'll send it as soon as I'm back. And yes, it was an absolute blast. If only all meetings could be that much fun, with that much dessert (!!!).
And you, my friend, are going to be such a good dad. HOT DAD! Oops. You're gonna be such a hot dad. :)
Sera

All those childhood tennis lessons were finally paying off.

. . .

Only Linda could pull off a white leather couch in a therapy office. The other two therapy offices I'd seen in my life had something in the oatmeal variety, worn and cozy and loved. They had the air of seeing some *stuff*.

Linda's couch had a different effect, with its contemporary comfort, tufted back, and mid-century wooden legs. The clean structure and modern flair. It both soothed me and made me want to be better, exactly like Linda did. Her room had the air of renewal, with the orchids, crystal tables, and amethyst rug. Every session, for me, held the hope of a mini rebirth, and I didn't care how *out there* that sounded, because it was entirely true.

My appointments with Linda were less frequent now, since my return to work in the fall. I came only twice a month, once with Coco and once by myself, and she'd been off for the holidays, so it had been a handful of weeks. I cherished her guidance so much and didn't plan on living without it anytime soon. Truthfully: I adored her. And I knew for a fact from Sam that therapists had favorite patients, so I not-so-secretly hoped I was hers. I could tell she liked me, too. No matter what, I knew she cared, for me, my family, our fate. I knew I'd disappointed her, more than once, but she never once let me down. She was just *so right* all the time. She reminded me of how far I'd come, and of how much less distance I now had to go compared to when she met me a couple of years ago.

Linda's ice-blonde hair was cut to her chin and her outfits always blended in with her scenery. Sophisticated, modern, and sleek. Today she wore extra-high-waisted houndstooth trousers with a tie-belt and a sharp white blouse. Red popped from the bottom of her black Louboutins, the only color on her whole body. She crossed her legs, tracing the air with one pointed toe.

"I'm so happy to see you, Sera," she said warmly. "You look fantastic. I love your boots."

I'd gone sassy today, channeling my inner Sage, knee-high boots and pencil skirt with a red ruffle blouse from Free People. "Oh my gosh, you too, Linda. I miss seeing you every week."

"I'm always here," she assured me. "How have you been? Tell me—well, tell me *everything*."

I reached into my briefcase and pulled out Coco's last drawing. "I know you always want to see these. This is Coco's latest, after a meltdown. The coloring has helped her so much. I cannot thank you enough. Drawing her feelings, using her calm-down place, showing me where it hurts on her body—all of it has been so incredibly helpful."

"I'm so happy to hear that," she said. "You're seeing real improvement?"

"Yes," I said. I was. It was hard; it would always be hard. But lately, things weren't feeling so hopeless. "Don't get me wrong. She's still a handful. It's tough. I know you see it. But things do feel more peaceful. Or maybe I'm getting more patient? Or at least less likely to blow."

I told her about the incident at the preschool, and she affirmed how we handled it. *Maybe we were making strides.* She thought it was an emphatic positive that we were taking steps toward a more unified co-parenting approach—and that, typically, this does take time. She predicted it would only get better from here. This relaxed my whole body in places I didn't know I was tensing.

She flipped back to some previous notes. "And how are the ten milligrams feeling? Does it feel like enough? Is it 'life-changing' still, as you said?"

The ten milligrams. I'd nearly forgotten. They were so built-in to my day. *Brew Nespresso, take medication.* A mild dose of an antidepressant. Only Sam and three doctors knew, for now, that I was taking something. It was a "baby bump," really, my psychiatrist called it, the smallest of tiny doses, but one that had changed my life. My existential heartache and torrents of tears had nearly ceased since I started the pills. *Had it been six months already?* My shame around the issue had slowly melted away, along with that of my divorce. Nobody else had to live in the body I did, with the prickly anxiety and moody brain chemistry. I'd officially been diagnosed with PMDD (psychotic PMS, basically) and anxiety the previous summer, which made me seriously consider medication once and for all, as Linda had urged for a while.

"I need to be creative when I go back to work," I had said to Sam. "Will it kill my creativity? Tell me the truth. I can't stand the thought of losing my spark."

"That's a fallacy," she explained. "Medicine doesn't kill creativity. *Depression kills creativity.* Nothing could kill your spark, Ser."

I had the prescription in my hands the next day. Under the care of my OB, Linda, and a psychiatrist, I was, well—I was on drugs, and I wouldn't change it for anything. It also made it easy for me not to drink. My pill and alcohol were not to be mixed. Especially for someone with my history.

"Absolutely," I told her. "I think I suffered unnecessarily since I was a teenager. With depression, probably anxiety. It's rampant in my family, but I just—maybe wasn't ready to see it for what it was. Such a darkness has lifted. I feel so *even.* I feel like myself."

"Which is *exactly* how you should feel. Please keep me posted, always, on how that's going."

"Of course."

"No side effects?"

"Not one," I marveled, and smiled. "Other than sanity."

"We're all a little crazy." She smiled. "I'm so happy for you. Now, let's talk more about *you.* Is there anything specific you want to discuss today?"

I blew out hot air in slow motion.

I didn't know where to start.

Should I tell her about my men? Were they really my men to tell about? At the very least, maybe it would bring me some clarity to *get it all out there*. Linda was all about "naming the thing," and I assumed this counted for men in my thoughts. For now, there they were—three charming, hot personalities riding the merry-go-round of my nervous system. I didn't hate it, for sure. But who was I, *The Bachelorette?*

I told her. In one big, sweeping soliloquy, I felt myself blushing and exhaling as I painted the portrait of my recent "relationships," if you could call them that.

I was on a dating app. *GASP!* I'd met a few other guys but now was only talking to Jack, who made me feel known and heard and smart and sexy and important and giddy. I didn't know what he looked like. I couldn't believe I didn't care.

In the throes of a massive work project, I was also forming an unlikely bond with the twenty-six-year-old heir of our company. *What?!* He was a bit of a socialite and modern business celebrity. We had a lot of fun together, and there was some hot tension brewing. He gave me butterflies, too.

And then Connor. I still had my bursts of missing him, absolutely, but wouldn't I, for a while? But then, yesterday. *Yesterday*. I was drawn to him in a completely different way and it threw me off balance a bit. I noticed him from an angle I'd somehow missed in the last thirteen years. Or maybe we were both changing? This change also did fluttery things to my stomach.

I might as well have clapped my hands as if dusting them

clean and letting the mess float to the floor. *Good luck with this, Linda! What do you think? Now. Tell me what to do!*

Linda was grinning from one shiny hoop earring to the other. Glowing, even. But silent. She pressed her lips before finally speaking. "Sera, I am so proud of you."

I scrunched my face. "Why?"

"You are exploring your feelings. You are sharing yourself, albeit slowly, with new people, new men. I think this is fantastic."

"Really?" I hadn't seen in that way.

"I've seen you so low, so despondent, so heartbroken—your confidence, your body image, your belief in relationships, shattered. I don't see that today. I don't see that woman here."

I picked some lint of my skirt as tears burned the backs of my eyes. I hadn't seen it that way, either. "But three men? I'm thinking about all of them lately, to be honest. I really am. It's so weird. Is it bad? Bad for me, bad in general?"

"Well, do *you* think it's bad? Aren't they just conversations at this point?"

"Yes, they are. Maybe I'm just not used to feeling—*anything*, except sadness. It's been so long. Maybe it just feels unfamiliar."

"As it would. You married Connor when you were twenty-four. And you guys had a hard road together. Your losses, his demons. Your depression, the distance between you. In the end, you fought for the marriage and felt abandoned. You've been healing. You're still healing. But do you really want to know what I think?"

"Obviously! Can you just tell me what to do?" I gave a half-pretend, toothy smile that said my prettiest please.

She winked. "Well, you know I won't do that. But I truly think this is great for you. I think you should keep exploring all three relationships—but as you do, I think you need to ask yourself one big question."

"What's that?"

"*Who is Sera?* Apart from a man, apart from anyone else's plan or approval, who are *you*? As a woman in her thirties, the mother of a wonderful girl with one special, albeit challenging marriage behind you, and the rest of your life ahead, who is Seraphina Lorenn? *What does she want?* Until recently, I'm not sure you were in a place to fully trust your own intuition. But I think you're there. I think you're ready to rise."

Was I, though? *Was I really?* "So just ... keep going? Find myself? *Follow my heart?*"

"You deserve to feel like the heroine of your next chapter, Sera. The fierce woman you are, being led by the powerful God I know you believe in. *You* are so powerful, filled with his light. And you are so very loved. I want you to start living your life and making your choices in full confidence of this truth."

I dragged my pointer fingertips under my eyes to catch the running mascara. "What about Coco?" I asked.

"What about her?

"I'm her everything. I'm her example. I'm not the kind of mom who wants to *date around* a whole lot. Even if it's not my body I'm sharing. I mean. *Yet.*" I didn't think I was ready for that—for kissing and holding and knowing. And yet, my body had begun telling me otherwise. I had been missing physical intimacy. Wanting to taste a man on my lips, to feel like a red-blooded female, and not just a tired mom. Jack, Graham, and Connor had all sparked new flashes of this, and it was breaking something open inside me.

"I think you're the most solid, courageous, loving example that Coco could possibly have," she said, folding her hands in her lap. "You're not talking to her about your dating life, right? You're not exposing her to a bunch of unfamiliar men?"

"Of course not."

"I have some homework for you then."

"What's that?" I was used to her small assignments.

She pushed her notepad shut. "I want you to have *fun*. You've been through so much. You have gathered more hard-won wisdom than you'll probably ever realize. Let loose. Enjoy yourself. And when, and if, down the line, you're ready to introduce someone to Coco? Let's talk about it first. I think that'll be important for you."

She really was always right.

"As for Connor," she continued. "You two had something very special, and I would never just say that. He was your first love, your husband, your 'soul mate,' as you've said, many times. I think you should lean into your unresolved feelings toward him just as much as you do with the new men. Don't stuff anything down. If you do, it'll come out sideways—as we've seen before."

I nodded, clutching her advice to my heart in a reverent fist. Her clock clicked to the top of the hour, and I leaned down to scoop up my things. "I feel so much better. Thank you. I know I need to tell Sam next."

"She'll support you. She always does." Linda knew *a lot* about Sam. I always wondered if they'd ever crossed paths in the OC therapy network.

"I can't believe I forgot to tell you!" I said. "More next time, but she's dating Beckham. As in my handsome, promiscuous boss. And I have *complicated feelings* about it." I rolled my eyes.

She angled her head, contemplative. "I look forward to it." She paused. "But—just remember. Remember how Sam has carried you. Think of where you'd be without her. Of how long Sam has been waiting for love, on her own journey."

I knew it; I knew it well.

"What am I always telling you?" she continued.

I recited it like a pledge. *"Life isn't always so black and white. I need to learn to embrace the gray."*

Beckham did love gray suits.

We rose and I walked to the door. I turned around before grabbing the knob.

"Linda," I said, in a surge of gratitude. "I know this might be weird, but—I just realized that I've never hugged you. I don't know if it's even allowed? But today feels big. I feel like I survived a war, and I couldn't have done it without you. Can you believe it? I lived!"

"You did survive a war," she confirmed. "And now? It is your time to thrive. I'm so proud of you, Sera. Also, I'm a big hugger."

It was just a few seconds, a friendly hug, meeting expectations for a normal patient-therapist hug, if patient-therapist hugs *were* a normal thing. But it felt more momentous than that. I imprinted the entire last hour into my memory.

Thank you, I said silently, holding her. *Thank you, thank you, thank you.*

"You're such a strong woman, Sera," she said as I disappeared into the waiting room. "We're all lucky to have you."

· · ·

My boots clicked on the path along the manmade creek that streamed through the mid-rise buildings. The Cascades complex was occupied entirely by mental health professionals. I also loved this about Linda's office. The whole space felt sacred and safe. To everyone in the waiting room or bathroom or coffee shop, I always gave a small nod. We were all there to grow; to humbly heal and to hope. I sometimes invented stories for the people I saw, based on the way they carried themselves, or the wonder or hurt in their eyes.

I halted, cold, when I got to the edge of the parking lot.

No.

It couldn't be.

It was. I'd know that black Audi allroad anywhere. First of all, you didn't see them very often, and secondly, I had clipped the corner of the right front bumper on our white picket fence four years ago. Connor had always been too stubborn to fix it. *You can't even see it!* he'd say.

Well, I could see it now.

I darted to examine the back view. I had to be sure.

The license plate frame. *USC on the top, UCLA on the bottom.* It cracked him up. He was so proud, and he always loved stirring that pot. You didn't see many of *those,* either.

What on earth was he doing here? Was he dating someone in the building? Visiting one of his clients?

Instinctively, I doubted either.

Connor was going to therapy.

. . .

Chapter

—— FOURTEEN ——

CONNOR

I touched the *snooze* button and exited Blinde, tossing my phone aside. Elbows on my oversized desk, I rubbed at the stress in my temples. Sera seemed fine with kicking our can down the digital road and keeping up with our dialogue for the foreseeable future. I was confident I would know if she were offended, and she didn't seem to be.

Phew.

But I wasn't dense; I needed a game plan here. To start, I could slow our pace, hopefully without seeming obvious. I could ratchet down the questions, reel in our voracious word count. I needed to buy myself a couple of weeks.

12:05 p.m. I had to get out of here. I'd moved my usual Monday evening therapy appointment to today's lunch hour because of my crazy work week. I looked down at the stacks of thick paper needing my time.

If you keep this up, Dad's going to cut you out of the will.

Mommy, what would happen to me if you and Daddy died in a crash?

He's spoiled, entitled, a trust fund kid. Can't you tell?

These were the human realities that ended up in my hands. I sat across from young parents as they ran through options A, B, C, and D, should the unthinkable happen, should they suddenly die. I had one mother break into tears because she *couldn't think of a single person* who would take her toddler boys in the face of tragedy. I had a married couple in their forties jump into a heated debate about life after death and free will, because the wife wanted the plug pulled, for sure, if she ever turned into a vegetable. *Take my organs!* she said. *Use them for good!* she said. I could still see the husband's shock. *How could you dare risk leaving us if there was even a chance?* he asked.

There were the companies, too, of course, allocating their funds for charity. I loved that part of the job. But the families lit the fire inside me. I saw me in them. I saw Sera. I saw Coco. I wanted to be the one who protected them and safeguarded all of their futures. They'd sparked me to start my own firm.

The timing for a new venture three years ago had not been ideal, to put it mildly. Sera was trying to get pregnant, again, despite the mounting tensions between us. She'd had two miscarriages in a year, and while she had little interest in *talking* to me, if she was ovulating, it was *game on*. Tigress unleashed. She would wear her most risqué lingerie, grab my tie at the end of the day, kiss my scruff, whisper how much she missed me when I was away at the office. *When did that stop being true?* I would wonder, sometimes, while pulling her body closer and feeling my own response. Of course, I never denied her. I'd have done anything to feel her against me, around me. Climbing onto me, craving me. Even if she only wanted me for my sperm.

Pangs of guilt or pain often flashed for me, during these interludes. Sometimes I saw images of other women that I tried to swat away like black flies. Sometimes I thought of our tender honeymoon and felt a cry fill my throat. Our marriage had become complicated, but at that point, I still believed in us, in my bones. Maybe we would get lucky, I thought. Maybe a baby that lived to breathe could superglue us back together.

My law firm, Murphy & Wilson LLC, began with my law school buddy Seth Murphy, me, and a fifty-eight-year-old grandmotherly paralegal named Josephine, with a pouf of gray hair and long floral frocks. She baked us cookies sometimes. Seth and I met as junior associates at the largest estate planning firm in greater L.A. As senior associates six years later, we hatched a plan in the copy room. We would start our own venture. Several big clients followed us.

On paper, our business plan was a dream. But every step became harder and more expensive than we had anticipated. We fronted our own money for overhead, branding, and other costs we didn't foresee. The financial squeeze put even more strain on my family, on Sera. Her eyes would fall when I said we had to eat out less or cut the Disneyland passes. *It's just for a season,* I'd say. *I promise you it will pay off, honey,* I'd swear. *Okay?*

Finally, today, we were into the black, succeeding—doing fantastic. The forecast was smooth and well-paid. Still, only now was I approaching my previous take-home salary as a senior associate. Since the divorce, Sera had needed to work to sustain our house, our lifestyle, our—yes, fine—*stability*. I thought it was good for her, anyway. She was a full-time stay-at-home mom for four years, and truthfully, she'd been incredible at it. Loving, patient, maternal, and fiercely determined. She formed a strong tribe of friends and even led a weekly mommy-and-me group in our house, mostly women like her, social, ambitious girls who never returned to work after maternity leave. Who approached their new call to mom life at home with vitality and commitment.

Sera shone like a firefly, making other moms feel better about the monotony that came with the magic—the package deal of parenthood. Both/and, hard/beautiful, heartbreaking/glorious, lonely/loud, day after day of their lives. Sera inspired her friends to embrace it all, the identity crises and the impossible joy. She thrived as a mom, she did, despite the cloud of depression and anxiety that followed her like a shadow, nipping the heels of her Sam Edelman tennis shoes. She was such a radiant light; it was hard to watch the darkness crash in. I wondered if any friends knew the depths of her struggles; even I sometimes forgot. Coco had no idea. Her happy mommy hung the whole sky.

Despite Sera's supermom status from any outsider's perspective, there was a bigger truth. I knew she missed having an outlet for all of the words swirling around in her brain. She journaled for hours in random bursts, sometimes looked online for jobs. She was constantly reading, devouring podcasts. I always figured she'd go back to work, someday.

12:10 p.m.

I stood. My piles were primly prioritized now for my afternoon of casework ahead.

I hoped Janine was ready for me.

. . .

I usually changed into casual clothes before therapy, so felt out of place in my custom suit, like a sixteen-year-old boy in a college interview, begging to look the part. Although maybe I did look more the part—*divorced thirty-five-year-old lawyer-dad*—today than usual.

Across from me, Janine wore a black sleeveless dress with beige snakeskin ankle boots. Sera would love her outfit and say something like: *Wow, she looks amazing.* Not *amazing for her age,* though; definitely not. She'd cut that out of her vocabulary from the time she had a baby, hit thirty, and people started saying this about her.

"I just want to look good, *period*!" she'd tell me. "It's so back-handed, don't you think? 'You look so good! *For a mom.*' 'You look so good! *For your thirties.*' Can't they just say, 'You look good'?"

Janine did look younger in a high ponytail and diamond stud earrings, but her smile held its old warmth. "How are you doing today, Connor? You look nice!"

Not nice *for a dad*. I'd take it. "I'm great, thanks. Sorry again for the schedule change this week."

She waved her hand. "It worked out great for me."

"Good," I said, suddenly desperate to get it all out there. I usually let her lead the sessions, but I couldn't hold it in anymore. "So, I have an update for you. Something, well—something big."

She smiled. "I'm glad you're here then."

"Me, too," I said. *No time like now.* "So. Here's the thing. I went on a dating app. Blinde?" I bit the inside of my cheek.

"Yes!" she exclaimed. "I know it. My nieces are on it. It's a great concept. Connecting through words, right?"

"That's the one."

My story tumbled out and onto the floor. I told her I'd quickly received messages from a handful of Blinde matches, one being, *oh,* my ex-wife. Boy Genius here decided to respond, not as myself, but as a guy named Jack, just to *see,* just to *play,* for a second. But now we were talking constantly. I was loving it, but Sera had no idea, which I was pretty sure made me evil. Especially because I felt fairly certain that Sera was loving it, too.

Was I the worst? *The worst.* A special corner waited in hell for me.

I also didn't know how to stop.

I'd been staring at the stray threads of the room's turquoise rug, mentally snipping them, tucking them back into place. As if maybe Janine could help trim and tuck me into shape, too.

She sat there with my words dangling between us, saying nothing at all. Her eyes were wide. Did she look … *perplexed*? Had I finally stumped Janine? Did I need to hide the scissors?

She spoke after thirty more seconds. "So you're pretending to be someone else," she said slowly, "and Sera thinks she's met someone new."

"I'm not really pretending, though." I lifted my eyes, pleading my case with them. "It's all me. Truly. Other than using a pseudonym—which the app *encourages*—I'm not telling outright lies."

She crossed her legs. "What do you mean by 'outright' lies?"

I felt my cheeks burn through my beard. "I don't make anything up," I explained. "Sure, I avoid topics, and I've told some fuzzy half-truths. But it's all me. Just me, as Jack Lawrence."

"What do you guys talk about?" Janine looked almost

awestruck. "She really has *no idea* it's—her ex-husband?"

"Absolutely no clue." Remorse filled my stomach. "We talk about everything, and nothing at all. Random trivia, fun facts, our favorite letters of the alphabet."

"So, sexy talk!" She smiled.

"*Totally*," I said, cracking a grin. "Definitely no sexy talk. I think I'd feel really bad if it got that far."

"Do you feel bad now?"

"Of course," I said. "Yes, of course I do."

More silence filled the room. "Let me ask you this, Connor. Why do you think you initiated this new line of communication with her?"

I shrugged. "Isn't it obvious?"

"Not necessarily," she said. "Maybe you felt jealous or threatened by the thought of her dating again. Maybe you were just curious. We know you've been missing her, so maybe it was a way to feel close again. Maybe you saw a way in. Or maybe you weren't really thinking at all—and now, here you are—invested."

My prop. I knew I'd forgotten something today. I had no place for my hands. My blue tie would have to do. I fiddled with the point at the bottom. "I think it might have started with a small combination of all that. But I think—"

I paused, looking her in the eye, slapping my hands on my thighs again.

"I think I wanted the chance for her to see me in a new light," I said. "Not as a disappointment, or workaholic, or whatever else made me lose her. Just me—just as I am. The way she looked at me, a long time ago.

"And she likes me," I went on. "Er—she likes Jack. I know she does. She thinks I'm funny, and smart, and she is so forward, and sexy. And now, here I am, not wanting to break her heart again. Gosh, *what is wrong with me*?" I burrowed my head into my hands.

"Nothing is wrong with you, Connor." Her rhythmic voice almost made me believe it. "You two *are* connecting. It's the whole premise of this popular app. It works. Our words bind us. Our words are the most incredible tool for connection we have."

Tool. *More like a weapon.* And I'd pulled the trigger myself.

"Your recent decision might be morally gray," she said. "But even our most powerful vices are there for a reason."

I sat with that for a second.

"Do you want this to go somewhere?" she asked gently. "In your ideal outcome—would you want Sera back, in your life? Romantically?"

I'd asked myself this ten thousand times in the last few weeks. I still didn't have the answer, and I told Janine as much.

"That's okay," she said. "You'll find your answer."

"Soon, hopefully," I said. "We have four thousand forty words until the moment of reckoning. The app makes you choose after that, based on their whole science of human connection. We can choose to meet—or say bye."

"Take all the time you can," she replied. "You both endured a tragedy together. The end of a marriage is a monumental, heartbreaking event. It is nothing short of a death. Your marriage is over. It's gone."

Geesh. *Thanks for that.*

"But," she continued, "That doesn't mean something new couldn't spring up again. You're doing deep work here. You've been unearthing all your mistakes and finding your way to amends—which takes great courage and strength. Either way, we're prepping the soil for your new beginning. Something new with Sera could always spring up. If you wanted it to."

I knew it wasn't that simple. What *would* Sera do if I told her? Slap me across the beard? Fall into my waiting arms? Call the freaking authorities?

She would—*for sure*—chop bangs.

What did my vices want from me?

"Where do you think I should go from here?" I asked, sounding more desperate than I intended. I usually left this office feeling cleaner and taller and better. Even in my best suit, today, I felt like the strings on that rug.

Wayward, pathetic, WHAT are we going to do with you?

"I think," she said, capping her pen. "You have four thousand forty words to find out."

. . .

Chapter

FIFTEEN

SERAPHINA

When was the last time I did this, *actually lay this still in the sun,* with a hardback book in my lap? My friends flitted around me like tropical birds, gulping down fruity cocktails. They dipped in and out of the rooftop pool, yelling, "She's getting married!" while pointing at Teagan, every chance that they got.

I couldn't remember when I'd last done this, but it was nothing short of sublime. We were one hundred percent closer to heaven up here.

Our spray tans and colorful bathing suits glowed like suncatchers in the cool winter shine. We were a sight to behold, an obvious bachelorette party, made extra-clear by our guest of honor prancing around like a red-headed beauty queen on her stage. She wore a white bikini, *bride* sash, and veil. I leaned back into my chaise lounge, sipping contentedly on my cold Diet Coke. I breathed, watched Teagan, and smiled. It felt ironic to me now that I'd embarked on my Blinde journey mostly to find a date for her wedding. A date on my arm would be wonderful, yes, but Jack had sneakily become so much more.

"Lucky son-of-a-gun," said Katelyn, flipping another page of *US Weekly*, nodding her big hat at Teagan. "She's so full of life. What a force. I am so happy for them."

"She really is," I agreed, cocking my head. I missed Katelyn the most out of all my mom friends. Partly because she was amazing, but also because she, more than anyone else, had made the effort to keep including me when I went back to work. Some of our crew had side hustles, as Instagram called them, but everyone was home with their kids. I never understood the great divide between full-time working moms and stay-at-home moms until I became the former. I used to think it wasn't a thing, not really, that *we were all on the same team!* That when it came down to it, no one cared, not really, on either side. *That women supported each other.*

But in the last several months, whether I liked it or not, my friends' daily lives kept on going, *and going*, without me. And, I supposed, mine did, too. The five of us had babies in 2015: me, Holly, Amber, and Payton each with our first baby, Katelyn—our mentor, we joked—with her third. A few of us met at infant music class, and we'd collected the others quickly at various mommy spots. Within a year, we were inseparable.

"What are we doing today?!" blinked the group text each morning, if we didn't already have plans. We did it *all* together. The cracked nipples, diaper bags, goldfish crackers, indoor trampoline parks, more collective tantrums from our offspring than we could count. The whole staff at Chick-fil-A knew us and our kids by name. "God bless you mothers," they said, every time. They boosted my pride and my joy on the hardest of days.

Those girlfriends had watched me struggle with Coco's mood bursts since she turned one. I trusted their input implicitly, and I needed them. We would be bonded forever because of those years, clutching to each other and what remained of our sanity. We worked so hard not to lose ourselves—or our keys, or our kids. We each lost all three, more than once, but it was always okay, because we were in it together.

While I didn't want to admit it, I knew things started to strain when everyone had their second babies—and then some, their thirds and fourths. Oddly, though, not with Katelyn, the one with the biggest brood. After my mom and Sam, Katelyn was the first on my doorstep after my first miscarriage at eight weeks, the one I passed at home alone, quietly, while sobbing into a bath towel. Connor had been at a client meeting in Century City. She brought me flowers, and lunch, and let me cry into her arms.

After my second one, who made it twelve weeks, Katelyn came over after my D&C and sat with me while my tears dripped down, more slowly and hushed this time. She brought a basket overflowing with heartbreak recovery items: chocolate, chick-flicks, tissues, popcorn, the shallowest magazines she could find. She recouped with me like we were thirteen-year-olds who didn't get a date to the dance. It was everything I needed and never would have known how to ask for.

When she came over after the third angel slipped from my arms, Katelyn brought nothing at all. No words, no gifts, could be offered. We sat in silence, and she rubbed my back as I stared into a stupor. I fell asleep in her arms. I still don't know who was watching her kids when she dropped everything in her very full hands to comfort me, every time.

My other friends kept their distance for weeks, which I understood. I did.

Mostly, I think, I did.

The separation and divorce didn't help.

In what seemed tornado-fast, our split had been finalized and I had gone back to work. Our group thread was quieter now, but I felt sure they'd graciously started another without me. Katelyn, though—she was my rock. She checked on me twice a week at the least. Our whole gang had become close to Sam and my college friends, but she was the only one who could make it this weekend for Teagan. I knew she'd probably also be the only who came to the wedding.

"You're quite the force, too, Kate," I said, eyeing her over my sunglasses, giving a whistle. "*You. Have. Six. Kids.* I still can't believe it. But you honestly should never tell anyone because they might stone you for looking like that."

My phone buzzed under my thigh. I'd turned on my Blinde notifications so I didn't have to keep checking my phone like a teenager. Jack and I had cooled it with the lengthy Shakespearean messages, but—you might say we went from tennis to ping-pong, and I was loving it more. Quick banter, snappy flirtations, random confessions. It felt more like texting now, and I couldn't get enough of him lately. We'd crossed over into new territory. I felt—dared I say?—like we were getting closer each day. I wondered if we could ever run out of words.

Jack Lawrence: How's the bachelorette party?

Sera Lorenn: Ahhh it's amazing! I'm so happy to be here. Lots of pretty girls!

Jack Lawrence: I know you're the prettiest.

Sera Lorenn: No, you don't.

Jack Lawrence: Yes, I do.

Sera Lorenn: What makes you so sure?

Jack Lawrence: I can just tell. I'm not blind!

Sera Lorenn: Creepy! Are you watching me?!

Jack Lawrence: I wish!

Sera Lorenn: LOL. Okay, Ryan Reynolds. Do you really look like him, btw? Because in my mind, you kind of do.

Jack Lawrence: That bodes well for me.

Sera Lorenn: Stop. So, do you?

Jack Lawrence: Kind of. Maybe! I don't know! You'll find out soon enough!

Sera Lorenn: How's golf?

Jack Lawrence: It's great. Have fun. I won't bother you again until Monday.

Sera Lorenn: Jack?

Jack Lawrence: Yeah?

Sera Lorenn: You're never bothering me. Xx.

"Who is making you smile like that?" Katelyn poked my forearm, yanking me back to earth. "Seraphina Jones. *Who is he?*"

Yikes. I really was smiling. *Big.* I pretended to wipe it off, but only ended up smiling bigger. "I don't know *what* you are talking about."

Sam strutted up to us then, fisting a raspberry mojito, wearing a lemon-yellow high-waisted bikini and white cat-eye oversized sunglasses. She looked straight off the *Grease* set but with a much deeper tan. She stooped to sit at my feet. "*Oooooh*, are we talking about Graham?"

My face heated up, and not from the sun. "No," I fumbled. Sam was the only one who knew about my trifecta. I told her a couple of nights ago. She was interested, warm, and supportive—just like she always was. I didn't give her enough credit. "I was messaging Jack on Blinde and she saw me smiling."

I tried lamely not to smile again.

"You?" Katelyn squealed. "You're on that thing? Geesh, who isn't, and where did it come from? Sounds like a sightless disaster, if you ask me. Like that awful new Netflix hit, *Love Is Blind*."

Sam giggled. "Why a disaster? Because Sera might be falling in love with a five-foot man? Or a werewolf? Although I have to confess—I'm obsessed with that show."

"Taylor Lautner wouldn't be the worst thing," Katelyn admitted.

"Jack is six-one," I chimed. "And he's been background-checked and Myers-Briggs'd and he went to UCLA. I think I really like him. And I know it sounds crazy, but I don't care what he looks like. I'm sure we'll meet in a couple weeks." I flipped back my golden hair, insisting to myself that everything I was saying was true.

"Come on." Katelyn sighed skeptically. "Connor was a total dime piece and we all know it. You're telling me you didn't partly fall in love with him because of those hot brown eyes and McDreamy hair?"

My stomach seized in reactive protectiveness. Connor was dreamy, wasn't he? *And what was he in therapy for?* Did he have regrets? Did he still love me?

No.

The topic was Jack, and how much *looks didn't matter.*

"Connor was handsome," I said, matter-of-factly. "He *is* handsome. I'll always think so." I directed my eyes to the pool, feeling a splash after Teagan's swan dive. She'd always been the type to be unfazed about getting her hair wet.

"Don't get sad, Sis." Sam patted my knee.

"I'm not," I said, smiling, meaning it. "There's something to it, though. Talking before you meet someone. I don't know. I am into it. I'm a believer."

"So does he ever—like—say *sexy* things to you?" Katelyn asked conspiratorially. She wanted the dirty details. Not that there were any.

"No!" I squealed, laughing. "It's not like that. I mean, that would be weird. Right? We flirt. We talk about everything. But crossing over like that with someone I've *never* met? I don't know. *No,* to answer your question."

She held her hands up. "I'm *just saying,* it's a new era, and God knows I don't know the rules." She had married at twenty-three, even younger than I'd been. I adored this about her. She and her husband, Matt, were still madly in love. They had that magic, that thing. Everyone knew we'd be watching them dance to Ed Sheeran at their fiftieth anniversary party someday. "But wait—who's Graham?"

I stretched my fingertips to the sky and let out a yawn. "Oh, *Graham Hamilton*. The Prince I work with. Who is *nothing* like I imagined."

"*Graham Hamilton*? The one from the tabloids who knows the Kardashians?" Katelyn never missed a beat of celebrity news, one more reason I loved her.

"He knows the Kardashians?" I was impressed. Even I didn't know that.

Sam nodded. "I saw that he went to their Christmas party the last couple years."

"Wow," I said. "Anyway, nothing much to report about him. We've been spending some time together on work stuff, and I think we're becoming friends."

"Men and women can't be friends," stated Katelyn.

"Oh, stop," I said. "Didn't you just tell me it's a new era?"

"Sure," she said, checking her manicured fingernails, wiping each tiny one clean. "We're finally progressive enough to know that it doesn't work. For instance—are you attracted to Graham?"

I hesitated, then nodded.

"I'm not saying you can't work together and have a great professional relationship," she clarified. "But actual, personal, close friends? Yeah—no."

Maybe she had a point. It didn't matter, anyway. "He's just a bright spot in my life right now. Work is crazy, and he's someone very high up at the company—clearly—who is fiercely in my professional corner."

"Is that what the kids are calling it these days?" Sam teased, squeezing my ankles and blowing me air kisses.

I pulled a massive fake smile, baring all of my teeth. "And how's *my boss* doing, Sis?"

Sam twinkled brightly, unbothered. "He's the best. I don't even know what to say. He is the sweetest, best guy I've dated in years."

Don't you dare break her heart, Beck, or I swear I will break your face.

I breathed and reached down for her hand. "I'm happy for you, Sis. I love you both. Seeing you both happy, makes me happy."

She looked up at me. "Really?"

I thought of the blush pink room we once shared for ten years, always plopping onto each other's beds to stay up past lights out, often wondering what it might've been like to have a brother. Beckham. *My brother?* I churned it around in my head.

"Really," I said. I was sure trying. *Hard.*

My phone was so hot it had stuck to my leg. I peeled it off to see it was one o'clock. "Should we order lunch before our facial appointments, ladies?"

"I don't know," Katelyn fanned her face dramatically with the menu. "*This is a really hard life.*"

As I picked up my own menu and debated between the salmon Caesar and sushi, I had to agree. It hadn't felt this easy in ages. I'd missed this. I'd missed my friends. I'd missed me.

. . .

While I admittedly felt on the edge of age-appropriate for a bandage dress, I also felt strong, alive, maybe even sexy inside of it, and my skin. Why not, after all? *Why not.* I was still in my early thirties, and the thing was surprisingly comfortable—over my Spanx, of course. We had all agreed to wear a different bright color while Teagan wore white. We didn't make her wear the sash and veil on our night out, agreeing that the dress and her glorious strawberry locks spoke for themselves, centering her in the middle of our attention and our vibrant crew.

It was the best spray-tan I'd ever had, from a thriving new chain started by one of our sorority sisters. *Honeyed.* Courtney Crenshaw was killing it, and none of us were surprised. The deep gold glimmered like candlelight against the hot pink of my dress. I felt lucky to have claimed pink. Yellow, lime green, orange, and blue were also among us. We piled out of our rides to the club like a happy package of highlighters.

Our heels clacked on the Hollywood sidewalk. I didn't know much about L.A. clubs—okay, I knew next to *nothing* about L.A. clubs—but even I'd heard of The Monroe and its art-deco, Old Hollywood glam. Justin Timberlake had opened it up last year, as a nod to Marilyn Monroe and the historic Owlwood Estate, down the road and up in the Holmby Hills, where she had spent plenty of time. Once a month, Justin *actually* performed and DJed. Not tonight. We weren't that lucky. But there might be another surprise celebrity performance, as there often was. Brynne, somehow, had found our group a way into the thrumming hotspot.

We approached the red velvet rope between the long line of girls and the current of Sunset Boulevard. Bandaged stunningly in her lavender, Brynne walked up to the bouncer, a brown-skinned, husky, bald twenty-something in a dark suit.

He was good-looking and crazy serious. She hushed something we couldn't hear, batting her school-teacher eyes. He looked at his list, then up at her, then over to us eleven. We pointed animatedly at Teagan to indicate, *Bachelorette!* He flared his nostrils and waved us all over.

As we walked in, I covered my mouth at the ambience and the crowd. Giant chandeliers glittered from the high ceilings and low, camel booths traced the perimeter, interspersed with curving couches matching my dress. Gilded mirrors and dramatic art decorated the walls, including several large canvases of Queen Monroe herself, black and white stills splashed with color. The dance floor was small, in the center, but pulsing and vital. It reminded me of college, grown up by a handful of years. The high-end vibe of importance was thick in the air. Neon lights flashed, matching our party, and pretty girls our age roamed the room with bright cocktails. There were also plenty of guys. Naturally, they, too, were gorgeous.

Brynne led us to an ample nook in the corner: "VIP Bottle Service," she called it. I didn't know this was really a thing, and we all took a seat, enamored.

"*Who on earth* do you know, Brynney Boo?" swooned Katelyn, crossing her tiny legs in her tiny, baby blue dress.

"I went on a couple Tapp dates with a part-owner," she explained. "We—um—*parted ways*, but he was *the nicest* man. And I do mean *man*. He was almost fifty. But he said if I ever wanted to come here with my friends—" She smiled and held out her hands, presenting to us the fruits of her dating.

I wanted to laugh and salute her—but my stomach was

suddenly stuck in the back of my throat.

I squinted.

No way.

Over next to the bar, he stood with two other guys, all of them talking to a curvy brunette in a beige off-the-shoulder number.

Was it?

It couldn't possibly. *What were the odds?*

He turned his head our way then—and I watched it tilt unmistakably before his face burst into recognition.

Well, well, well. If it wasn't my prince in a black-shirt-and-jeans suit of armor. My butterflies hammered their wings.

Graham Hamilton in casual clothes. Graham Hamilton out of the work role. Graham Hamilton on a Saturday night.

Graham Hamilton making a high-speed beeline right for our table.

Oh gosh Oh gosh Oh gosh.

"Hey, guys," I interrupted with urgency. "You know Graham Hamilton? The Paris Hilton of my company?"

With wide eyes, they nodded, like—*duh.*

"*He's coming over here,*" I hissed, making a visor of my right hand to shield my face. I felt unmistakably thrown, and self-conscious suddenly in my super-tight dress and huge curls.

Sam bounced in her seat. "Oh my gosh! *She knows him,* you guys. He has a crush on her." She shot up her hand, *waving,* enthusiastically. I grabbed her wrist, to no gain.

"*Sera?*" Graham stood at the edge of our table, radiating sex appeal and adorable curiosity with his grin, his hair extra-messy tonight, two-day stubble dotting his jawline and chin.

"Hi, Graham!" I said, my pitch several octaves too high. "I'm here ... for a, uh ... best friend's bachelorette party. This is Teagan, and, uh, all our friends."

From the center of our circle, Teagan thrust her hand out. "I'm the bride! And oh my gosh, I am *such* a fan. We're doing our honeymoon at Palmeras."

He folded his arms and rocked, smiling. "Amazing choice. That's the best of our Mexico properties. Have Sera email me. I'll upgrade you guys."

You could feel our collective swoon.

"She wants to dance with you," Teagan continued, reaching to grip my wrist.

I shook my head. "No, no. We're here for girl time. It was so fun to see you, Graham—"

I was powerless. My friends grabbed, pulled, and *shoved* me out of our VIP situation to a towering Graham, waiting to hold me up with his hands, which were strong and rough, I noticed. You know, for an *Ivy League* flower. He pulled me into a hug.

"Buy you a drink?" he asked over the house music, guiding me toward the bar. "Tonic water? Cranberry spritzer? A snack? Whatever you want. This is so wild! What are the odds?"

That's what I'm saying. "Tonic water is perfect," I said, watching him place the order with ease. "What are you doing here? Do you come to this place a lot?"

"I guess you could say that," he said. "It's kind of the spot of the moment."

I didn't know how to feel about this. From the gentler, downhome-boy side I'd seen of Graham, part of me pictured him home, binging Netflix, alone on his Saturday nights. Fewer supermodels surrounding him. Clearly that was my inner mother with her naïve wishful thinking.

Was I a little bit jealous?

We climbed onto two open barstools, holding our drinks. This felt so wildly out of context. I was fighting hard for my bearings. I took a sip of my drink and savored the cold fizz in my mouth.

"Looks like a fun bachelorette," Graham said over the music, drawing in his amber liquid.

"The best," I said.

"Do you get to do stuff like this often? With your girlfriends?"

I shook my head. "Hardly ever. I haven't in months. It feels *so good*. It's even more special because it's so rare."

He inched closer. "You look incredible. Hottest mom— *maybe*—I've ever seen."

I pushed at his shoulder playfully, refusing to be intimidated by the dozens of notably *non-moms* filling the room. "Not so bad yourself." His outfit was actually perfect, completed by rugged brown boots fairly high on his ankles.

"This old thing?" he teased. "I only wear it when I don't care how I look."

My stomach again. He knew *It's a Wonderful Life.* One of the best movies. *Ever.*

"George Bailey, I'll love you till the day I die!" I laughed.

"You want the moon? Just say the word and I'll throw a lasso around it and pull it down."

He was so freaking adorable. "You really *do* know the movie."

"Just trying to be a nicer Mr. Potter," he joked. "Changing the world with my riches. Kidding. Obviously."

It was funny because it was true. I scooted closer myself now. *Relax, Sera, you can calm down.*

We continued to banter, and chat, first about movies, then about our nights, before briefly touching on our Jackson Hole pitch in a couple short weeks.

"I bet you're so cute in snow clothes," he said.

"Not really," I said. "When I snowboard, it's hard to tell if I'm a man or a woman."

He laughed. "I find that *hard* to believe."

It might've been my imagination, but I sensed he was trying not to look at my body, in the most flattering way, not a creepy way, and it made me gulp. I looked down nervously at my drink. It was undeniable. I was so fully attracted to him, in that raw, kinetic way I had not felt in years. I heard Katelyn in my ear. *You two CANNOT be friends.* I remembered that she was surveying my every move now.

When I looked back up at him, I noticed how close our faces were. I then felt his hand on my knee, where heat shot straight up my thigh. *What were the rules between us?* He wasn't my boss, not really. I was *very much* in this moment.

It seemed like an awful idea.

But that didn't keep me from melting into him when his soft, hungry lips met my own. I kissed him back, and moved closer, and stroked his hand on my leg. His tongue slipped, just barely, into my mouth, and I breathed back into his. He tasted like whiskey; he smelled like pine. I wanted his hand to move higher.

Coco. Connor. Jack. Work.

YOU.

You don't even know what you want. THIS IS AN AWFUL IDEA.

It took everything inside of me, but I pulled away, and sat still. And then crashed my forehead gently to his.

"*Ugh!*" I sighed, sitting up, sobering up, feeling suddenly sad.

"That's *it*, right there!" he exclaimed. "The response every guy hopes for when he finally kisses the girl he's been dreaming about." His eyes held some hurt, maybe, but he was smiling.

He'd been dreaming about me?

"No, I loved it," I assured him quickly. "Too much." I sighed. "I just—I don't think it's a good idea. I mean, do you? We work together."

He shrugged. "We don't *technically* work together."

I couldn't help but smile. "I think we pretty clearly *work together*. We are pitching the actual biggest wigs at the company together in a couple of weeks."

"Well—*I'm* the biggest wig at the company, if you're going to make me play that card." He caressed the tops of my fingers, which I hoped he couldn't notice were shaking a little.

That smile was *murdering* me.

He tucked a strand of hair behind my ear. "I don't think that's what this is about."

I shrank back, grabbing my drink again.

"Maybe not," I admitted, a few heartbeats later.

"Maybe you're not ready?" he guessed.

I chewed on a piece of ice. *Thank you, God, for this ice.* My anxiety needed a crunching place.

I looked up at him. This adorable boy, all of twenty-six, the world of his eyes, with his experienced lips and completely electric hands.

"I think," I said. "Maybe not. But, oh gosh—*this is so bad. Does it have to be weird now?*"

He grabbed both of my hands and kissed them right where they met. "I don't let things get weird," he promised. His practice in dealing with women was obvious. "And I especially wouldn't with you. I know things are complicated—and I like you. A lot. But I respect you more."

"Okay, then," I said, letting go, slowly, mostly relieved and a twinge devastated. "Okay, Mr. Hamilton. I'll email you this week? We can pretend this never happened?"

"You can pretend all you want." He grinned, swirling his tumbler. "I'll be playing it on repeat in my mind for—at least a month."

This. Charmer.

I sipped the last of my bubbly water and smacked down the glass on the bar as if I'd just taken a shot. Graham stayed on the stool as I stood between his legs and grabbed him for one more hug. I pecked him once more on the cheek.

"Bye, friend," I said into his ear. "Have fun tonight, okay?"

"You, too, Sera."

I felt him watching me leave.

. . .

I'd returned to the booth with both cheeks blazing and my

legs barely willing to get me there.

"Oh. My. *Gosh*!" squealed Sam. "Did you guys really just kiss? Right here, in front of all these people who are—I don't know—at least C-list celebs?"

"Wow," I said. "That boy can *kiss*."

Questions sprinkled on me like pepper, but I explained. I explained how much I wanted to keep exploring things with him, on so many levels, but mostly that I felt like I shouldn't. If work wasn't involved, it would be different. If I didn't have a daughter, it would be different. If I didn't feel stronger feelings currently for a guy I was talking to on a dating app—and still sorting through my Connor Conundrum—it would be different.

Who was I, the Bachelorette?

We danced, we celebrated, several of the girls exchanged numbers with aspiring actors and models. When our night of revelry started to slow, and the moms among us could hang no more, I waited on the curb with Teagan, Katelyn, Brynne, and Sam for our Uber.

My head still throbbed to the deep bass of the music and to the depth of Graham's kiss.

Did that really happen?

I felt woozy and warm, as if I were filled with drinks. I climbed into our ride, a black Suburban, behind Teagan, who needed help hoisting into the center bench seat. She wasn't tipsy, per se. *Okay*. She was beyond tipsy.

"That place was *amazing*," she gushed. "And Graham Hamilton, are you kidding? *Wow*. He is even more gorgeous in person. How did he taste?!"

I smiled and buckled her seatbelt. "Sweet," I said wistfully. I doubted she would remember this in the morning.

"Ser?" she asked.

"Yes, buttercup?"

She waited a beat, seeming cautious.

"Where'd it go wrong?" she asked in a drawl, tugging at the edge of her dress. "I'm so in love with Ryan. I am obsessed. How could I ever not be? Tell me what not to do. Or what to do. How can we stay married forever?"

Something both soft and concrete swelled in my stomach. We had been close, like sisters, since college. This moment, in fact, reminded me of several when I'd been on sober patrol in our sorority days. *She has the most beautiful hair*, had been the first thing I'd ever thought about her when she showed up dressed like Ariel for our Disney exchange with Sigma Chi. She had always been tough and strong, but she was rarely this vulnerable.

I thought, for my friend, and I breathed.

My phone pinged in my lap just then and Coco's face grabbed my eye. She smiled hugely in a shiny red booth, holding a kid-sized milkshake piled with whipped cream and topped with a cherry. *1:45 a.m.* What in God's name was Connor still doing awake? Another photo popped up, a selfie of them. Connor grinned, Coco beamed. They held up breadcrust with a glassy lake and flock of ducks as their backdrop.

> She really missed you today and made me promise I'd send you these. Hope you ladies are having a blast.

I sat with it. *Huh.* Did my heart just squeeze with the slightest disappointment that there were no emojis or exclamation points in his text? Was I still wanting a little more from him, after the other night? I shut my eyes.

Too many men.

I reached up to stroke my friend's pretty hair, which remained curled at its soft ends.

"Never stop letting him see you," I said, finally, sighing. "Life is hard, Teag. Challenges are going to come. It's just a matter of what yours will be. But if you stay connected, and talk—*really talk*—every day, even for fifteen minutes, you'll keep hold of each other. Give him a chance to see all of you, even the parts you don't like. I think we started sliding downhill when I started shutting him out. Also, you have to learn to forgive."

She said nothing, head on my shoulder; still.

I glanced down to see that her green eyes had fluttered shut.

I kissed the top of her hand and squeezed it tightly in mine, thumbing her pear-shaped diamond inside of its halo.

. . .

SIXTEEN

CONNOR

Arms outstretched on the park bench, I leaned back, breathing in the clear Sunday afternoon. My sister, Isla, and I watched our kids climb on the sunbathed playground, the best in Orange County, I thought. Built into the side of the Back Bay, it overlooked the shimmering body of water that was surrounded by teeming wildlife within this city-protected sanctuary in the middle of Newport. So few people were aware of this park, and I didn't spread the news. It felt like a secret, a pocket of ethereal nature with breathtaking views.

We held our lattes. As usual, Isla had packed the best snacks, so Coco and her cousins took turns bounding toward us for reinforcements. Pirate's Booty, organic gummies, mini-muffins, string cheese.

"Coco seems so great," Isla observed, tearing open a pack of the gummies and popping one into her mouth. She wore her brown hair mid-length, wavy, always down, untouched by products or heat, and never a stroke of make-up. I loved her this way. She didn't need any additives. Her skin was almost distractingly pure and so were her sky-blue eyes. She looked like me, except for our eye color, everyone said. "Calmer maybe? She hasn't cried or screamed once today."

Playdates with Coco were usually a mixed bag of sweet exploration and really, *really* big feelings, a seesaw of friendship and *"Dadddyyyy! So-and-so did this to meeee!"* I was forced into the most gentle, present version of myself I'd ever had to muster, and it often left me wondering how Sera had done it—*day in, day out*—for four years at home with few breaks.

Today with Coco felt different, though. Pleasant, even. Dared I say tranquil?

"She really is," I said. "Sera's been taking her to this therapist for months now, and I'm amazed at how much it's helped. The littlest things. She's a 'highly sensitive child,' as we've known for a while, but they're also going to test her for anxiety and OCD."

"Oh, wow."

"Yeah, it sounds kind of scary, but—I don't know. It's Coco. She's so special, right? We want to be the best parents we can. And would either of those diagnoses really surprise you?" I half-smiled, shrugging. I didn't care what the labels said. I'd always adore my girl and give everything I could to love her and know her.

"I guess not," she agreed. "I'm impressed, though. You guys are doing such an amazing job with her during all this. I can't imagine how hard it's been."

"Yeah." I swigged my latte. "Brutal. It kills me to have only the weekends with her, and not tuck her in every night. I try to make the most of it, though. I even took her golfing for nine holes yesterday. She loved it. Her focus is insane for a four-year-old."

"Basically five," Isla reminded me.

I felt the stab of a reminder that Sera wouldn't be there to celebrate. She was working so hard, though, to make the birthday special. A tea party at our house—*their house*—on the actual day, a Wednesday at four o'clock, with all of her little best friends. Her mom and sister would run the show, but I would be there, of course, maybe as the Mad Hatter.

"You guys will be at the party, right?" I asked.

"Of course," she said. "Wouldn't miss it."

Isla fell quiet then, and I thought I saw something upset, conflicted maybe, flash across her smooth face. She watched her oldest, Cara, seven, swing across every one of the monkey bars like a champ, but she didn't clap and holler, like usual. She didn't shout her mama-bear, "Way to go, baby!" or "YEAHHHH!"

Her eyes fixed on the water below us.

"Hey," I bumped the side of her shoulder with mine. "You okay?"

She frowned and glanced at me, skittishly, before biting the lid of her coffee. "I have to tell you something."

My pulse sped, and I looked at her kids. *Which one? Something must be wrong with my niece or one of my nephews, so which one, and how could I help?* I put my hand on her back and squeezed.

"I'm here, Sis," I said. "Whatever it is."

"No, it's not like that," she said. Gosh, she was frantic. I could practically feel her pulse through the neck of her sweat-shirt. "I just—I have to get it off my chest. Remember a few weeks ago, you asked me to promise you something?"

I reached back into the archives. *So much had happened* in the last few weeks. Janine sessions, work insanity, not to mention, *oh,* I was secretly internet-dating Sera.

I remembered the night of my date with Hailey.

Isla calling.

You have to tell me if Sera meets someone.

No. *No way.* There was absolutely no way. Sera was dating—er, is that what you called it?—Sera was "into" *Jack.*

Thus, Sera was into *me.*

"I do remember. About Sera? I made you swear you'd keep me informed?"

She nodded, rapidly. "I'm so sorry, Con. I wanted to tell you in person."

Of course, though—Jack! Maybe Sera had told my sister all about *Jack.* It was totally possible. "Isla, *this guy*! I am so into *this guy* I met on that dating app without any pictures. CAN YOU EVEN BELIEVE IT, WHAT DO YOU THINK, could it be lasting true love?"

Everything was just *fine,* I told myself, seven times.

"Go on," I said to Isla, feeling unsteady. "She told you she met someone?"

"Well, not exactly."

Huh. "What does that mean?"

"We haven't talked much lately. I know she's really busy at work, and juggling everything with Coco, and the birthday party—but Drew saw her. Out. With a guy."

Someone might as well have socked me in the gut with a bat. *What?* Who? *Wait.* We'd never said we were exclusively flirting and baring our hearts, but—I don't know. It hadn't even occurred to me that she might be dating other people. Which, of course, was her right.

So why did I feel so sick?

Isla fished into her diaper bag. She pulled out her phone, swiping and tapping to a text from her husband. She held up a picture. "Look."

I'd know Sera anywhere, and the picture was surprisingly clear. I recognized immediately that they were at Water Grill, where I'd taken her for her thirty-first birthday. The place had recently opened back then. She was still pregnant and sick.

In the moment I held in my hands now, Sera tilted her creamy blonde head back, laughing, looking sexy in a low-cut, long-sleeved black work blouse. From behind, across from her, a guy who looked tall from the back, darker blonde, in a black suit jacket, reached across the table to her dessert.

You could feel their chemistry in the photo.

I hadn't seen Sera laugh freely like that in years.

She was radiant. Possibly smitten.

We always shared two desserts.

I dropped the phone back in my sister's lap. I was spinning, and hurt, feeling impossibly stupid, all of it jammed in my throat. Drew clearly captured what he thought he was seeing—my ex-wife, moving on. As I should've been doing for months.

Well, what the hell was Sera doing with Jack, then? *With me?* Blinde-writing me constantly like she cared? Was I a distraction? Filling a void? Just *a friend*? How many men was she talking to?

Hold up. *Had she slept with this sandy-haired, dessert-stealing idiot?*

No. She wouldn't. I knew she wouldn't. But even the thought of them touching toes under the table made me want to go jump in the bay.

I leaned forward, head between my legs, digging my fingernails into my scalp. I thought, for a moment, I might accidentally cry. Isla rubbed my back, just like our mom would have done, our whole lives, if she had ever *cared to be an actual mother.*

"I'm so sorry," Isla said. "I'm so, so sorry, brother. Did I do the right thing, telling you?"

I blinked at the concrete. "Of course. I wanted to know. I'm just—I need a second."

I went on a date with Hailey, didn't I? That didn't go anywhere. We could've easily kissed in the parking lot. I even could've taken her home. Everything going on in my mind that night was so much more complicated than it could've, perhaps, appeared—two adults, in their prime, sharing guacamole and personal details, bonding over delicious tacos and the best band of all time. Then again, that was before I started talking to Sera on Blinde.

I needed more time with this. I didn't know how to feel, so I imagined what Janine might say, and decided to feel it all. The confusion, jealousy, rage. Most of all, though: just loss. I felt the weight of reality settling in. To Sera, I was: (A) some guy on the internet, and (B) the ex of her past. I was, decidedly, *not* the guy hearing about her day, with her actual sexy voice, telling her everything would be okay, noting how pretty she looked in this cute outfit, or that.

I was not the guy taking a bite of her *cake*.

I never would be again.

"Thank you, Sis. Thank you for telling me."

Coco ran toward me then, throwing her arms around my neck in an enthusiastic, little-girl choke. "Can you take me to the bathroom, Daddy?"

I hugged her tightly before standing up, brushing off my thighs and taking her hand. It was so dainty, for how strong she was. "You got it, Cokes. We'll be back, Isla."

On our way to the restroom, high in the clean blue sky, I saw three black birds flying together, forming a pointed arrow, upward and north, before one of them veered to the left, away, and alone.

· · ·

Chapter

SEVENTEEN

SERAPHINA

I could admit it with (almost) no shame. I was, officially, not Forever 21. Even with no hangover to cure, I was still feeling the 3 a.m. Saturday night come this Monday morning. Thankfully, Connor had done me a favor and kept Coco for one more night, dropping her off at school for me early today. I'd needed the extra recovery time.

And coffee. *Get me more coffee.*

The exhaustion was worth it, though. Our Sunday had been the perfect end to the perfect bachelorette weekend. We brunched, we shopped, and we hailed our limousine home. I sat by Sam in the back of the limo, and we thoroughly dissected my club kiss like only sisters could do.

"This is a big deal, Ser," whispered Sam. "You haven't kissed a guy besides Connor in—*fifteen years.*"

When she put it that way … *Well, dang.* "I know, I know. But honestly? Does it have to be such a huge thing? Maybe I should be out there kissing *more* people."

"And if you want to? I will support you. A thousand percent. But why do I feel like that's the last thing you want to do right now?"

I sighed, wishing as I had for most of my teen years that I could *just be that girl*. But I knew it. I knew I couldn't. I got attached. I had never been able to make out with guys and walk away casually.

Except for maybe this one time with Graham when my heart was so clearly elsewhere.

"It's just too much right now," I said. "And working together? I can't. I actually wish I could—have you seen him? But truly. I can't, Sam."

"I get it," she said, grabbing my hand and squeezing it.

It took two sisters forty-five minutes to determine once and for all that we were both glad that it happened, we wished it could happen again, and that it was probably best if I released one of the *three* single men swirling around in my thoughts these days.

"How was the actual kiss, though?" she asked. "Because it looked *smoking hot*."

I exhaled. "It was the hottest, Sam. I think I probably needed it."

At the top of my day's to-dos, I had to email Graham today to set up our run-through for Jackson Hole. I couldn't figure out what to say.

Hey Graham – Wow, WE KISSED! LOL!

So, Saturday night, huh? You're such a good kisser! ANYWAY!
What day/times are best for you next week?

Dear Graham: Following are several times proposed for our
Jackson Hole social media run-through. Sage will be present
as well. I hope you had a nice weekend.

So many choices! Like I said. Stumped.

Coffee! That's right. I stood and smoothed out my skirt.

"Oh!" I jumped, grabbing my chest, at the sight of Phoebe,
our top boss and global manager, filling my doorway. It was only
half past eight. She usually wasn't here until nine, and she rarely
ever came to my office. Hers was way down the hall, three times
the size of mine, and fit for *Architectural Digest* with its urban
modern décor. I was slowly proving myself back at Hamilton, but
I was still considered one of the *little people*. Phoebe, meanwhile,
was running our branding worldwide.

Why were her eyes red and puffy?

She was trembling, then still. Her complexion was the color
of chalk.

"Phoebe? Are you okay? Come in, come in." I motioned to
my couch and sat at my desk again, but she shook her head and
stayed planted right where she was.

"Something's happened," she said, sucking in a breath.
"Beckham. His brother. The twin who lives in L.A. He—"

She continued, "Brad died. Early this morning. He had a
heart attack."

What?

What?

"What? No. No, no. Are you serious?" I covered my mouth.
Beckham and his brother were the most symbiotic, closely

connected brothers I'd ever known. Brad had been in the office many times over the years, and I'd been to happy hours and work parties with him. Even Connor had met him. He looked *exactly* like Beck. Maybe slightly less obsessive about his personal style. But handsome, and so very funny. Engaged to the love of his life. Their wedding was in two weeks.

"Yes." Phoebe smoothed down her shiny red hair. "Very serious."

Why hadn't Beck called me or texted? *Why Phoebe?* But I knew the moment I wondered. The air in his lungs had been vacuumed out of his chest. He had just lost an appendage. He wanted to make one work call, and Phoebe was the perfect candidate to deliver the message to us with brevity and precision.

I had no words. I actually had no words.

"A heart attack?" I mustered. "He was thirty-seven years old. How can that even—"

"It's devastating," she finished. "They're doing a full autopsy, of course. Can you tell Sage? I'll tell everyone else."

"Of course," I said. "And anything, everything—I'm here, Phoebe. What can I do? What can I take off his plate? I assume he'll be out indefinitely?"

"At least a few weeks, yes. And it's actually good fortune— ah, I suppose—that you're already leading the Jackson Hole trip. But I'll need you for other properties. And some stuff on the global side. Beckham had his hand in a few Europe and South America projects."

I didn't know that. Good for him. "You've got it, Phoebe. Anything. We can meet later this week if you want."

"That would be good. Check my calendar and send a meet–ing request."

I opened Outlook right there.

"One more thing," she said, crossing her arms on top of her purple sheath dress.

I froze my mouse and looked up. Her piercing eyes were so green. "Anything."

"You're doing a fantastic job, Sera. On every call. Every draft I've seen. I know—" she paused. "I know how hard it is to do what you're doing. To pick yourself up. To be there for your daughter. To do it all. I wanted to say I'm impressed. And that we're lucky to have you."

She bowed her head briefly, and tightly smiled. And then, as Phoebe marched away, I realized how very little I knew about this woman's personal life. I had vague recollections of two teenage kids and a second marriage, but not much of anything else. One thing I did know, however, was that she was sparing with compliments. I would take this one to heart.

And I would carry my friend, the way he had carried me.

I picked up my phone to see it illuminated with five texts from Sam.

Sis, call me. Oh my gosh. Did you hear?

Beck's brother?

He had a heart attack.

In his bathroom. Early this morning.
Driving to Beck's now.

CALL ME!!!!!!!!!!!!!!!!!!

First, I had to text Beck. What was there even to say? I told him how sorry I was. I told him that my heart broke. I told him that I cared for him like a brother, and that I was here. That I'd always be here.

The first ring didn't even finish ringing before Sam picked up. She was calm, as she tended to be in a crisis. Abnormally quiet, too, despite her fast and furious texts. I think she was speechless, like I was, when it came time to speak.

"Sam," I said firmly. "I am so sad and so sorry for Beck and their whole family. But I want to say something else."

I could hear her nodding.

"Forget anything bad I ever said about Beckham. Forget my hesitations about you guys. Forget what I said about him not being good enough, or not believing enough, or any of that being a thing."

She nodded again.

"None of it matters. He needs you. I think he might love you. Just be there for him. Okay?"

"Thank you, sister," she said quietly. "I love you. Will you take care of everything at work? He was mumbling something about London. He's in shock, but—"

"Don't let him think about Hamilton for one more second. It's done, it's covered. Hug him for me. It's handled."

Now it was my turn to breathe.

I *hoped* it was handled.

. . .

I didn't need the caffeine anymore. Feeling shaken enough, I called Connor, and it made me feel close to him, however briefly. Tragedy always had a way of cutting through dances of awkwardness. Brad had been a lawyer, too. Entertainment, but still. They always had plenty to talk about it. I knew he would want to know.

Connor told me he'd love to come to the service, if there would be one, if that wouldn't be weird, or that he'd be happy to help with Coco while I went for us. I promised to keep him posted, wondering silently if I ever wouldn't want to hear Connor's voice amid major disaster. *Time doesn't fully heal wounds,* I thought. It just smoothed the incision. Eventually. If you were one of the lucky ones.

I closed my eyes, elbows on my desk, heels of my hands on my brow bones.

I was back in January 2018.

We were walking briskly, Sam and I, on a chilly gray Saturday morning, when I felt the first sharp pain. I'd never felt anything like it, not in my labor with Coco, not in my first two miscarriages, not in my entire life. I knew in my soul right then. *Something was not right in my belly.*

We kept walking, though—another lap around Balboa Island, past the darling sailboats and picturesque oceanfront mansions. *We kept on walking*, a misstep for which I'd never forgive myself.

If we'd raced to the hospital at the first sign of danger, could we have altered history as I knew it? Would Connor and I still be married? Would we have a baby boy?

It haunted me still. Less often.

But I still wondered.

At the end of the next lap, I doubled over in pain in front of a garishly modern glass house. I cried out, guttural, wide-eyed, seizing my sister's hand. A small crowd gathered around me and my seventeen-week pregnant stomach, which already looked more like thirty. I always carried early and huge. That's when I saw the blood start to seep through my turquoise yoga pants. Sam called the ambulance fast. They arrived even faster. I blacked out on our way to Shore Hospital.

"How many weeks?" the medic had barked. I couldn't speak. I heard Sam tell him *four months* before everything faded to black.

I didn't dream during the three hours I lost forever. You hear those stories about meeting Jesus and being sent back to earth. Spending ninety minutes in heaven. Or, at the least, seeing your life flash before your eyes, like a series of movie previews. I wish I had something profound to report from those minutes, but they only would ever be blank.

When my eyes finally opened again, my first thought was: *I feel empty*. I looked down, and sure enough, my ripe belly had softened already.

"She's awake," I heard Connor say. Dark circles ringed his eyes.

A nurse in blue scrubs with deep brown skin and a nose ring came to my bedside. She explained what had happened to me and told me her name was Esther.

Placental abruption.

Emergency surgery.

Heart stopped beating.

We don't really know.

0.5 to 1.5% of pregnancies.

You were hemorrhaging.

Had to save you.

Lost the pregnancy.

Didn't have to do a hysterectomy.

You're okay now.

"Would you like to hold your baby?"

Baby. *My baby.* Of course, I would like to hold him.

I nodded, groggily, ill. *This is a dream.* Right?

"Ser, you're okay—I'm so glad you're okay," Connor choked. He stroked my hand inside his. I stared at him blankly, the picture of what had happened slowly pixelating before me.

Wrapped in a cream-colored blanket with baby-blue stripes, my tiny boy was placed in my arms, all seven perfect ounces. I wept. I wept like I never had before and know I will never again. *His skin is so shiny*, I remember thinking. *Iridescent, like glass.* Eyebrows and nose and fingernails exquisitely formed. He was so fetal and pure, curled into a tuck.

"Does he have a name?" Esther asked. I was warmed by her phrasing and inference. My human soul, and my son, cuddled there in my arms.

I nodded, not looking at Connor. *I got this final say.*

"Deacon," I said, voice breaking. "It means servant, and messenger. Sent here to teach us something."

For all of my lifetime, and all of my words, the ones I'd been paid well to write, our hour with Deacon is something I won't ever be able to crystallize into language. He was an angel, simple and pure. *Sent here to teach me something*. I was still searching for what. I would repeat every second of that fated pregnancy, ten times over, if it meant I'd get that hour with him. He was part of my fate, indeed, and I would love him forever.

Connor and I both kissed his forehead and passed him back to Esther, who'd kept a gentle distance, head bowed. After she took him from us, to prepare him for his final journey, I heard her voice softly praying on the other side of the curtain that divided my hospital room.

"Lord Jesus Almighty, into your hands, we commit this soul, this sweet little baby boy. May he rest eternal in the loving arms of his Savior, who gave him life, and now takes him home, to never know sin or pain on this earth but rather life and joy abundant forever. And be with his mama and daddy, Lord, watch over them, Jesus. They're gonna need it. By your grace and your mercy. Amen."

Connor and I would have a good three months together after that. Our delicate boy, the ache and experience, brought us closer for a brief time. My body healed from the trauma while Connor doted on me, going through the motions. Friends brought us food and flowers. We binged *Parenthood* on Netflix, and every restaurant on DoorDash. We read to Coco, did puzzles and crafts. Sam and my mom saved us during that time—they were over, or helping with Coco, every second they weren't tending to the top necessities of their own lives.

But when they left, and the casseroles stopped, and it was just me and Connor again, within three more months, we were more miserable than we'd ever been.

My real nightmares began, and so did the end of our marriage.

. . .

Chapter

— EIGHTEEN —

CONNOR

" Thank you," I told the barista, nodding in acknowledgement of the wonder that a church had a full-service *barista*. This café was legitimate, filled with tables and surprisingly crowded for a Tuesday at 6:48 p.m. College kids appeared to be studying, and staff members seemed to be meeting. One woman in the corner looked to be crying into her muffin, and I wanted to give her a hug. Two men in another corner were praying. The glass-wall view looked onto a clear baptismal pool the size of a half-court, and beyond that was a dark-water lake bleached in milky moonlight. I'd heard about Crossfire for years, and now I knew why. This place was more city than church, but also felt strangely like home.

Gripping my lavender latte—I knew it was girly, but I was intrigued, and *no one had to know what my cup held*—I opened my phone to the property map, in search of the Upper Room. *Perfect.* It was a quick elevator ride up from here, and I was a few minutes early. I took a seat to check Blinde.

I had held *big plans* for punishing Sera after hearing about her date caught on camera. I gritted my teeth when she'd asked me to take Coco an extra night after Teagan's bachelorette party. Usually, I didn't mind, but this time, I flung a litany of unspoken insults her way as I texted back:

> Sure, no problem!

How's the giant dessert-stealer doing? Did you meet anyone in L.A.? Maybe Jack will casually ghost you and let's see how you feel about THAT, huh?

I knew it was petty. At least I had held it in. But at the very least, I'd planned to pull back on Jack and play it cool for a couple of days. Let her miss him. Let her wonder why her online boyfriend didn't message her eagerly come Monday morning, as had become our usual. Let her question and stew. I'd been ignoring my other matches, but maybe I'd go check them out.

I wondered how Hailey was doing?

I tried to wonder how Hailey was doing.

But then, out of nowhere, Sera had called me, and told me the news about Brad. My stomach had dropped. I could still see his face—the kind you didn't want to be threatened by as a guy, but that made you definitely, secretly want to ask how it felt to be that good-looking. He looked exactly like Beckham, of course; they were identical twins. But also, Brad was distinct. His whole essence was so much less—squirrelly? Talkative? Perfect? Less stylish, yes, but he conveyed such a sincerity. Also, I was fascinated by his job in L.A., negotiating high-profile music contracts and diving headfirst into scandals. I only hung out with him twice, at some Hamilton gatherings, but I remembered him clearly. He was someone you didn't forget.

Sera was understandably shaken. I suspected this meant her workload would spike, so she was probably stressed, in addition to the heartbreaking tragedy, especially with her trip coming up.

Plus, I still had to step back—like a man—and figure out exactly how I was going to climb out of the ditch I had dug. No matter how you looked at it, here we were with, at the very least, a real online friendship. I decided it was not the best time for Jack to be a big jerk. I had my guard up now—I hated that she was seeing anyone else—but all I could do was stay focused within our relationship(s)—*yikes*—and hope we'd rise to the top. I would block out the noise, like every good *Bachelor* contestant had modeled.

So Monday afternoon, I messaged her, as if nothing had happened. We had a quick conversation before signing off, and the rest of the day, she'd been quiet. Which was good. I was still trying to stall our word count until I made a decision.

Jack Lawrence: Hi, you! Happy Monday! How was the rest of the weekend?
Sera Lorenn: So good! So fun!

Pause.

Sera Lorenn: Today is weird, though. Super sad. My boss's brother died. Super suddenly. Heart attack. He was only 37. :(
Jack Lawrence: Oh my gosh. I'm so, so sorry. That's awful.

Sera Lorenn: I know, right? I didn't even know that could happen in your 30s.

Jack Lawrence: Ugh. I'm so insanely sorry. Can I do anything?

Sera Lorenn: Nah. It's okay. I mean, it's not, but ... Ugh. How are you today?

Jack Lawrence: Oh, I'm great. Just working. Well, I mean, not this second.

Sera Lorenn: Lol. Let's talk about something fun. Ask me something weird. About ... I don't know. Childhood.

Jack Lawrence: Okay! Let's see ...

Pause.

Jack Lawrence: What's the weirdest thing you were obsessed with as a kid?

Pause.

Sera Lorenn: It's frightening how many answers I have. But—I think I'm gonna go with my lucky rabbit's foot. Feet? Gosh, I *collected* those things! How. Disgusting. Did you ever have one? Why did my mom let me carry those monsters around?

Jack Lawrence: Hahaha. No. I did not. But my sister definitely did.

Panic. Sister. Had I mentioned a sister yet? Shoot. Breathe. Sigh. Lots of people had sisters, I reminded myself.

She clipped right on. *Thank God.*

Sera Lorenn: I actually believed they were lucky. I also never stepped on cracks or walked under ladders. What about you? Favorite weird childhood thing?

Jack Lawrence: Hmmmmmm. I think I'd have to say Pogs.

Sera Lorenn: HA! OMG, I forgot about Pogs!!! But, um, they weren't weird. They were awesome.

Jack Lawrence: Right? I had the most serious collection of slammers.

Sera Lorenn: We should bring them back. Pogs. Not the rabbit's feet.

Jack Lawrence: Done.

Sera Lorenn: Well, I should probably go. Work's gonna be extra crazy for me in the next couple weeks. Talk soon?

Jack Lawrence: Yep.

Sera Lorenn: Okay. Have a great day. Xo.

That had all been earlier today, and I still didn't have any new messages. I decided to leave it alone, though. I figured it wouldn't hurt to not only give her space after such a weird day—but also to let her miss Jack. *Just a little.*

· · ·

The Upper Room was enormous, with lofted ceilings and high oak beams. There was a stage, so I imagined the space was also used for events. Tonight, though, it felt more like an AA meeting. There was a small table, with coffee and tea and cookies and Styrofoam cups, and a ring of folding chairs in the room's center, mostly filled up by this point.

Janine, I thought. *Where on earth have you sent me?*

A bald older man in a lumberjack flannel and glasses walked up to me, smiling. "Welcome!" he said. "I'm Roger."

I grabbed his hand. "Connor," I said. "Is this Renegade?"

"Sure is. We're happy to have you, son. Come sit!" He had a strong Southern drawl.

I ambled over, assessing the crowd. *All ages. All shapes. All sizes.* It was as if Roger, or whoever, had plucked the most eclectic male sampling available to represent our kind as a whole. One thirty-something in a blue suit was handsome, black-haired, clean-shaven, looking sufficiently bored. One well-muscled Hispanic man in a tight black t-shirt was artfully sleeved in tattoos. One white kid looked no older than twenty, skinny and blond, with acne.

This was going to be interesting. A night with these guys, *about intimacy.*

I took a seat next to the tattoos, because of the way his eyes sparkled. He smiled as soon as I did.

"Frank," he said, grabbing my shoulder. "Welcome."

"Thanks, man," I said. "You've been coming here a while?"

"Six months," he said. "Every week. It's not what you think. You'll like it."

"What do we talk about?"

He shrugged. "Whatever we want. Whatever is blocking our relationships, or our lives, you know? Wait. You need a workbook."

Oh. *Did I really, though?* "Okay."

He returned with a spiral-bound book that read simply *Renegade*[2] on the front, by Clive Able, PhD. I immediately flipped it open, landing on a page titled *Intimacy's Intricacies.*

Men always want to be a woman's first love—women like
to be a man's last romance.
— Oscar Wilde

You could say that again.
I skimmed on.

Healthy intimacy is meant to be both expressed and
received emotionally, intellectually, socially, spiritually
and physically within our relationships. This is true for
both men and women. Without healthy intimacy, pursu-
ing sexual gratification is like pouring water into a bucket
with holes. It will never satisfy a man's heart.

I pictured a spaghetti strainer and all the images I had poured
into it over the years, their shiny allure and toxic residue leaking
out of the bottom. I considered these various aspects of intimacy,
too, and where Sera and I had gone wrong. It seemed to me that
we had crumbled in every category, one at a time.

Roger stood in the middle of us, while several more members
sat down to fill out our gang.

"Welcome, everyone," he said warmly. "Please help yourself to
the coffee and the chocolate chip cookies my wife made. We have
some new members, so how about we all go around and introduce
ourselves—and say, if you want, what brought you here?"

Here we go.

I tried to memorize each man's story. Frank had served
time in jail for domestic assault, and his ex-wife had been gone

for years. He found Jesus in a bar in 2015 and had been sober from drugs and alcohol since. He was single and had restored his relationship with his fifteen-year-old son.

The pimple-cheeked blond was also new. His mom had made him come tonight because she "freaked out" over what she found in his browser history. *Been there, boy*, I wanted to tell him. I also wanted to look him in the eye and say, *Stay. Fight this now. Your whole life will be better.*

I gave the CliffsNotes of my story when my turn came. I had a history with porn, I guess you could say, since I was twelve. My wife and I divorced a little over a year ago, and it was a big factor in us falling apart. I was feeling disillusioned by it lately, but curious about digging deeper into the power the stupid thing had held over me for so long.

The group had no official format—Roger was the clear leader, though, and a skilled facilitator. He mostly opened it up to questions and sharing after our introductions. If one thing was clear from this group, it was this: We were all looking for love and acceptance but had wrapped ourselves around the wrong things one too many times in our quest. We were misguided, but not evil men.

Our stories were all very different. Roger had been married for thirty-eight years, but six of those, he said, "were hellfire and brimstone, my friends." He cheated, he lied, he drank; she left, she met someone else—but Roger went back to fight for her after he turned things around. Now they had five grandchildren, renewed their vows every five years, and did what they could to help save shattering marriages. Especially those with young kids, or alcohol issues.

The handsome business guy was a self-proclaimed sex addict, particularly, lately, on all of the dating apps. The ones you signed onto to find a fast, easy hook-up, to go chase the hit in real time. He had a wife and two kids. None of them had a clue.

I kept my eye on the young kid, Brody, with his eyes so darting and downcast. Isolation and pain emanated from his thin body, but I could also feel fear. *What had happened to him? Where would he go from here?* I wanted to tell him it wasn't too late, that it was never too late.

I was fascinated by these men's stories and humbled by our commonalities. Frank and Roger were my easy favorites.

After sixty minutes of sharing, Frank recited the Serenity Prayer as most of the guys nodded along. I'd never noticed the prayer's simple power. Then again, perhaps I'd never heard the whole thing. The serenity to accept the things I cannot change, the courage to change the things I can, and the wisdom to know the difference."

I stayed after to grab a cookie and say bye to Roger. I also wanted to ask him something. I walked up when he was alone. "Thank you for this, Roger—for doing this. There are some stories in here."

"Everyone has a story," he said. "It's a matter of how much we're willing to share." He seemed so sweet and so Southern. It was hard to imagine him cheating and raging and, to be honest, fighting like hell for his wife.

"Can I ask you something?" I shifted from foot to foot.

"Course, son."

"How did you know it was the right thing, to get your wife back? After she'd already left? Six years, you were apart? That's a long time."

"Well, she was only gone for two," he explained. "Six were bad. But yeah. Why? You thinking about chasin' down yours? Because I'll tell you, you gotta be careful with that."

Huh? Not the exactly the "go get her" pep talk I'd hoped for. I dug my hands into my pockets. "I'm not sure," I sighed. "It's complicated."

"Always is."

"I'm trying to figure it out. I guess I'm just—looking for clarity and direction."

"Well, this group will help," he said. "Before you go running after her, though—you gotta be sure you're right. In here—" he pointed at his temple. "And here." He thumped on his chest. "Don't you go there unless you're *sure* as the day is long."

I listened. I knew he was right. "Your marriage, though," I asked. "Since you've been back together. It's been good? Strong? You guys are—happy?"

His grin broke out then. I felt him study my face. "There's a lotta people 'round here who'll say, 'marriage isn't about happiness, it's about holiness.' But I think that's part crock. I think a healthy marriage is, by definition, happy, a lot of the time."

"Well, I like that," I said.

"We're not perfect, Alma and I. We got issues still, like everyone else. But we're stronger than ever, and happier, too. And we've known well this second time that neither of us going anywhere. Not soon. Not ever again."

Not ever again. "Thank you," I said. Thank you so much. I'll be back when I can."

"Open door, son. Come whenever you'd like. In the meantime—I'd tell you to get nice and quiet. You can't hear your answer unless you clear out the noise. And, whatever you do, don't miss pages fifty-eight through sixty in there." He tipped his head to the notebook on my seat, resting under my phone.

I nodded. I promised I wouldn't.

. . .

I was still nursing my lavender latte—it was delicious, if lukewarm by now—so I found a table at the café again and opened up the *Renegade* book. I flipped to page fifty-eight. Not too surprisingly, it was the chapter on porn.

Porn's Illusion of Pleasure Hides the Pain

Some Numbers on the Problem's Severity:

- Every second, 28,258 users are watching pornography on the Internet
- 40 million American people regularly visit porn sites
- 35% of all internet downloads are related to pornography
- 2.5 billion emails sent or received every day contain porn
- Every 39 minutes a new pornography video is being created in the United States
- The industry's value is estimated at $16.9 billion in the U.S. alone.

It wasn't that the statistics themselves surprised me—it was just jarring to see them all in one place. *$17 billion?* Then came the section on its destructive influence on families and marriages:

- Pornography use increases the marital infidelity rate by more than 300%
- 40% of "sex addicts" lose their spouses
- 58% suffer considerable financial losses
- 33% lose their jobs
- 68% of divorce cases involve one party meeting a new partner over the internet, while 56% involve one party having an "obsessive interest" in pornographic websites.

Geesh. Was all of this true? It didn't seem like a church or a PhD would lie about something so serious, but it felt a little extreme.

At the same time, though—*did it?* Even my own divorce supported the claims.

Next came the page with the negative impacts.

Unrealistic expectation of what women should like, do, expect, feel. Objectification of women. Porn turns sex into masturbation. Desire for new and different partners and types of sexual experiences. Heightened association of violence and coercion with sex. Feelings of remorse, guilt, and low self-esteem. Decreased sexual arousal to "normal" stimuli.

Here it was, in my hands, whether I liked it or not. Evidence of everything I'd always suspected, if I was being unflinchingly honest—and everything Janine had confirmed.

I'd lost the taste for my latte. I was ready to shut the book for good when one more line grabbed my eye:

To My Porn-Watching Dad,
From Your Grown-Up Daughter:

I didn't know if I could take it. I did, though; I took it. I took every word. It left me silent, and sick, some lines searing more than others:

It seemed very hypocritical to me that you were prohibiting what movies and music I let into my mind—yet here you were consuming this junk on a regular basis.
I became acutely aware of your wandering eye whenever we were out and about.
I saw you, Dad. I always knew. I just didn't say anything. Your behavior communicated to me that I would only ever be beautiful and accepted if I looked like the women on magazine covers or billboards.
I learned to have less and less faith in you until I couldn't trust you anymore.
No girl should ever have to wonder about the man who is supposed to be protecting her and the other women in her life.
Your porn watching has hurt my relationship with my

husband all these years later.

I struggle with intimacy.

Porn doesn't just affect you.

Did you ever really love Mom? Mom is so funny, and sexy, and cool. Why wasn't she enough?

I pray you can find a way past this, Dad, and that you— along with the millions of men who struggle with this— will someday open your eyes.

. . .

The night was colder than when I'd arrived. I slam-dunked my paper coffee cup into the trash can and speed-walked along the path. I felt jittery and unbelievably sad. I didn't know where I was going, but I was craving fresh air.

The sidewalk wove past the baptismal pool and the lawn before winding down to the lake. The stars glinted high above me.

Coco had been too young to know what I had been doing, during the worst of our marriage. *Right?* Yes. I was totally sure.

But she wasn't too young anymore. I needed to make a hard turn and stay on the right side of the fork. Married or not, I needed to keep moving on, toward being a better father than mine had been. I knew he had done his best, and I had compassion for all of his demons. But, at the end of the day, he'd chosen them over me. And ultimately, they killed him. They killed him in cold blood.

At the shore of the lake, rimmed in willow trees and manicured greenery, I stopped at the sight of a boulder. It looked like the kind of place people probably paused to think or, maybe, to pray. A quote was imprinted into the stone:

God buries our sins in the depths of the sea
and then puts up a sign that reads:
No Fishing.

—*Corrie Ten Boom*

I looked out onto the water, glasslike, reflecting the trees. I remembered reading Corrie Ten Boom's biography as a kid, *The Hiding Place*. She was famous for having the courage to hide Jews in her family's home during World War II. She risked her life. She poured out her love. She put others above herself. She also lied, and bribed, and forged, to protect the Jews she kept safe. Corrie fudged the line to do the right thing.

Maybe things weren't always so black and white.

Then again: Some things were.

I reached down to pick up one of many round rocks on the ground, nestled there in the mud. I brushed off the grime, and I gripped the stone. I lifted my face to the sky. *Is anyone here with me? Because, God, I can't do this alone.* I flung the stone into the water, as hard and far away as I could.

I heard the plop echo and watched its ripple effects.

Down, down further,

It sank.

I felt a sharp breeze and zipped up my jacket, feeling him in the wind. *Son, my son, I'm here. Always here. And you don't need to ever fish here again.*

I remembered a passage from scripture about a woman, ostracized, judged, pointed out for her heinous wrongdoings—she was caught in adultery. In front of a gathering crowd, Jesus wrote something down in the dirt that none of us will ever read. Jesus stood by her, shocking everyone, taking the woman's side. It was impossible, gracious love—the kind at which religious people turned up their noses.

Let he who has not sinned cast the first stone.

I pivoted, and I walked away.

I believed it could be my last.

. . .

NINETEEN

SERAPHINA

The PowerPoint presentation lit up the conference room. Sunshine also slanted inside and onto my spread for the morning. I'd grabbed us water bottles and stopped for my favorite muffins and scones on the way, from the bakery by Coco's school. This run-through was serious business. We needed hydration and snacks. Sage and Graham would arrive any minute.

I heard a knock on the glass door. "Come in!" I said without looking up.

"Hi, Sera."

Sage's voice croaked, and I snapped my head. She didn't bound into the room with the zest I would've expected today. This presentation was a huge deal—especially huge for her, as an intern, because it was *all her*. We wouldn't have this pitch without her, and it could mean everything for rebranding The Bentley.

"Sage?" I asked. "Oh, no. What happened. Don't tell me someone else died. Gosh, that sounded worse than I meant it to—"

"No, no," she said quickly, tiptoeing into the room before pulling out a chair from the conference table. In a gray sleeveless dress that showed off her sinewy arms, she sat and folded her hands on the table. *Much too professionally.*

What was happening? Another Jenga piece in my life stack could *not* be pulled out right now. I'd already had to cancel one order for Coco's tea party cupcakes and place another, plus call in the balloon order, all before nine in the morning. Planning a five-year-old's birthday party that you wouldn't be attending was harder than you might think. I pressed my fingers into the bridge of my nose.

"I have an opportunity," she said, and my heart dropped.

Of course, she did. She was leaving me. It was only a matter of time. I'd always known she wouldn't stay here forever. But why today, *why now, pretty Sage?* I needed her.

I really did.

"Okay," I managed. "Tell me more? You got another job?"

"No way!" she said. "I love it here. I'm not leaving. I mean— unless you fire me after you hear what I'm about to tell you."

Cautious relief cascaded over me. If she wasn't leaving, then what? Oh, Sagey girl, *spit it out!* "What's going on? You're freaking me out!" My professionalism was slipping onto thin ice, but I didn't care at this point.

"Nordstrom contacted me," she said. "I would've said something sooner, but I didn't think it could possibly be legit."

"Nordstrom? Sage! Um, that's *huge.* For what?"

"I know it's big," she said. "And it gets better. They want to partner with me on a new fashion line. By me, for my demographic of followers. I will have full creative license, but it will be a Nordstrom brand. We'll come up with the name and the looks and everything, together. I honestly still can't believe it."

My heart exploded for my intern even as I knew what this meant for me. She was on her way up and out. She was special, and gifted, a one-in-actual-millions gem. She deserved this, so much.

"This is *insane*, Sage! I am so proud of you. But you want to keep working here? How? How's that even going to work?"

"Well," she continued, "I would have to cut down to two days a week."

"That's fine!" I practically screamed. "Of course. Anything. We'll make it work."

"And—" She licked her lips and ticked her nails on the table. "They need me in New York next week, for a fashion show at their new store."

There. There it was. I blew out the breath I'd been holding. *Thinking, thinking.*

"If you tell me no, Sera, if you tell me it's this job or that—I'll go to Jackson Hole. Without a doubt. You're such a mentor to me, and I don't want to let you down. But this is a crazy break for me, so if there's any way I could—"

"Go," I said. "You need to go to New York."

I looked at her there before me, and I saw so much of myself. The world was her whole big treasure chest, and I wanted to see her open it and let the diamonds and pearls slide through her fingers as she sorted through where they could take her. I'd known it before, but I knew for certain now, that my days with Sage were numbered. Some people were meant for greatness, spinning on a next-level plane as the rest of us couldn't stop watching, those souls designed to create, the ones meant to be shared with the world. Sage was also the best writer I'd ever known at her age, and she'd always have glowing reviews from me. And from everybody at Hamilton.

Her eyes grew wide. "Really?" she breathed. "Are you sure? Am I—do I—can I keep working for you?"

I smiled. "Of course, you can. But I think we both know you're on your way to bigger and better things."

Next thing I knew, she was holding my neck in a hug. "Thank you, Sera. Thank you so much."

I hugged her back, closing my eyes, before holding her out at arms' length. "I need you today, though, okay?" I put my hand on her head and squeezed my eyes shut. "I wish I could just *download* everything from your brain to mine, in case they stump me with a question about the algorithm."

She laughed. "You can totally FaceTime or text me or call me, *any time*, all week. But yes. Today, let's do this."

"*Ahem.*" Graham cleared his throat from the doorway, holding a giant red box tied dramatically with a pink bow. "Am I interrupting?"

I sighed. "Sage can't come next week, but it's fine, no big deal, she just struck a deal with *Nordstrom*, the only department store that's ever mattered."

He looked from Sage to me and then back to Sage again. "Well, good thing I brought chocolate!"

He set down the box, and there was a small enveloped card attached. *Seraphina*, it said. "Mr. Hamilton," I said. "What is this?" When we finally got around to arranging this meeting, after we'd all processed Brad's death and Beck's sudden departure, Graham had been a professional sweetheart and perfect gentleman. Since I'd been tied up, he had been the one to email me first after our kiss. It was all business, until the end:

> By the way, I had a *moment* with this super-hot mom at a club in L.A. Saturday night. She can kiss like she can write.
> Then again, I'm pretty sure it was all just a dream.
> Best,
> Graham

"Tomorrow's Valentine's Day." He smiled. "So this is for you girls, from *the company.*"

"Which, obviously, equals you," Sage jabbed.

I didn't care. Sage was leaving me and I needed *chocolate.* I set aside the card and pulled at the end of the ribbon.

"Just you and me, kid," I said to Graham as caramel filled up my mouth. "Sage is going to walk us through everything. We'll be fine."

"Please don't call me kid." He pretend-winced, grinning, and reached to fleck a piece of chocolate from the side of my mouth. "But, yes. *Of course*, we'll be fine! Let's get started, shall we, ladies?"

. . .

After three run-throughs with Graham, I spent the afternoon with the presentation up on my desktop. I clicked through it until four o'clock, when the slides had officially blurred together and I desperately needed a break. Graham's card was still staring up at me. Perhaps it was time. I popped another dark chocolate into my mouth and shredded open the envelope.

Sera,

I wanted you to know how thankful I am that I had the privilege of joining forces with you on The Bentley. The hotel means so much to me, and there's no one I'd trust more to handle it.
Proud of you.
Mom.

Sincerely,
Hamilton Properties

He was such an unbelievable sweetheart, and so widely misunderstood. To have the confidence and maturity to proceed like he had, after getting bluntly rejected right to his face? He was special. I was thankful, too. We had our pitch in the bag. I shouldn't even be worried.

But, of course, I still was. I wasn't nervous so much for the presentation, but rather for the massive amount of intel I'd have to gather by myself during the week. Usually there were at least two of us—taking the notes, snapping pictures, collecting current marketing collateral, attending the meetings, trying the restaurants, all of it. I was dizzy just thinking about it.

I picked up my phone. I had a new message from Jack.

Jack Lawrence: Having a good day?

Sera Lorenn: Eh …

I didn't mean to be dramatic, but it was precisely *"eh"* with the ups and downs, and the foreshadowing of completely losing my Sage.

Jack Lawrence: Uh oh. Penny for your thoughts?

Why did men love to ask me that? It sounded like something my grandpa would say, charming the gals at his nursing home.

Sera Lorenn: Well, I have a huge work trip next week …

Jack Lawrence: Yeah?

Sera Lorenn: And I found out my intern can't come. She was going to help me big-time. I'm on my own now, and I'm also probably going to lose that intern forever, and I'm obsessed with her—it's a lot. Also busy planning my daughter's birthday party, which I have to miss next week.

Jack Lawrence: Man. That is a lot. Where's the trip?

Sera Lorenn: Jackson Hole, Wyoming. The Bentley Hotel. DON'T GOOGLE ME! I basically just told you my specific profession and workplace.

Jack Lawrence: BRB, I'm gonna Google you.

Jack Lawrence: Oh.

Jack Lawrence: Wait.

Jack Lawrence: YIKES.

Jack Lawrence: That's what you look like?!?!

Sera Lorenn: OMG!!!! STOP!!!! DON'T TEASE ME!!!!!!

Jack Lawrence: :) No Googling. I promise. So, what do you have to do there? Writing? Interviews?

Sera Lorenn: Kinda. More like 100 stories and group interviews every day. It's a marketing trip. I have presentations and dinners and I have to take notes on the property so I can help our whole team "paint the picture."

Jack Lawrence: Makes sense.

Sera Lorenn: Sorry. Venting like crazy. Just spinning a little.

He went silent then, as happened sometimes. I was thirsty anyway. I grabbed my marbleized Hydro Flask and headed for the kitchen to fill it. When I returned and picked up my phone again, I saw a list of four messages:

Jack Lawrence: So. Hear me out. What if I came on your trip with you?! I wish I could ask this in person so I didn't seem like a creepy weirdo. But, we've got to be approaching 4,040 words again, right? And we want to meet at some point. Right?

Jack Lawrence: Oh no. You're quiet. I spooked you.

Jack Lawrence: Sooooo, some weirdo stole my phone and suggested he FLY TO WYOMING to meet you. I am SO SORRY about that.

Jack Lawrence: Unless you're into it, in which case it was totally me.

I stared at my phone, flipping the idea over and over, until it burned the back of my eyes. I squeezed them shut and pressed my middle fingers into their corners. *No.* Maybe? *What in the actual?* Was he serious?

Sera Lorenn: Are you for real? Like actually serious?

Jack Lawrence: 100%.

Jack Lawrence: Unless you hate it.

Sera Lorenn: LOL. You're killing me!

Jack Lawrence: I've had a crazy month but work just came to a halt. I have the time, I have the money, and I'll get a separate room, obviously, in case you think I am hideous.

Sera Lorenn: I couldn't possibly.

Jack Lawrence: I don't know. What if you're crazy hot, and I'm crazy—average?

Sera Lorenn: LOL! Stoppppp.

Jack Lawrence: I'll really help you, though. I think I've proven that I have impeccable grammar.

Sera Lorenn: That you do!

Jack Lawrence: And a very observant eye. And a business mind. I'll run around and take notes or whatever you need. I'll be the best intern you've ever had.

Was I crazy for entertaining this idea?

Was I even crazier for thinking it could be *fun*?

I didn't want to fly with him, though. What if—what if it *was* a big disappointment for both of us, a huge, massive old blind disaster, and we had to *sit next to each other* for an agonizing three-and-a-half-hours?

Jack Lawrence: Hello?

Jack Lawrence: Oh no.

Jack Lawrence: Gone Girl.

Sera Lorenn: Lol. You're hilarious today. I'm here.

And I had made a decision.

Sera Lorenn: Let's do it!!!!!! Oh my gosh, let's do it. You have to fly under the radar, though. I don't want the company knowing I'm meeting my internet boyfriend.

Jack Lawrence: Did you say boyfriend?

I could feel his smile, and I smiled back.

Sera Lorenn: Ah! You know what I mean. :) Okay, though. WOW. I get in Sunday at 6 p.m. Take a different flight though? Let's meet at the hotel.

Jack Lawrence: !!!!!!!!!!!!!!

Jack Lawrence: That's perfect. I can't come until Monday, anyway.

Sera Lorenn: And how about no more messaging until then? It'll add some mystery. What do you think?

Jack Lawrence: I like that. I mean. I think I do. Might miss you, though!

Sera Lorenn: You, too, Jack. You, too. Message me when you land? We can meet in the lobby.

Jack Lawrence: Wow. This is happening.

Jack Lawrence: See you soon?

Sera Lorenn: See. You. Soon!!!

. . .

I picked up Coco from school and would have her with me until Sunday, since I'd be gone the whole week after that. After much debate, we decided it would be easiest for Connor to stay at our house, to keep Coco in her routine. He would sleep in the guest room. I didn't care, either way, if he slept in my bed—it had been his, too, for years—but he suggested it before I thought of it, which felt respectful and sweet. I couldn't help but wonder if therapy was changing him deeply.

I took Coco to pizza for dinner, our favorite spot with creative toppings and packs of clay for the kids. Coco adored that clay.

"Are you excited for your tea party?" I asked.

She nodded, patting the yellow into a pancake. "I'm so excited! I'll miss you, though, Mommy."

I squeezed her wrist. "I'll miss you, too, baby." *More than you could possibly know.* "Gramma and Daddy are going to send me lots of pictures, okay?"

"Daddy said he'd be the Mad Hatter!"

"He'll be *such a good* Mad Hatter."

After tucking her in, reading her *Runaway Bunny* and scratching her back for twenty minutes, I kissed the top of her sleeping forehead and padded downstairs to the kitchen. Her backpack sat on a barstool. I unzipped it to pull out her lunch pail.

As I did, a piece of legal paper fluttered down to the floor.

I squatted to pick it up.

Dear Ser,

I swallowed, feeling a thick, heavy ball begin to tickle the back of my throat. The words were in Connor's handwriting. I skimmed to the end. Sure enough:

Love,

Connor

He hadn't written me a letter in years. But I knew as soon as I saw the length of it, and several words that popped out, that this letter had never been meant to land in my hands. Coco. *That Coco.* She could spell my name now. Did she see my nickname on it? Did she steal this from his apartment? *Did Connor give it to her?*

No. He didn't. He wouldn't. It wasn't like him. This delivery had arrived in my hands in one ridiculous turn of fate.

I set it on the island counter and set to brewing myself a decaf Nespresso.

Should I read it?

Should I toss it?

Should I text Connor and tell him I found it?

I cupped my mug and snapped up the letter.

We spent fifteen years of our lives together, didn't we? I deserved to read what he had written, about me. *To me?*

I snuggled into the couch with my fuzzy white throw and the lengthy handwritten memo. I inhaled sharply and read:

Dear Ser,   *January 15*

That rhymes! Kind of. I'm nervous. I hate that it feels so awkward to write you a letter. Do you remember when I used to write you notes? I know you have them some-where. Or did you burn them after I left? Can't say that I would blame you. I wonder what they even said. It's sweet to think about, isn't it? Also incredibly sad.

Well, I know you're not going to believe this, but—
I'm actually going to therapy. Right?! It's a lot to cover in
writing, but I reached a point where I couldn't live with
the pain in my chest anymore, and it wasn't getting better.
So I did something that probably betrayed your trust and
I want to say that I'm sorry. I called your sister and got
a couple of recs. Please don't get mad at her. I begged.
I was desperate. I'm sorry. There! You have two whole
apologies and I'm only two paragraphs in! Just kidding.
Maybe I shouldn't joke.

I just sat here for another seven (whole) minutes
(definitely not in heaven) and I'm having a hard time
knowing what to say next. So I'm just going to dive in.

First and foremost, I want to say that I'm sorry, Ser.
I haven't said that to you outright, but I am saying it now.
Our love, our marriage, our time together? Well, it was
the best thing that ever happened to me. I don't know if
you do this, but I look back and try to pinpoint when we
lost our way.

Was it the first time you found my browser history in
year three? I'll never forget that look on your face. I
don't think you ever really came back to me after that,
not in your innocence and your fire. You never stopped
making comments about not measuring up. You carried
it, the weight and the images. It's possible you still do.

I could never persuade you that all of those issues have never been about you.

Or was it year five, when Coco was born? Neither of us could have known exactly how much she would scream. Only the two of us will ever understand that it really was 24/7, that screaming can make you insane. That a being made from pure love can sprout and twist like a vine between you, twisting around you and making you choke. We love her, more than we love anything. Obviously. But that first year of parenthood nearly strangled us.

And yet, we survived to see years six, seven, and eight, which brought three different babies that never took a breath on this earth. I lost more of you with each one, but mostly the son we held, our little messenger angel. I stopped knowing how to talk to you, officially, after that. You stopped letting me in. You started to recoil—that word, like they always say about miserable wives—at my slightest touch. I lost what I had left of you, and Coco became the only thing that held us together, until even she couldn't do that. It was always too much for a child.

I know it's possible you blame yourself for your drinking and mood spells when your pain became too much to bear. It's true that I can't count the number of times I came home from work, or woke up next to you, and all I wanted was to know you again or to hold you or see you there. But I truly felt like the Sera I knew was gone, and it broke my heart. I know you were hurting, though. I was, too. I just want you to know that I don't blame you for wanting to numb all that pain. I did the very same thing. Just with a different substance.

More than anything, I want to tell you that—while our fights were hideous in the end—it haunts me that I was the one to break your heart first, with my stupid habit, and send us down a dark path. I wonder—if after your miscarriages, if you could've looked at me the way you looked at me on our wedding day—if things would've turned out differently. If I had dealt with my problems earlier, gone to therapy years ago, even before we were married?

I wonder. I do.

In the end, you were the one with the last bit of fight in you. You started getting better. And I was so happy to see it. By then, though, I felt like I didn't know you. I didn't know us anymore. I felt you were better apart from me; I was not doing well by that point. I couldn't stand the thought of hurting you even more than I already had.

So I left, because it was easier. Because I wasn't brave enough to keep fighting.

I'm not writing you this because I want something from

you, or because I expect any sort of response, or for any
reason other than giving you the long-overdue apology
you deserve. I smashed us to pieces, Ser.

I'm writing to tell you I'm sorry for breaking your heart. I
pushed you into a situation I know you never imagined. I
know you've always hated divorce. I know it has crushed
your spirit, and I promise it's crushed mine, too.

I want to move forward in peace, and that's why I'm writ-
ing you this. Supposedly I have to walk THROUGH my
stuff before I can move BEYOND it. Though all I want to
do is go BACK and be 100% less of an idiot. I was selfish.
I was nearsighted. If I could go back to our marriage, I
would. I would see you. I would look harder. I wouldn't
chase the wrong things. I'd hold what was right in front of
me. I'd choose you every time.

Remember the Friends *episode where Rachel writes Ross*
an eighteen-page letter about their relationship? She says
that they can get back together if he agrees to everything
she has written. "Does it?!?!" she asks. Clearly, he hasn't
read it—it was so long, it put him to sleep. But he wants
to be with her, so he agrees, YES, it does! Whatever that
means! She hugs him, ecstatic. Only later does he find out
what he was admitting—that sleeping with someone else
was, in fact, a betrayal. That their entire breakup was his
responsibility. Yes, it DOES sound like I can admit that!

Naturally, Ross is irate. Of course, he revokes his acceptance of the long letter. Because, for the hundredth time: "WE WERE ON A BREAK!!!"

This is a reverse of that letter. Also long. Also might put you to sleep.

(Are you still awake?!)

The only thing I'm asking you to accept is my heartfelt apology. I want to say that I'm sorry. I'm asking if you can forgive me.

Does that sound like something, by any chance, that you can consider thinking about it, from anywhere in your heart?

"Does it?!?!"

Okay. That's all.

Love,
Connor

. . .

Chapter

— TWENTY —

CONNOR

66 Thank you," I breathed, "for meeting me so last minute. I'll be out of town on Monday now, and like I said—it's an emergency."

I wondered if Janine had any idea how much she had grown to mean to me, in these short weeks. *Was I really this guy?* Was I really the guy who couldn't make a *life choice* without first consulting his *therapist*? Did my socks actually match today? Did I really remember my sparkling water, my prop? I believed this was what we called *progress*.

"No problem," she said kindly, tucking a strand of hair behind her ear. She wore a chunky white sweater today with her chestnut hair down and curled. She was truly a woman of many looks. I still wondered sometimes if she fought crime on the side.

"What's on your mind?" she asked. "Tell me everything."

I spilled it all. I told her what *that rascal Jack* had done, proposing a crazy blind meetup in the middle of nowhere. I told her I was flying to Jackson Hole on Monday to meet Sera, and how this offer had felt so right at the time, but that now I was spinning out.

In three days, I was flying to a snowy five-star hotel. To meet my ex-wife, who might or might not despise me—I honestly didn't know.

And I would say *what*, exactly? That Jack was me this whole time? That hopefully we could laugh about it? That I loved her madly and wanted to get back together? I explained everything to Janine, which was to say, I told her I didn't know, I didn't know, *I didn't know what to do.*

Did she have any advice? Or maybe a manual of where to take it from here? That would be so great, *thanks!*

Janine blinked and pulled her mauve lips together. She was so comfortable with these long silences, but they always pushed me toward the edge. "Do you remember, Connor, several weeks back, when I first told you about the three layers of mourning someone you have lost?"

I focused.

The actual person, the version of yourself, the time together.
"I do."

"We covered the first two at length," she said. "What we haven't discussed is the period of time you spent together."

This was veering off track.

Back to the Wyoming train wreck, Good Doctor.

"I guess my question for you is—do you want that time as a couple to be over, or do you want to revive it?" she asked. "Last time, we discussed how your old relationship died—and you weren't sure if you wanted to revive it or not."

"That's right," I said.

"Right now, Connor, I want you to picture your whole life."

She held out her arms in a timeline. "Sera will always be part of it. But do you want to renew a romantic relationship? To spend the rest of your time with her as your partner? I want you to ask yourself if you can honestly picture a new marriage with Sera."

The thing was?

I could.

I did.

But I didn't know if *she* did, and here I was, for the ten-thousandth time, truly not wanting to hurt her.

Would she be furious at me when I showed up? Would she slap me? I knew she liked Jack—a lot. That much seemed clear to me. And we seemed to be doing great lately. But flying to Jackson Hole carried huge potential to pummel her heart to the ground, while humiliating myself. Not that this was about me. But I cared about protecting us both.

"If it were up to me," I said slowly, "yes, I would fly to Jackson Hole. I would explain that it had been me all along, and I would tell her I love her. I would tell her I want her back."

"Have you bought your plane ticket yet, or booked the hotel?"

I shook my head.

"And who's watching your daughter while you go do this?"

I didn't love this part. I knew Sera was already breaking down over one of us not being there to celebrate Coco's fifth birthday. Both of us missing the party? It might be unforgiveable. Then again, did the ends justify the means if our absence brought the three of us back together again? The risk felt worth it to me. I'd have to hope it wouldn't land Coco here on a therapy couch as a teen. *The Mad Hatter didn't show up to my birthday. Oh.*

He was also MY DAD.

"My in-laws would have to do it," I said, sighing and shifting. "It's not ideal, because it's her birthday, but I know they'd make it super special. They adore her. Plus, she's resilient."

No one ever said the *Parent Trap* mission was easy.

"It Takes Two," after all.

Janine held back any comments on my childcare plans.

"So, you want this, Connor?" she asked, adjusting her glasses. "You're sure? You think you're ready for a new life with Sera—as the husband and father you believe you can be? Leaving behind the things you know eroded your marriage?"

I'd never been more certain of anything, and all I could do was beg for the strength to keep going, keep walking, keep *moving*, as I left my old ways behind.

I wasn't sure where Sera stood.

But I would fight to find out.

"I am," I said. "I love her. I want to be a family again. I'll take the risk. I've already survived the worst. I didn't fight for us when she needed me to. So, this is me. Fighting. This time."

Janine folded her arms, smiling broadly.

"Then I think," she said, "you need to get on a plane. Go get your wife, Connor."

Go get your wife.

. . .

PART THREE

Knock

Chapter
TWENTY-ONE

SERAPHINA

The Bentley was even more transcendent in person. Fluffy, snow-covered mountains were laced with ski runs and trees. The massive hotel was nestled at the base of their majesty, timeless and grand, as expected. The friendly staff delighted me with an exuberant welcome into the lobby, where flames crackled in the rustic stone fireplace. Fresh hot chocolate was served on a silver buffet, with shortbread cookies and a lavish charcuterie.

I could get used to this.

I arrived Sunday evening as planned, after a weekend packed with as much pre-birthday magic for Coco as possible. We went to Disneyland on Saturday. She turned into Belle at the Bibbidi Bobbidi Boutique, where magical cast members made over girls into their princess of choice: hair, makeup, and, of course, the full gown, complete with a special birthday button. We waltzed around the park for the rest of the day. Coco looked and felt like a queen.

"You're five, my baby," I kept saying. *You're five.*

Theme parks were hard for her, usually, with all the stimulation and crowds, but she amazed me for those eight hours. I was calmer than normal when she did have one meltdown, when her updo became too tight underneath her tiara. It gave her a headache, sending her into hysterics. She screamed, and flailed, while people watched on, wide-eyed and whispering, worried.

For the first time in a long time, though, I didn't care what they thought. My cheeks usually blazed as I shot up apology glances and broke into a full sweat. Today? I had eyes only for Coco. I was at Disneyland, with my perfect girl, and didn't we all know the migraine-of-death caused by too much hairspray and bobby pins? I held her close and rocked her, on a bench right in front of the castle. I let her hair down and tousled it gently. "There, Sweetie," I said. "*Much better.*"

We had brunch Sunday morning, with my parents, Sam, even Beckham. He was emerging slowly and accepting what had happened as truth. Coming to terms, in his way. He'd had several rock-bottom first days of physiological shock. He looked like himself today, though; just thinner, and wearing jeans. I could tell from his and Sam's body language that the tragedy was bringing them closer. The autopsy had determined cause of death as a widowmaker's heart attack, caused by a total blockage of the left anterior descending (LAD) artery that wraps around the heart. *Widowmaker* because of its deadly outcomes, due to the location and extent of the blockage. As Brad's twin, Beckham would need to have serious cardiac testing and full-body scans, to make sure he was okay. If they located anything suspect, there were preventative treatments. I hated that he was enduring this, but glad that he wasn't alone. I'd miss Brad's service during my trip, but Beck insisted I not worry at all. Sam would represent for us both.

Sam and Beck were darling, I had to admit. Adoring, too. It was a time when I was so glad to have had it so wrong. The way Beck looked at her? You didn't see that every day. It was the way my dad looked at my mom.

When everyone else fell out of earshot, I pulled Sam aside and told her about meeting Jack. I wanted to tell her in person so I could read her face in plain sight. I sensed a small hesitation before she flashed a big smile. "Um, *wow*!" she squealed. "He must be super into you. To fly all that way? Gosh, are you nervous?"

"Yes—and no," I said. "We've talked so much already, you know? But I admit it. I want to look *the very best I've ever looked*."

I had already texted Sam pictures of my planned outfits for almost every day of my trip. I needed her sister opinion. It wasn't the easiest to look both stylish and professional in the snow, but boy, this mama would try.

"Well, it's a given you're going to look hot," Sam said. "Your outfits are on fire. He's going to fall all over himself. This is crazy, though. I just hope he's cute. What if you have no attraction?"

I shrugged, smiling playfully. "Or what if I can't keep my hands off him?"

What I hadn't told Sam—or anyone else—was about the letter from Connor. I read it at least seven times. I cried the first time, through every word. And the second time, and the third. Then the tears finally stopped, and I sat with how *unfair* it felt. Why didn't he have those words when there was still hope for us? And where did this leave us now? I wanted to tell him I'd read it. I felt fairly sure about that. I wanted to look in his eyes and see if he meant what he said. Did he want to go back? Did he really spend time thinking about it?

But what if we could?

We couldn't.

I'd shoved the letter into my jewelry box and out of my mind. *I had packing to do.* I'd worry about it when I returned from Jackson Hole. I texted Connor from the airport runway.

> Thank you so much for this week. Text me pictures and updates, especially from the party! Really appreciate it. Hugs!

Graham Hamilton wouldn't arrive in Jackson Hole until our presentation day: Wednesday. My schedule before then was busy, but spotty. I had random pockets of free time to fill. During these, I planned to luxuriate in the spa, live in my hotel room, watch romantic comedies, and order the whole room service menu. At least twice. It was my job, after all.

Monday morning had included a tour of the whole property with the current general manager, Enrique, who was highly sophisticated and knowledgeable. I learned that seven U.S. presidents had stayed at The Bentley, in the Penthouse Suite, which practically knocked me over when I walked through its doors. At four thousand square feet, it was quarters fit for a king. The wrapping balcony gave the best views of the mountain resort, and the two-story suite was really more like a mansion. I loved that the furniture and décor felt luxurious and original, some of it royal, even. Overstuffed red velvet chairs, elegant parlors, ornate crystal chandeliers. The carpet and fixtures needed major updating, yes, but I made a note that the old-world charm and detail suited the property. It wouldn't be up to me, but I could cast my vote for keeping a lot of the original pieces and simply balancing it out with modernity. I thought we should focus on keeping the unbelievable bones.

Finally, now: *Monday evening was here.* Jack had sent me one message to tell me his flight was landing at four. He told me what he vaguely looked like, and to search for him in the lobby at seven. We planned to enjoy our first dinner together in the nearby casual grill.

My stomach would not stop flipping. *I had gone completely insane.* I met a faceless guy on an app and let him fly here to meet me. Anxieties over my safety did cross my mind, but, then again, I was looking for a guy with brown hair and a black Patagonia puffer jacket. How dangerous could he be? There was security all around. If I saw someone unhinged coming at me or reaching to pull out a knife—well, then, I would just scream.

More than anything? Most of all?

I felt like I had nothing to lose.

Settled into my stately room, I looked in the mirror one final time. I wore a white pom-pom beanie on top of my blonde hair: curled, sprayed, shaken loose. I puckered my lips with my favorite pink gloss. I'd gone medium on the eye makeup. Dramatic enough to make my eyes pop, but not dark enough to be overshadowing. I wore a white oversized sweater, cozy, long on my arms, tucked into the front of my dark-wash, high-waisted jeans. Taupe booties completed the outfit. Clouds of perfume, Chanel Chance.

Ready as I'd ever be, I grabbed my crossbody purse and blew myself one final kiss.

. . .

The elevator doors opened straight to the lobby, with its aqua-and-brown patterned carpet and towering wooden beams. I exited toward the fireplace on the far side, scanning the room as I walked. Guests bustled in and out of the high-traffic space, on their way out to dinner, or back to their room after visiting town.

I saw him.

He was wearing a dark-gray beanie and warming his hands by the flames.

Was it him? I didn't see anyone else in a black puffer jacket, and I thought I saw some brown hair.

This had to be him. I drew in a breath.

As I got closer, though, I halted short. Next to this man was a little girl, and he reached to pat her head.

Jack didn't have a child. *Did he?*

No.

The girl wore a fluffy purple jacket with a brown faux-rabbit-fur collar.

The jacket I'd bought last year.

She turned around and saw me before I could process and bolt.

What. In. The.

Actual?

"Mommy!" Coco sprinted into my arms and flung hers around my body. "Mommy, *Mommy!*"

The man turned around and took off his beanie.

Brown hair.

Patagonia.

He looked a little, come to think of it, like Ryan Reynolds.

Smothered by our daughter, I looked up at him, frozen. He smiled—and I knew that anxious grin. He might pass out from his nerves.

I, however, was not smiling.

I gently pried Coco's hands off my neck and kissed her cold cheek. I stood up.

"What are you guys doing here?" I asked, flatly.

I wanted him to say it. I wanted to hear, from his actual mouth, *what he could possibly say.*

He exhaled and walked toward me. "Almost a month ago," he began, before pausing for several long beats. "I heard about a dating app that didn't allow pictures and focused on deeper connections. I loved the sound of it, and so, I signed up for Blinde. In my first batch of matches, the final name I saw—it was you, Ser."

Me. *Jack.* Connor. *What?* The room swirled fast, but he stayed still.

"You sent me a message," he continued. "You sent *Jack* a message—I chose to use an alias. And I freaked out when I heard from you. I didn't know what to do, so I thought—hey. *What would it be like to message her?* Just once. Or twice. But then, I didn't mean to—but I fell in love with you, Ser. I fell in love with you all over again. As Jack. I'm Jack. Jack—is me. It's been me this whole time. I'm here, and I wanted to tell you—"

"No." I cut him off, holding up my hand like a firewall so *he wouldn't come any closer.* Heat was creeping up whole body, ready to explode onto my face. "You can't be."

He walked closer and reached out his arms as if for a hug, but I yanked away, harsh, fast. "Wait," I stammered, arranging these pieces into the full-puzzle picture. "You lied to me? Pretended to be someone else. That was—*you? This. Whole. Time?*"

I started replaying our conversations. *Went to UCLA. Wanted more kids in his life. Small family business.* What else? I was dripping in his slimy half-truths. I tried to think of what else, but then I realized—most of what we had shared had been about nothing at all.

It was nothing, Jack was nothing, *we had nothing at all.*

"Why would you do that?" I breathed, livid, embarrassed, *so confused*, reaching to wipe a hot tear. "I—I told you things. I told *him* things. Why would you? How could you do that to me?"

He suddenly looked like he might cry, too. "You messaged *me*, Sera. You were one of the first girls to message me, and the only one I ever responded to. But I never planned to let it go anywhere."

"And yet—" I spread my arms, presenting the massive lobby in snow country. "Here we are, Connor. *Here we are.*" The edge of my voice cut sharp and clean.

"We started talking, and we started *connecting* again, Ser. And *I missed you.* Okay? I missed you. I loved you. I do love you. Think about it—it was all me. You liked me. I know you did! And I never really lied to you."

"Ha!" I threw my head back and cackled. "Never lied to me. That's *funny*, Connor. That's *real* super-*duper* hilarious. You know what your problem is?"

I knew it. I knew the familiar rage bubbling up in my chest, and I knew this was going somewhere I didn't want it to go. I knew I was going to pull out my words like a sword and slice through Connor and make a scar on his soft heart that I could never repair.

And I didn't even care.

"You don't know what *truth* means. You are incapable of having a real relationship. First the internet girls—and now, what, *me* as one of your internet girls? This is insane behavior. You need help. You need *actual*, serious help. It's a good thing you're going to therapy. Yeah, I saw your car in the Cascades parking lot. I'm scared of you, Connor. I have to go."

Shaking, I bent down to kiss Coco's nose. "Baby, I'm so sorry you had to hear Mommy and Daddy fight. I'll maybe see you tomorrow, okay? Mommy needs to get some sleep."

I ran to the dark wood elevator. "Hold the door, please!"

I slid inside and watched the doors slice down the middle of my heartbroken family.

Hadn't we been through enough?

· · ·

Chapter
— TWENTY-TWO —

CONNOR

Well, that went well.

Over the weekend, I'd run through every potential scenario, every upset version of Sera, every elated version of Sera, and everything in between.

And yet.

Her response was still worse. In one grand gesture, one single swoop, I'd managed to resurrect the Sera I'd only seen a handful of times. So fuming, hurt, angry, and shocked that she had nothing else to do but pull out her harshest words, like darts on fire, and thrust them right at my face.

"I'm scared of you, Connor."

Bullseye.

I didn't drink, but I needed something. I felt a tug on my sleeve.

"Daddy, Mommy is *mad*," Coco said, peering up at me, brown eyes wide. "I don't think she likes this surprise."

Oh, little sweetie. *Ya think?* I pulled her into me. "It's okay, Coco. Mommy loves you. She's angry at Daddy. Want to get a cheeseburger?"

She nodded. Her beautiful head was so small protruding

from her oversized parka. She looked more like her mom every day. "Maybe Mommy needs a time-away," she suggested. "Sometimes my body tells me I need alone time. I always feel better after."

"I think that sounds smart, Coco Bean. We'll give her some time, okay?"

I held her cold fingers in mine and led us to the Wolf Grill. We had our room until Saturday, but we could easily fly home before then. I ticked through the week in my mind. We could even be back in time for her birthday tea party Wednesday.

If I hadn't canceled it all.

Why had I done that? Confident fool. I'd had to loop Sera's mom into my lovesick bonanza, because there was no other way. I might've left out the part about catfishing Sera on a picture-free dating app—but I did tell her I loved her daughter, deeply, that I was going to fight for her and try to win her back on her work trip. She cried when I told her. She wept. She clasped my forearms, looked in my eyes, and said, "You never stopped being my son."

We'd stay through most of the week, I decided. There was plenty to do, and I had to make it special for this precious five-year-old girl who had done nothing to deserve two parents who *couldn't get it together*. None of this was her fault. I knew Sera would probably also want to see Coco again. We hadn't been to the snow with her since she was old enough to feel the full magic, throw snowballs, catch drifting flakes as they fell.

Would Sera want time with me? *Ha!* That was another story. I might have to carefully hide. Shove Coco into the hallway and have Sera scoop her up, covert-ops style. We'd have to get creative. I didn't picture Sera wanting to see my face anytime soon. I was officially, now, where I started. On the other side of enemy lines.

. . .

The grill's bison burger medium-rare with Tillamook cheddar was the best burger I'd ever had, no question, and I inhaled two Arnold Palmers. Our table rested under a frosted window overlooking the ski slopes.

"Do you want to go up the gondola tomorrow?" I asked Coco, as we finished up. "Those little baskets carry people all the way to the top." I pointed outside, tracing the mountain in the air with my finger.

She shook her head fervently, brows furrowed. "No way! Too scary! What if we fall?"

"We're not going to fall," I promised. "That really big rope holding everything up? It's called a *cable*. It's made of *metal*. It can't break."

She glanced down, biting the straw of her Shirley Temple. "Some things break anyway, Daddy."

It pierced me. It pierced me that I couldn't argue.

After dinner, we went back to our room. I'd sprung for the South Tower Suite that included a master bedroom, kitchenette, and full separate living room with a pullout couch and TV. *Just in case.* Just in case things had gone differently tonight and Sera and I needed some privacy.

Had I actually pictured us in here together? Kissing, maybe?

Spooning and smiling? *Fine*. My conspiracy had come crashing down, but I couldn't regret that I tried. Our suite was even yellow, by happenstance—Sera's favorite color since she was a kid.

Coco begged to sleep with me in the noble king bed, and I couldn't resist her plea. I lay with her until she nodded off, her lashes fluttering like hummingbird wings until they, at last, fell still. I flicked off the lights, pulled the door closed, and picked up my phone before plopping into the embroidered couch that looked like it belonged in Versailles.

I needed to call my sister before I zoned out to whatever movie might be on demand. I didn't want to dwell on what had happened tonight. It hurt too much and didn't feel real yet, anyway. I'd face my real life tomorrow. Or maybe at the end of this trip. I didn't see any harm in enjoying some winter fantasy time with my daughter, in making her feel like the most special girl in the universe, despite all her parents' issues.

Isla picked up after three rings. "Oh my gosh, I can't wait another second! How'd it go? What did she say? *Ahhhhh*! I feel like I'm watching a movie."

My hollow silence said everything. As soon as I heard her voice, my throat began to close in on me, along with the lemony walls.

"Oh, Connor," she said softly. "No. Not well? Bad? What did she say?"

I exhaled, loudly. "She hates me, Isla. She can't believe I would lie to her like that. She thinks I'm scary and awful and—in so many words—I can go straight to hell."

"No."

"Yes."

Now she was quiet, but her breathing presence a thousand miles away still made me feel less alone.

"It's okay, Sis," I said. "I tried. I wanted to give it one last fight. I've been working so hard on myself, and we've been doing so great together and with Coco, and I know it sounds crazy, but—we had something on this stupid app."

"I believe you," she said. "I do. And it wasn't stupid. Don't say that. And don't be too hard on yourself."

"Thank you," I sighed. "Hard not to be."

"Maybe she was in shock. Did you think of that? Maybe she needs a moment."

Of course, I had thought of it, but I wasn't holding my breath. That look on her face. My least favorite look in the world. I'd broken her trust. *Again.*

"Yeah," I said. "I mean, we have a child together. We'll have to get past this no matter what. I just—"

"No. Don't lose hope yet. Give it a couple days."

She hadn't seen what I'd seen. She didn't know Sera like I did.

I remembered some words Sera's dad had given us in the depths of our infertility: a reminder that it was never in our control. He said that obsessively gripping particular plans often ends up squeezing the life out of them, and ourselves, hurting everyone more. That often the things we want to keep clutching most tightly are better left to the wind.

When I think I've surrendered, I surrender more.

I came here to fight, and I did. But it was probably about time to forfeit.

"I'll keep you posted," I said.

"I'll be praying, Con. Text, call, any hour. I'll definitely talk to you on Coco's birthday. The kids want to sing to her. We love you."

I managed a smile. Surrendered more.

"Sounds good, Sis. I love you, too."

· · ·

SERAPHINA

There was never a more gorgeous meeting room. One high wall was entirely windowed, which made it feel like we were looking out into a snow globe. Light flakes floated and swirled outside in front of the three-dimensional backdrop of the rugged mountain valley and the other curving side of the lodge. Moose, elk and buffalo heads decorated the walls between landscape artwork, refuting my lifelong insistence that taxidermy was freaky. In this conference room, it felt elegant; it felt strong. I kept returning to the same word in my branding copy drafts, but this lodge was nothing short of *majestic*.

Yesterday, Tuesday, thankfully was my busiest day of this week. I didn't have time to wallow in dismay over the death of my online boyfriend and the deception of my ex-husband. It was all so bizarre. My mind was still, two days later, bending its way around the ordeal.

I'd swiped back through my every conversation with Jack, *every comma and word*, and the strangest thing was—Connor hadn't been wrong. I didn't understand how it was possible, but he'd hardly told any blatant lies. White lies, sure. UCLA was for law school. There were omissions and deflections for days. The whole saga was a charade—but the building blocks weren't total fallacies.

Even worse, Connor's humor, his charming flirtations, the random facts about his dreams and regrets—it pained me to say that *it was all new information.* At least new to the me of today. We talked like that in the early days, sure—when I was nineteen years old, when we didn't have a care but each other. We would make out until four in the morning and share random facts between kisses. But that was so long ago. *How much do we change over time?* When was the last time, during our marriage, I had asked him something creative, or funny? Or, for that matter—personal? I didn't want to fish for the answer. I knew it would hurt my heart.

We'd exchanged a few texts the morning after our lobby showdown.

> How long are you here?

> Until Saturday. Unless you want us to leave.

> No. I want to see Coco. I'll text you.

We communicated again, early this morning, only to establish that I'd see Coco this afternoon.

"Hey, girl, *hey!*" Graham waltzed in with his briefcase,

breaking my funk, looking princelike in his black peacoat. "*Y'all ready for this?*"

I laughed. "Feeling nineties today, are we?"

"I *was* born in 1993."

Um. Was that possible? Quick math said yes.

I'd kissed a nineties baby.

"I'm excited," I said. "Eight board members and Phoebe, right? Everyone's coming?"

"They are indeed," he said. "Phil Abel and George Wheeler will be at the head of the table. They've been here the longest. They'll be the hardest sell."

No pressure. "Got it." I circled the giant table, placing Hamilton water bottles at each seat. The staff would be catering lunch to us at noon, after we finished presenting. Which would be delightful if they loved our pitch! Perfectly awkward if they detested it.

"You okay?" Graham asked, pulling off his coat and draping it onto a chair. "You look—I know women hate when we say this, but you look tired. Maybe also distracted."

My neck burned, and I rubbed under my eyes. *Did I? I wonder why. Maybe because I. Can't. Sleep.* I waved my hand. "Nah, I'm good. Just a little nervous for this."

"You sure?"

I groaned as I fiddled with the presentation remote, triple-checking that it was working. There's no way I planned to say anything to Graham about my latest development, but here he was—so sincere—and, well, my teammate, right?

"Maybe I'm not so sure," I said. "It's a long story, but—my

ex-husband? He's *here*. At The Bentley. He wants me back, I guess. He came here to tell me he loves me."

"Smart guy," Graham smiled. "I'd want you back, too."

"Stop," I said. *Or don't*. I never got sick of his compliments. "I'm trying to push it out of my head. I'm just thrown."

Graham came over to hug me, smelling even more American mountain man than he usually did. I let him hold me. I was craving the human contact. *Who would've thought?* The Prince had become an incredible ally and friend. I'd have to tell Katelyn that she'd been wrong with her theorizing about men, women, and friendship. Or maybe it was, simply, rare.

"Let's get through this," he said. "And then, let's get you to the spa, and make sure your week is filled with things to help you figure this out."

"I don't hate that plan."

"Remember when we kissed?"

"Graham, *stop*!" I laughed.

"Made you laugh, didn't I? It's a start." He tilted my chin and patted my head. "Chin up, buttercup. And the board is going to love you."

Graham could've given me more warning. Phil Abel, George Wheeler, and the rest of the board were not intimidating—they were *impenetrable*. Full white heads of hair, for all but two hairless board members, every one of them poised in a black suit and tie. I hoped I was fancy enough in my simple pantsuit from Ann Taylor Loft. I personally thought our presentation was engaging, and funny, and smart—but their faces reflected nothing. Their expressions were icy cold, which was appropriate given the weather, but disheartening, nevertheless.

Then there was Phoebe, of course, ever the classy redhead in her striking white skirt suit, with nylons. I felt manly next to her when she hugged me hello—but the hug was a nice departure for her. She'd thawed a little, I thought, in the wake of Brad's sudden death.

Once we had clicked through the twenty-three slides, regaling them with our plans for the influencer partnerships, social ads, digital marketing, plus a teaser of our taglines and content—we had a smaller presentation on Friday to hash through the words in great detail—I breathed. *We did it.* In well-practiced choreography, Graham and I had done the darn thing. We'd suggested our bold ideas for this icon of a hotel.

I was ready for my concluding remarks.

"Gentlemen, and lady," I nodded at Phoebe, smiling. "The Bentley holds an incomparable place in the heart of America. Since 1890, the hotel has shined as a beacon of timeless luxury, beautiful nature, unmatched service, and prime amenities. There is no resort property like it in the U.S. From its crisp autumns to its white winters—" I gestured outside to the storm. "To its bright springs and spritely summers, The Bentley gives its guests more than a simple vacation. It gives them memories to last a lifetime—at a historic destination so many will only dream of experiencing."

I paused, locking eyes with George Wheeler as he stroked his chin, then shooting my gaze to Phil Abel, resting his chin on a tightly balled fist.

I had their attention now.

You've got this. Don't stop. Keep going.

"Some things are special enough," I continued, "to deserve a fresh, critical update—a second lease on their full potential. This doesn't mean we don't love the original bones. It means we *do* love them. We adore them—we need them. It means that we believe so strongly in the foundation of this resort that we want to do everything in our power to bring it into a new era. To build on its past—and pave the way for our future. We think the plan we've presented today will reach the most people in our existing demographic—as well as the next generation. We think it will set the bar for the future of Hamilton, with this—" I turned to Graham proudly.

"With this incredible man at the helm." I smiled at him. "Thank you for being here today, everyone. Thank you."

I clicked to the closing slide, a spectacular photograph of the property in its full glory against the mountainous backdrop. Six words overlaid the image:

Old World. New Style. The Bentley.

It took me several moments to realize they were all clapping. *Clapping.*

For me. And for Graham. For our pitch.

George Wheeler stood at the front of the room, and the rest of the board followed his lead. They were giving us a standing ovation. I glanced at Graham, mouthing, "Thank you. Thank you for everything."

To the pitter-patter of their enthusiastic applause, I rewound my own message within the walls of my quieting mind.

It means we do love the bones.

To build on its past—
and pave the way for our future.

. . .

I had the rest of the afternoon free, and I was grateful, especially because it was Coco's actual birthday. Despite everything, the ultra-bizarre turn of events meant I got to spend this landmark day with my half-decade girl. We had a date at the hotel ice cream parlor at one, and I wanted to make it to the fitness center spin class at four thirty. Partly for research, partly to let off some steam. Connor would take Coco out tonight to the hotel's fine-dining restaurant, Woodstream. She would undoubtedly be the only five-year-old there, but I still loved the idea. That precious girl deserved it.

Connor delivered her to me at Snowcone like a phantom on eggshells—*in, out*. His face told me he was *ready to talk* when I was, but I was not. Not yet.

Snowcone was heaven for both of us girls. Everything was bright white and black—hexagon patterns, white-quartz counters, beveled-subway-tiled walls. The dining tables were small, and round, flecked with sparkles, circled by bistro chairs. The menu was divine, with house-made gelatos, exclusive coffee drinks, fresh pastries, handmade chocolates, and, of course, signature snow cones. I ordered an affogato and Coco picked a mint-and-chip snow cone. Daddy's favorite flavor. *Subtle.* They put a birthday candle into the top of it, per my request, and lit the tiny hot flame.

I sang to her at our table, clapping my hands together. Our coats were on our laps, keeping us warm. I was so proud of this girl. How far she had come this year, the hardest yet of our lives.

"Happy birthday, Coco Baby. You're *five*!"

She beamed. She blew out her candle with gusto.

"What'd you wish for, Sweets?"

She scooped a small mound of her treat. "You know, Mommy," she said.

I sipped my espresso, perfectly sweetened by the vanilla gelato. "No, I don't," I said, shaking my head. "Tell me!"

"If I tell you, Mommy, it won't come true."

"*Ooooh*," I said. "Then you don't know the Mommy rule. Mommies don't count. You can tell Mommies *anything*."

"Really?"

"Totally."

"*Wellllll*." She sounded so mature with her *well*s. She looked up at me from her cup, eyes open, intent. "I want you to love Daddy again. He loves you, Mommy. A lot. I want you to love him, too."

. . .

I barely made it in time, clicking myself into bike 33 as the clock struck 4:28. It felt lucky, the thirty-three. My favorite number, my age. It was one of the few still available. I had wrongly assumed an afternoon spin class at a mountain resort would be undesirable, empty. Every bike was filled up.

"Have you ever taken Ken's class?" asked the woman next to me, brightly. She was roundly built with kind eyes and a high brunette ponytail. Probably in her mid-forties, she wore a baggy t-shirt, which was refreshing. Lots of girls in here wore only sports bras. I was somewhere down the middle with my tight Zella top and high-waisted, magical leggings that really did *suck it all in*.

I shook my head. "I haven't! It's my first time to the resort. You?"

"Oh, yes," she said. "He's *the best*! You're gonna love it. It's like a dance party, with the spirituality of yoga. You know? I'm Sharon."

I accepted her high five. "I'm Sera." I did know. It was precisely why I used to be obsessive about my spin classes, especially while I was healing after my first two miscarriages. Once my body was ready, I would ride and look ahead as the pain dripped out of my pores.

"Who's ready to go to *church* to-*day*!" yelled a man's voice from the back.

Applause thundered. Women hollered. I noticed there were no men among us today. Only Ken, who jogged to the front of the darkening mirrored room, wearing full neon spandex. He looked Korean, crazy fit, super cute, black hair waxed into spikes. His energy was electric. I cranked up the gear on my bike.

The first song was, in fact, an upbeat remix of "Take Me to Church," by Hozier, which felt meaningful. It was incredibly motivating.

"*Grind into it, ladies*!" Ken shouted. "Turn it up. Start slow. We're going to build on this. By the end of this song, it should *burn*."

Okay. *Yeah*. It had officially *been a while*. I could barely breathe by the end of the final chorus.

"Take off some of that sugar, babes. It's time for us to go *fast*."

I loved the next song. *I loved it so much,* but I'd never heard it anywhere but my own random Spotify playlists. "Broken Arrows," by Avicii, taken away too young.

Now as you wade through the shadows that live in your heart / You'll find the light that leads on / 'Cause I see you for you and your beautiful scars / So take my hand, don't let go / 'Cause it's not too late, it's not too late! / I see the hope in your heart.

My legs spun faster than my mind could whirl, and I tried to let everything go, as Ken was instructing. His playlist was out of this world, and so were his motivational nuggets. They felt so personal, raw. Sharon was right. *He should be running a SoulCycle, or his own studio, in a major metropolitan city.* But he seemed so happy here.

"Right now!" he shouted. "Right now. *You,* Seraphina. I want you to ditch every little thing that is tearing you down, hurting your heart, and holding you back. Whatever it is, I want you to leave it behind."

Did he really just call me out? I'd heard of instructors doing this, but it had never happened to me. My body hadn't been challenged like this in months, and the rigor, combined with his words, were forcing an unexpected bulge of feeling into my throat.

I pedaled faster. I twisted my gear. I fixed my eyes in the mirror. *How far you've come, baby girl.*

"Fight for more freedom, more power, more love!" Ken yelled.

I saw Connor, his back to me, there by the fireplace. *Waiting for me.* He was waiting.

"You will find it—I promise!"

Did I already have it? For so long, he was right there, in my arms, in my house, in my bed. When did we lose each other?

"What does it feel like to fight, ladies?"

It felt like giving Connor a piece of my mind—that's what it felt like to fight. How dare he? How dare he, *that liar*. And why had I never been good enough back when he had me?

"What does it look like for you to let go?" Ken's voice fell gentler now.

But what if I had always been enough, and I was the one who didn't know how to believe it?

"Keep going. And going. *And going.*"

I heaved, and I wheezed. I looked so much stronger in the mirror than I felt right here on my seat. But I was doing it. *And I wasn't stopping now.*

Maybe I hadn't known myself, so Connor couldn't possibly, either. Here I was now, though, *doing it.* I was writing to provide for my baby. I was good at it, sharing my words to make my mark on the world. I was letting myself feel, and *cry.* I was opening myself up to love.

I was loving myself.

Seeing me through the eyes of God.

My purity, and his power.

A woman doing her best.

"Fill your rib cage with air—and *rise*!" bellowed Ken. "Let your shoulders slide down your back. Lift your head higher, *move faster.* Don't look to the right or the left."

One of my favorite songs came on, and I heard a laugh-cry escape from my chest. It was "Old Thing Back," with Ja Rule.

It was crude, absolutely, but also filled with saxophone music and lyrics that reverberated inside me. I used to run to this song, for miles.

I heard something about going *blind*, between the blunts and the hoes.

I shut my eyes, *and I saw*, as muscle memory took over the physical ride.

I saw Connor on the front steps of my sorority house, he and his group of best friends each holding a rose, the sisters all watching as strangers stopped to clap, too. He walked up to dip me into a kiss, and gave me his final rose, as everyone else blurred away. "I love you so much, pretty girl." I felt his lips on my neck again.

I saw him grab my hand as Coco's head crowned. "We're parents," he cried, eyes glazed. "*You're going to be such a good mom.*"

I saw him, *night after night after night*, trying so hard to connect, me repeatedly shutting him out, his patience through so much pain before finally letting me go.

I saw his tears dripping onto Deacon's soft head, pleading with me, *I don't understand.*

I saw him with his phone, his computer, Blinde open, doing everything in his power to *fight for me*, win me back.

Ken's voice was a tide, surging high.

"Are you going to reach deeper than you ever have before? Are you going to pull the self out of you that you've never had the courage to share?"

Yes. I was. *I am.*

"Dig deeper. Push harder. *Go longer.*"

Okay. *I'm ready now.*

"Demand more courage than you have before. Girl, *go*! I see you! *Keep going*!

"Ride for the change. Push for the healing.

"Shine, baby.

"*We're going home.*"

Stunned to my bones in the hotel lobby, taking in Connor and Coco, hadn't exactly been my Meg Ryan moment. How many times had I seen *You've Got Mail* and not whatsoever seen this coming? "I wanted it to be you," she says in the end to Tom Hanks. "I wanted it to be you so badly."

I didn't want it to be him; I never conceived it was possible. Here at last, though, was my answer. Maybe I had to lose him, to find myself.

But it had always been Connor.

It never stopped being him.

. . .

TWENTY-FOUR

CONNOR

Knock, knock—knock, knock, knock.

Pop, goes the weasel. I startled, checking the clock from my perch on the fancy couch in the den of our suite. Awfully impressive room service, even for this kingdom. I had called in my order—a nightcap, some apps, and dessert—fifteen minutes ago. Coco had crashed right after our special dinner, now tucked away in the king bed again. She loved every bite of the unreal meal, and her behavior had been imperial. She seemed so grown-up tonight in her rose-pink, long-sleeved dress and the low braid I'd managed to twist. She seemed exactly five. *My girl.*

It was almost eleven, but I wasn't tired, and I was hungry again. Fine dining did that to you, giving $200 dinner portions fit for a cat. I'd found *Friends* on repeat on TNT. I turned down Ross's voice, insisting that he was *fine* over margaritas. Ser and I used to love this episode. I'd seen it a hundred times.

"Coming!"

I swung the door open, and stiffened. I was sure, in that moment, that she'd never been more beautiful. Her tight black dress and thigh-high boots, under a burnt orange coat, didn't hurt. Neither did her red lips, fuller now than the night we met.

But her eyes. They were dark, and sexy, and warm, and something had dropped from them. There was a layer—*gone*. They were asking me something.

But what?

"Ser?" I wasn't sure what to do.

She stepped forward, cautious at first. She pressed the door shut behind her.

"I found your letter," she said. "The one you wrote to me? About me. Coco brought it home in her backpack. Did you know that?"

My eyes widened, then narrowed. My mouth fell open. *How did she do that?* I'd left it on the counter, where I stack bills and my lists. Coco was so proud lately of knowing how to spell both our names. "I did not," I gulped, "know that."

"Did you mean it?" she demanded. "What you wrote? And what you said Monday—you love me? You came here. You talked to me, *all these weeks*, and you've been working on yourself. So—you want this?" She touched her heart and then mine. "You want us? Again? Right now?"

I took a step toward her. "Yes," I said slowly. "I meant every word."

I paused. *Words*. They really were everything, weren't they? I had to choose mine carefully here.

"But I don't want this, right now," I continued. "I want this forever, Ser. I'm never leaving again, and I'm not walking away from this knowing I didn't put everything on the table. You're it for me. You're all I want."

She started to cry. "I can't lose you again, Connor," she whispered. "I can't lose us. I know I messed up, too. But I don't want to hurt anymore. Can you promise not to hurt me again? I loved you. I loved you so much. *I love you.* I love you so much."

"Hey, hey." I pulled her into me, breathing the scent of her, snowflakes and perfume. "I wouldn't be here if I wasn't sure. I love you, Ser. I never stopped. And this time? I promise you."

I felt it then, her lips on my mouth, soft but also urgent, and hard. I felt her need for me, want for me, immediately, in a way I knew I never had. My body crushed into hers, and I reached to peel off her soft jacket. I was fine with slowing things down, *way down*, but she didn't seem to want that, and so I wouldn't complain. I pulled her over to the couch, plopped down, while she slid off her boots. I pulled her onto me, and she straddled me in her tights. I hiked up her dress to her waist.

She pulled away for a second. "You were so sexy as Jack," she whispered into my ear.

I laughed, panting a little. "I am Jack. You just hadn't seen that side of me."

"Well, *Jack*," she said. "I'm going to take advantage of you. And I think our first time is going to be *hot*."

"Are you going to sing me all the names of the U.S. presidents?"

She giggled. "I'll think of something better."

"Already the best I've ever had," I said, hearing her moan as she started to kiss my chest. I felt her warm tongue and her teeth on my skin, and it was heating me up.

I breathed. She was here, I was here, this was real, *we were real together*, again. Pulsing and biting and craving. I put my hand between her legs, on top of her tights, and started to rub, while she rocked into me gently, then faster.

"Keep doing that," she whispered. "*Keep doing that.*"

There was nothing between us anymore.

I mean, once I ripped off those tights.

There were no images. No more cold shoulders. No booze, no betrayals, no cruel words we'd choke on later. No apps, no computers, no screens. No separations, no lies.

It was all stripped, and here we were.

Clear-eyed, naked, and known.

. . .

TWENTY-FIVE

SERAPHINA
SIX MONTHS LATER

"*Thank you*, Piper Maddock." I exhaled, leaning back into my beach chair, sipping my virgin piña colada. All the screensavers and calendars and promises in the world that, *yes*, the water really *is* that color—did not do this heaven justice. The sand was white, and the water was turquoise-clear. Even as you stared into it, you almost didn't believe it. But here we were, for a full week in August, lounging in Bora Bora. Compliments of our cupid, to whom we owed the rest of our lives. Otea—the name of our hotel and a well-known Tahitian dance—was probably the only non-Hamilton property that could actually blow me away. It was independently owned and operated, but you never knew. Maybe Graham would want to acquire it someday. Each room was a spacious hut perched high above the water.

Teagan had prompted me to submit our outrageous love story. Sure enough, on the Blinde website home page, among the small-print selections at the bottom—next to *FAQ*, *Guidelines*, *Press*, *Privacy Policy*, *Careers*, and *Events*, there was a *Contact Us* option. If you clicked on that, it led to another page, where you could press *Share Your Blinde Love Story.* You could upload a video or a full-length write-up. I decided on both. We filmed a brief interview, with Coco—and I tapped out a 500-word write-up. I wrote what we'd learned. I wrote how we'd used the app. I shared how it changed the course of our journey, and our view of human connection.

The next day, an unfamiliar "213" number lit up my phone while I was walking the Back Bay. I almost sent it to voicemail but snatched it up on a whim.

"This is Sera."

"Sera!" crackled a voice. Our connection wasn't the best. "This is Piper Maddock. From Blinde?"

No. Teagan? Brynne? Beckham? Who was behind this prank?

"Uh—" I scratched my head underneath my ponytail, slowing my pace.

"My team emailed me your video—and honestly, I can't believe it's true. Are you guys for real? Please tell me your story is true."

Could it be?

"Yes—yes!" I squatted onto a bench. "Connor, Sera, and Coco? I know it's crazy, but it's totally, 100% true."

"So you're back together?"

I smiled. *Oh,* we were back together. It had been the most deeply loving, connected, sexy few months of my life, on the springtime day of that call. We'd kept Connor's apartment for a full month, decided to "date" for a while—which was amazingly hot, to date your spouse in that way, after living together for years. I wouldn't let him sleep over, but we kissed and laughed and explored each other like the young kids we used to be, but with more chemistry and passion than ever. After a handful of weeks, though, Coco started to pester us.

"Daddy, can you please move back into Mommy's room? I want you to be home."

He moved back the next day, and we celebrated with a French toast feast. We ate a huge cost on his lease, but we considered it a worthy price of admission. We went to city hall in July. Although I felt strongly that we were already married in the eyes of God, we wanted to make it official. Before God, the State of California, and our out-of-her-mind-happy flower girl.

"Yes!" I told Piper. "We are very much back together. We're doing great. Honestly, we can't thank you enough."

"I'm just *obsessed* with this story," she oozed, and then paused. "You create something. You know? And it's a risk. The market was saturated with dating apps, everyone told me. But people are really connecting with it."

"Because it's special," I told her, lifting my face to the sun. "You've built something you should be proud of."

"Thank you," she said. "So much. So, I have something to ask you, something to tell you."

I liked her. "Of course."

"First, would you guys be open to letting us film your story, for the website and our social media channels?" she asked. "You guys are so darling. Nothing long. We want to do something like what you submitted. We just want to shoot it professionally."

Ummmm. "Yes!" I blurted. "Wow, yes, of course." Connor might not love it, but he would do it for me. I was becoming ecstatic. *Was this for real?*

"And, secondly, as a thank you, and congratulations, and part of the publicity, yes—I want to send you guys on a trip. To either Mexico or Tahiti. You pick."

My eyes almost dropped out of my head. "Are you serious? This—*this* is for real?" I held out my phone to look at the number again.

"I'm for real, if you're for real!" she said. "My assistant will send you an email right away. Thank you, Sera. Look for the details and check your calendar for a trip in—say—July or August."

"As in, this July or August?"

"Yep. Talk soon! Thanks again! And congratulations. To all of you."

So, here we were, the week of our would-be ten-year wedding anniversary, celebrating our reunion in the ultimate way.

Our new relationship was not perfect, or anywhere near it. Neither of us would pretend so. Even with the new excitement, fire, and relief that we were a family again, we had significant work to do. Both Janine and Linda had agreed that they couldn't be objective enough to see us together, so they referred us to a new, young male therapist named Darren.

Darren was amazing and had young kids himself. Neither of us had seen a male therapist before, so it felt like fresh, fertile soil. A new season, all around. For the first time, in open air, we begun to voice the frustrations we each felt ruined our marriage the first time. We dug back into our deepest pains and biggest frustrations. We were still in that process, and it wasn't always fun. Darren suggested we stay in couples therapy for a full year, and we didn't argue. We made a weekly date night of it.

Sometimes, we gushed effusively during the sessions, blinking our eyes at each other. Other times, both of us yelled. Once I threw down my HydroFlask.

Sometimes, we left the Cascades compound feeling hopeful. Renewed and whole. Other times, we barely spoke, arms folded on our way to the parking lot, wishing we drove separate cars. All of it was essential, though. As true as we knew how to be.

As for life around the house, it was like I'd slipped on my favorite pair of old sweats, pulled from the back of my drawer. But they somehow smelled new and fit better than ever, despite how much I had grown.

We split duties and spoke kindly, most of the time; we listened and kept no score. He hugged me from behind while I made Coco's lunches, asking for mundane details about my day. I spooned him as we fell asleep. When we fought, we fought out loud. As fairly as we knew how.

Teagan and Ryan's midsummer wedding had been a wine country dream. Connor's presence felt as natural as the sun dipping into the vineyard, spraying the huge sky orange. I shimmered like a disco ball in my sequined dress. "I don't want this to sound backhanded," Connor said into my hair. "But you're even prettier tonight than you were on our wedding day."

Connor snapped me back to Bora Bora as he stooped down into his chair, holding out two giant cheeseburgers. "Lunch!" he announced. "These better be good. They were forty-five dollars apiece."

"*Yum*," I said. "They look sublime. And I don't think Piper will notice."

We chomped and savored our lunch, and I looked down at my belly.

Still flat.

I hadn't told Connor about the new doctor I'd found, a couple weeks after Jackson Hole. I was due for my annual gynecological exam, but didn't want to go back to my OB. I saw her, of course, after my seventeen-week miscarriage, for the healing and checkups, because it was the easiest option. But since then, every visit had felt upsetting and painful. I couldn't have one more test in that place, one more bit of bad news, one more conversation to discuss the odds of me having more babies. I was thankful for her guidance in identifying my mental health issues, but I needed someone new.

But then I'd found my angel, Dr. Askari. Her warmth, her manner, and her unbelievable knowledge. She was a brilliant obstetrician who integrated traditional Western medicine with Eastern and holistic practices—acupuncture, herbs, and unconventional theories. She also ran various mainstream tests that *my OB never had.*

"Miscarriages are common," had been the refrain from my old OB's massive group practice. "Try again. It'll stick when it's meant to be!"

It'll stick. How I hated that expression offering "hope" of a viable pregnancy. What were my babies, bubblegum?

And, how was it that those doctors could find *nothing*, nothing at all, when my heart had been shattered three times—yet dozens of my friends walked around with armfuls of children and zero losses to count?

Dr. Askari found something, in her first round of tests. A double gene mutation that, yes—was linked to blood clotting, miscarriages, and placental abruption, to name a few things. Carriers of the gene also faced a massively increased risk of anxiety, depression, addiction, and PMDD.

I cried. I broke into tears, right next to the fiddle-leaf fig in her serene room. So much of my life clicked into sense during the summary she rattled off.

How had no one else caught this?

And, would Coco carry it, too? Yes, most likely, she would. In fact—she probably did. The mutation was also linked to child anxiety, OCD, ADHD, and hypersensitivity.

But there was treatment. *There was hope*, for Coco, and me. Dr. Askari put me on a full regimen right away, a plan to even out my hormones and balance my system. If I ever became pregnant again, she was confident she and her team could hold my hand—with fertility shots and vigilance—and guide me, hopefully, finally, to a happy, healthy, full-term, air-breathing baby.

"You're quiet," said Connor. He grabbed my giant coconut to steal a swig of my drink. "*Penny for your thoughts*? How did you not know, by the way, that it was me—when I said that to you on Blinde? I thought for sure it was over."

It was a great question. I sighed. "What can I say? Jack was good. He was *real good*."

We watched the water lap lazily up onto shore.

"I have something to tell you." I grinned and placed my hands on my stomach.

It was still mostly flat.

He knew it. He knew it immediately. "Really?" He breathed. "Are you sure?"

I nodded. "I think it's a boy."

. . .

--- EPILOGUE ---

CONNOR
SIX MORE MONTHS LATER

She did it, that fiery girl. Sera accomplished one of her biggest dreams. You're holding her book in your hands. This is the most honest story she's ever told. Though it is, of course, not only her tale to tell. It is a marriage story, which always has exactly two sides, to hold up to the light like a prism. The colors dance, the shadows fall. All of it is worthy, and true—but the truth can look radically different depending on where you stand.

This is us. Our crash, our rise. The fight of our lives and our love. The way we see our relationship.

Channeling her fierce inner journalist, Sera spent hours interviewing me for my vantage point in this book. Of course, we had every single Blinde message and text to draw from. *Never write anything in an email that you wouldn't mind seeing on the front page of the news.* Sera wrote my chapters, with searing accuracy, but I edited them for additional detail and a clearer rendering of my personality. You can't be a lawyer without a grasp on the written word, and I had fun bringing my old-man self to the page. Additionally, Janine was very important to me, and I wanted to get her right. Between Sera and me, I think we nailed it. I am so proud of Sera. I am so proud of us. This project was not always easy, as you can imagine. In the end, though, it healed us both.

Our story caught fire, you might say. Piper Maddock, now a dear friend, can be thanked for this. In addition to the trip to Tahiti, if that weren't enough, she told many of her friends in all kinds of high places about our journey with Blinde—out of her own romantic excitement more than anything else. I've learned that people perk up their ears at stories of love, particularly of love that has been through the trenches, that maybe lost its way for a while, but found itself once again. We all really want to believe in it. We want restoration, and hope, the possibility of forever, of absolution from the secrets we buried alive a long time ago.

I think maybe we all want to believe that, against every odd, despite our own unlovability, witnessed in nightfall and pain, there exists a higher love to cast out our deepest fears. Love we can give and receive, wholly and purely and daily, through every triumph and flaw. We can be seen, and fully adored. We can return safely home.

Before Sera and I knew it, we had a segment on the *Today* show, and *Ellen* wanted to meet us. She put together a hysterical video parody called, "OK, Catfish!" and everyone in the audience roared. The appearances landed Sera a book deal. Our story went to a major six-publisher auction. Sera could leave Hamilton if she wanted, but I think she'll be there a while. The job brings her so much joy. She and Beckham now share the manager title. Sage's fashion line is about to launch, but she left Hamilton recently, with Sera's final nudge. I think those two will be friends for a very long time.

Best of all, next week, I'm taking Sera on the surprise week-day date of her lifetime. Piper got us into the taping of *After the Final Rose*. Not only that. Piper's college roommate is a *Bachelor* producer. Chris Harrison is calling us onto the stage, and we're doing a two-minute interview. We have tickets to the cast afterparty on a rooftop in downtown L.A. Sean and Catherine will be there. So will Trista and Ryan. Sera is going to flip. Never mind that she's eight months pregnant. Nothing could keep her from this.

Piper has always adored us, but we earned extra favor with her at *Forefront Magazine*'s annual "30 Under 30" party. As lead female honoree, Piper invited us to attend, and Sera thought— *just maybe*—Piper might hit it off with her male counterpart for the year: a certain Prince with a worldwide footprint and a genuine heart of gold. Sera introduced Graham to Piper excitedly, as if she were lighting a flare. She swiped the match, dropped it, and walked away, smiling. I'm not sure they've spent a night apart since. They're in the tabloids sometimes, hotel royalty and tech's unstoppable softie.

Speaking of matchups, Beckham and Sam are getting married this summer, at the Mirabelle in Laguna. Sera pulled some strings. It's not what the family imagined, Sam falling madly in love with someone who doesn't believe like they do. But I'm growing to think that maybe some of us *do* believe, the very best we know how, without fitting into a category. Maybe we're on a journey.

Maybe it takes something big, something shattering, to yank the floor out from under our feet and render us to our knees. They go to church together on Sundays. Beckham remains wary of labels, but he says he's encountered an invisible presence of strength on his path of grief. He says he prays all the time. I don't know if he's said: "the prayer." *Jesus, come into my heart.* I also wonder if—more often than we could possibly realize—Jesus is already there.

Sera's a little worried about her maid-of-honor dress, since we'll have a four-month-old. Never mind the stress of a newborn. What is she going to wear? She's already gained fifty pounds, but I'd honestly never know if she didn't mention it. I love watching her move around the house, making (six!) pancakes for Coco or tapping away on her laptop. Overall, she is far less concerned with the weight gain this time around. I think she's too busy thanking God for the miracle growing inside her. Everything is perfect, and healthy, with Sera and with the baby. She's monitored closely, with extra appointments twice weekly, but somehow, we both feel peace. She carries it all with such grace. Where she was once anxious, and insecure, she is now steadfast, and sure. I'll spend the rest of my days reminding her how sure I am, too. I can't believe how much I love her. I can't believe she took me back. I can't believe we're having a son. I can't believe we're having *another* son. We are naming him Jack.

Coco is thriving in school, in therapy, and more than ever at home. She continues to teach us with crystal hindsight and present clarity that the connection between our flesh-and-blood bodies and rawest emotions can teach us more than we realize. *That sensitivity is our superpower.* That we can listen. We can know.

Several weeks into first dating all of those years ago, I realized I hadn't probed into Sera's full name. "*Seraphina*," I asked. "How did your parents pick that? What does it mean?"

"It's biblical," she explained. "In Hebrew, it means *fiery-winged*. It originates from *seraphim*." With a smile, she added, "They're the most powerful angels."

I saw it then. I see it now. Her power, her beauty, her blinding light.

Vanquishing both of our demons.

Seraphina Lorenn Jones has taught me more than I could ever express here. More than anything, though, she has restored my faith in myself and my belief in forgiveness. She has reminded me to look up.

Ask, and you shall receive.

Seek, and you shall find.

Knock, and the door shall be opened to you.

Great love does not always see straight. Sometimes, I tell you: It's blind.

But one thing's for sure. Love sees what matters, and forges on anyway. It keeps no record of wrong. Unbelievably, it never fails. On the blackest night, when death has come, love rips the veil between earth and heaven, once and forevermore.

It brings us morning.

It gives us life.

Once blind.

But now, we see.

. . .

Amazing grace! (how sweet the sound)
That sav'd a wretch like me!
I once was lost, but now am found,
Was blind, but now I see.

—John Newton

As he went along, he saw a man blind from birth.
His disciples asked him, "Rabbi, who sinned,
this man or his parents, that he was born blind?"
"Neither this man nor his parents sinned," said Jesus,
"but this happened so that the works of God might
be displayed in him."
—John 9:1-3 (NIV)

While Jack is now a proper name in its own right, in English it
was traditionally used as a diminutive form of John.

ACKNOWLEDGEMENTS

I used to marvel a bit at the length of the acknowledgements tucked into the backs of books. *Does it really take that many people to make a book happen?* The answer: Yes. But my deep-down dreamer took the wondering further. *As a writer, an artist, a human being: What must it feel like to have that many people believe in you and your work?* The answer: Well, I can hardly express it. But right here, I'm going to try. I have so many people to thank. Without their collective alchemy of encouragement, brilliance, and unflinching honesty, this book would not be in your hands. They are the ones who kept believing in me when I struggled to believe in myself.

But foremost, I have to thank *you*! Whoever you are, wherever you are. You just spent time with a whole cast of characters that was birthed from within my soul. Were they fun? Did you laugh? Did you feel? Did you cry? *Gah*, I hope you just loved it. Writing a book has been my life's biggest ambition since I was four, and it wouldn't be possible without many factors—but most importantly, without readers. Thank you, for being mine. I have dreamed of you. I have prayed for you.

I would absolutely love to hear from you if you ever want to drop me a line!

And now, first up: The love of my life, my Douglas. The reason I believe in marriage, in men, in soul mates. You moved heaven and earth to help bring this book to life, babe. Thank you for supporting me through the countless late nights, the days away, the incredible highs, and the heartbreaking lows. You, my husband, have carried me. Additionally, I have a sneaky feeling some might read this book and wonder if, just maybe, any of it was inspired by our own experiences. The answer: Well, you'll just have to wait for the memoir!

Next: Mom and Dad. Thank you for leading, guiding, and launching me—for always seeing a book in me. You are my heroes of love, pillars of faith, and foundation of all that I value. From my earliest memory, I wanted to write. You did not scoff at this passion or quell this gift or blink when I wanted to study it at the graduate level. You gave me pencils, and laptops, and books. You make every word possible. All I want to do in this life is to make both of you unbelievably proud. To take the seeds you have given me and plant deep roots with my time here on earth. You have watched me toil for a very long time with this project. I hope you're filled with joy seeing it flourish.

Brad, Heather, David: My siblings and my first friends, forever the final opinions I care about. Your influence is stamped on this book. Brad, you made me keep going. You reminded me on the darkest days that *this is just the beginning*. Heather, my sister, licensed marriage and family therapist: Everyone's loving Janine. I am quick to tell them that the therapy chapters of this book—*while certainly not certified or written by an actual expert, guys*!—were often crafted with extreme care based on theories you shared with me. "What would you say to Connor if he said X?" was a recurring conversation of ours. Thank you, my sister. Thank you. David, you know it's coming: *graduated number one in your class at Harvard Law School in 2018*, when I was a million months pregnant but still flew my pregnant ankles there. I knew from the get-go that Connor would be a lawyer, and that you would lend me your brain. Thank you for all of your insight. You're the baby of the family we all can't stop looking up to. As for Wendy and Tyler: You guys positively shattered the mold for siblings-in-law. I don't know how you put up with all of us and our not-so-momentary insanity, but I'm sure glad that you do!

Allison Sanden: My very first reader. You were the perfect person to read those awful early-draft pages. You devour sixty-plus books a year, so I knew you were being sincere when you said you saw something magic in mine—because you also said it needed some work. I worked hard, and we did it! Thank you for making Seraphina who she became. You pushed me further into my writing with your critical feedback, and more importantly, further into myself. I love you so much! I'm so glad Doug stalked us into being your lifelong best friends! You're the Martha Stewart to my mad scientist forever.

Molly Kelley: You're my oldest friend, my ride-or-die, and one of the first people who heard my idea for this crazy novel. In my driveway. After a night out at Javier's. "What do you think?" I asked sheepishly. "I think," you said, "you need to go write this book. But like, right now. Before someone else does. And because I am dying to read it!" Thank you for being the best, and also one of my earliest readers. And always the other last guest to leave every party.

Devon Daniels: I started calling you my mentor, jokingly, maybe a year ago, soon after we met. But then one day it just became the truth! I quite simply couldn't have done this without you. You held my hand each literal step of the way. With nothing more than a mutual friend in common, you took me under your wing. (Although she is one *exceptional* mutual friend: Kirsten Storm, thank you for ceaselessly cheering me on from absolutely day zero.) You were the literary soul sister I needed in 2020, Daniels, and the insider-boss-lady-friend who has showed me the ropes of this industry. I'll keep saying it: I owe you unendingly. And 2021 *is our year*! Just ask Jessica Simpson!

To the other author friends and friendlies of mine, who have encouraged and helped me however you could, without any hesitation: Rebecca Serle, Bethany Turner, Jedidiah Jenkins, Camille Pagán, Riley Costello, Shannon Leyko, and Ashley Rodriguez. From DMs to coffee dates, long emails and LOLs, to my ongoing awe of your work: What a privilege to be truth-seekers and storytellers with every one of you.

Bryan Edward Farmer: There's so much of you in Beckham, and he is 100% inspired by our special bond and unforgettable antics in cubicle land. Our funny and meaningful conversations, both out loud and via Office Communicator. I *did* have to make him straight so he could fall in love with Sam, but he's all yours, BEF! And to Aaron Joseph Farmer, August 10, 1976, to September 28, 2016: Rest in peace, dear twin flame of my cherished friend. You are so loved. You are so missed. I know you're so proud of your brother.

To Mr. Zirretta, my high school English teacher, the best teacher to ever live. Thank you for affirming my flair for writing, and for giving me a love of great books. Also thank you for telling me that I was the *second*-best writer you'd ever taught. That hilariously honest qualifier made me know that you meant it. I still think about it today—and wonder what that other chick's up to! JK, JK. Anyway, *Jane Eyre*'s still my favorite book! There's no way I would be a writer (or love twisted novels so much) if it wasn't for you.

To Janet Fitch, #1 *New York Times* bestselling author and my favorite professor of all time by a mile. Thank you, also, for calling out what you saw in me. For telling me I was "talented" in the elevator of our classroom's building. Not that I recall it in vivid detail or anything! I will never forget the moment of hearing my heroine say she thought I was great. Everything I ever learned about great fiction writing I learned from you.

And now, to the ridiculously talented team of professionals who came into my life in Q4 of the weirdest year ever, and suddenly made it awesome for me. Drew Tilton of Asio Creative, there is no question in my mind that God ordained our collaboration. I'm bummed I couldn't work for you a couple years ago when we first met, but I'm *so thrilled* that I had your info! Anyone looking to self-publish, ever, needs a Drew in her corner! We'll just call him my agent because it's basically what he is and also it sounds cool. Thank you, Mr. Tilton, for everything. You kept me on task, buoyed my confidence, and prayed before every meeting. I hope this project is our first of many together. Truly. You made it a blast.

Jessica Snell, your edits fine-tuned this book into something far more pristine and sparkly than it was before hitting your desk. You get me, my voice, my heart. For this, I truly thank God. You forgive my love of constantly trying to flip clichés on their heads and capitalize just about everything. I cannot thank you enough for the way you enhanced my writing and this book's message of redemptive love.

Natalie Johnson, you know I'm crazy about you! Your interior design of the book, your gorgeous rebrand and web work, every meeting we've had. You bring such a calming, warm focus to my ever-spinning ideas. You're the definition of wonderful.

Zak McIntyre, I still can't believe you took my ridiculous stick-figure sketch and brought it to life in this breathtaking cover. You've been a dream to work with since our days at CBRE, but you really knocked this one all the way out of the park for me. Thank you for giving my book a cover by which I'm thrilled to let the world judge it.

Kimberly Kirkhuff of Kimberly Hope Photography, you have been there to capture my life's most significant moments for quite some time now. Thank you for putting me at ease in the photos I needed for this new chapter. For making posing solo less scary! For making me feel like an author. You are a sister. You are a queen. The very best is ahead.

To my entire launch team, listed after this section, *I am so blessed by you guys*. Thank you for being the most darling and loyal hype squad there is. For reading my novella-emails. For deafening me with your cheers.

To my three daughters: My sun, my moon, my star. Emerson, Hadley, Reese. You are my reasons, my one-two-three hug, the trifecta that leads me home. Over and over again. What a privilege being your mom. What an honor watching you grow. I am enchanted with you, my very own little women.

Finally, but foremost: Thank you, Lord, the mighty God of my whole existence, from whom all blessings flow. Every good and perfect gift I've ever had is from you. Thank you for dictating this story to me so generously so that I could give it away to the world. We had fun, didn't we? When I wasn't yelling at you, of course. I'm still so sorry about that. You are so utterly faithful, when I am so utterly lost. As always, I'm speechless at your plan and provision. You prevail, you conquer, you chase me down. You transform with your radical love. Thank you for giving me fingers to write. For giving me eyes to see. I can't wait to see what you've got up your loving sleeve next.

XOXO,
steph

LAUNCH TEAM

Alana Andrews

Lauren Beaney

Jennifer Blossom

Kaley Brandon

Carlie Buys

Courtney Cano

Katelyn Cheo

Beth Ciemenis

Erin Clark

Kristin Clousing

Julie Dunbar

Chelsea Edmonston

Sue Fielder

Hope Flatt

Courtney Frei

Nic Gaudet

Whitney George

Blaire Going

Jill Gunderson

Ashley Hall

Allie Harris

Melissa Hess

Karen Hobbs

Allison Huff

Brittney Hurley

Allison Isakson

Laura Kang

Marci Kimura

Wendy MacGinnis

Mariah McDaniel

Mindee McDonald Metz

Kristen McIntyre

Jen McNeely

Haley Miller

Melissa Nienhuis

Shaheena Patierno

Brittany Peterson

Celina Shwam

Susanna Szkalak

Stephanie Tiss

Alyssa Wuestefeld

Kristen Whitmore

Hillary Winningham

Jessica Wrabel

NOTES

1. *The Highly Sensitive Child: Helping Our Children Thrive When the World Overwhelms Them,* by Elaine N. Aron, Ph.D. (New York: Broadway Books, 2002).

2. *Rescuing the Rogue: Free to Forge Intimate Relationships that Last,* by Randell D. Turner, Ph.D. Note: Statistics and quotations in Chapter 18 all came from this published workbook. Some lines from the passage "To My Porn-Watching Dad, From Your Grown-Up Daughter" were also pulled, paraphrased, and included. The original, full-length letter appears in the workbook.

Made in the USA
Monee, IL
24 April 2021